Mercy, Merci

Mercy, Merci

Jean Edwards

Jean Edwards

To order additional copies of this book, contact:
Xlibris Corporation
1-888-795-4274
www.Xlibris.com
Orders@Xlibris.com
40249

Maine incorporated with Massachusetts in 1691
Maine became a state in 1820.

Saint LAWRENCE RIVER

RIVIÈRE-du-LOUP
FRIENDS OF JESUS CONVENT

Long Lake

Square Lake

QUEBEC

Eagle Lake

SAINT JOHNS RIVER

ST. CROIX RIVER

ST. STEPHENS
CALAIS

KENNEBEG RIVER

PENOBSCOT RIVER

(GEORGEANA)
Augusta

BANGOR

BELFAST

MACHIAS

PORTLAND
(FALMOUTH)

THOMASTON
FRIENDSHIP
Pemaquid

SACO
BIDDEFORD

monhegan Island

Bangor was called "Kadesquit" by the Indians
Later "Condeskeag".

What once was, no longer is; what was not, is here today but will soon be gone. As the earth turns and the seasons change, so changes all that was and is and all that will come to be.

Merci

Pezhik Onindj

FORWARD

Having searched many accounts and legends associated with the Jonathan Buck monument in Bucksport, Maine, its mystery could be determined as mystical, imaginary, or merely an intriguing characteristic of the stone from which the memorial was created. With the many conflicting stories, (witches curse, revenge of an innocent, Indian lore of missing legs, etc.) I have aligned my thinking with that of Tim Sample and Steve Bither as written in their book "Maine Curiosities", that one can draw one's own conclusions and thus fabricate a story of the possible.

The book by James Kirby Martin, "Benedict Arnold, Revolutionary War Hero", proved to be an invaluable reference in confirming my suspicions that perhaps the much maligned turncoat had been a victim as much as a perpetrator. While the Continental Congress put forth ideals of equality for all, those ideals seemed to have been breached in favor of the rich and privileged, much as we see in politics today. How lives are changed by the shortcomings of those in power as well as the bandwagon effect that follows their lead, must be continually examined and corrected if we are to have a country that lives up to its rhetoric.

I am presenting this work of fiction built around historical events of the eighteenth century. Many of the characters actually lived and their contribution (although in many cases based on historical fact), are, nonetheless, simply added to facilitate the presentation of the lives of the less fortunate of the period and the struggles they endured in the building of a new nation. The lives of the famous are well documented in the archives of history, but the common people and their trials are often neglected. Using history and adding imagination has brought this story into being, hopefully to the pleasure of all who choose to read this book.

Some events are repeated demonstrating the different vantage points or views of the characters.

References:

Don't Know Much About American History, by
   Kenneth C. Davis
Encyclopedia Americana
Maine Curiosities, by Tim Sample and Steve
   Bither
Webster's Third New International Dictionary
Benedict Arnold—Revolutionary Hero, by James
   Kirby Martin
The Folk Remedy Encyclopedia, FC&A Medical
   Publishing
New Choices in Natural Healing, Edited by Bill
   Gottlieb, Editor in Chief, Prevention Magazine
   Health books
The Internet
The General Henry Knox Museum
Dorlands Illustrated Medical Dictionary

Special thanks to Colleen Cox for assisting my memory with old time methods of sugar-maple tree tapping and willow whistle making, Lindsay Cameron and Jeanine Milinazzo for portraying "Merci", Lindsay and her brother Matthew for allowing their baby pictures to portray "Aiyana" and "Andrew", Jon Ross Caron for portraying "Lone Wolf" (Pezhik Onindj), Chris Utley for portraying "Jeremiah", Gloria Cookson for allowing her registered black on black Appaloosa "Lucy" to portray "Chevalier Noir", and Donna Herkel for allowing her dog "Fred" to portray Rudy. I would also like to thank Ed and Samantha Kennedy for their assistance with my computer skills, (or lack thereof.)

Buck Monument

The Curse

Many have lied and many have died
And many a story been told,
Some of it true, but it's up to you
To find truth as the pages unfold.
If it's love that you seek you will find it
Along with betrayal and grief,
And as you peruse through these pages
Perhaps you will change your beliefs.
So open your eyes and open your heart
And grieve for the sadness found here,
For love is as fleeting as dust in the wind
While the curse of revenge perseveres.

Chapter I

1756

In Quebec City, high above the St. Lawrence River where the Ursulines' Monastery and Convent was established years earlier, a brave young nun sought and gained audience with the Bishop, and with great courage made the trek through the narrow streets of Sault au Matelot and Sous le Cap, past the brewery and on to the Notre Dames des Victoires chapel to voice her request.

"Your Eminence, I and my fellow Sisters wish to establish a convent in the northern tip of the territory called "Maine", a part of the Massachusetts colony. We wish to provide refuge for travelers and to promote Christianity among the trappers and natives of the area. We would greatly appreciate your indulgence and support in this endeavor. Our cause might be unorthodox but we feel there is a need until a church can be established at Rivie`re-du-Loup, and hopefully our convent could eventually become a true church of the diocese."

"Sister, I commend your ambition but you are obviously unaware of the dangers such a venture would present."

"We trust in our Lord and Savior to guide and protect us. We have prayed without ceasing for guidance and truly believe it is our calling. We will gladly brave any danger and ask only for a minimum of help and your Blessing."

The Bishop rose from his chair and strode to the window overlooking the river, hands clasped behind his back. He felt that granting this request was unwise, that there would be no way a few Sisters could survive in the wilderness, let alone accomplish any good, and that his compliance would probably seal their doom. On the other hand, nothing was impossible if God willed it. Being an instrument of God was not always a comfortable position. After a long moment he turned, walked back to his desk and sat down.

With quill in hand he moved a sheet of paper to the center of the desk and with a sigh of resignation, began to write. Sister Margarite remained very quiet, hardly daring to breathe. The Bishop continued to write for what seemed an eternity, and with many dips into the ink well, he at last sprinkled sand on the writings and sat back in his chair.

"Very well, then, but be advised I consent with much trepidation. I have written an order for guides and builders to assist you, but they will return in two years and you will be left to become self-sufficient. This is all I can offer you at this time. Our priests make regular visits to Rivie`re-du-Loup and they will check on your progress."

"Your Eminence, it is more than we could have hoped for and we are thankful for your assistance. We will do all we can to prove your generosity well deserved. You will be forever in our prayers in gratitude for your faith in our endeavor."

With that, Sister Margarite left the Bishop and within the week, supplies, guides and workers had been assigned to the making of the new outpost of the church, and the long northeasterly trek to Maine had begun.

CHAPTER II

1758

The eight monks and workers had quickly cut timber and built sturdy cabins by the stream that gurgled its way to Eagle Lake. The ground was rich and moist, perfect for the crops they would be planting, the abundance of smooth stones found there were made into chimneys and the compound had quickly taken shape. The buildings were arranged in sequence, facilitating easy access to all sections in winter. With the Sisters' quarters at one end, the chapel in the center and a long shed for storage at the other where wood stacks were protected from the weather, it contained an apartment above where the workers had quartered. The final building was a large barn with a loft in two sections, one for hay storage and one for travelers. Three healthy cows grazed in the cleared field and a sturdy steer had been brought for plowing in the spring. In a separate fenced pasture four bleating sheep nibbled tender grass sprouts to convert into fluffy wool coats while two brown and white goats with small bell-like tassels on their cheeks frolicked in the front yard and kept the area in the front of the compound clean and neat. A small secure hen house was also built with an attached scratching yard for six hens with a cock to keep them happy, together providing eggs and a cheerful good morning with the rising of the sun. The barn was a large safe haven for all the animals at night. It was, indeed, quite a commune.

The Sisters were appreciative of the help in building their compound, but relieved when the workers left at last and they could adjust to being on their own, with a promise to the church that their mission would help all in need that might come their way. With all the problems, dangers and anticipated work that would lie ahead, still, the Sisters were jubilant. They were free from past agonies, they were serving a loving God who accepted them as they were, and they in turn accepted the challenge of doing His work. Truly, they served a merciful God. They decided to call their mission the "Amitie le Christ," ("Friends of Jesus").

1760

At the small French convent near the Canadian border an unwed mother had screamed for mercy as she lay dying, and in her dying it had been granted. The Sisters believed she was naming the child while thanking God that the infant lived, and not just a plea for absence of pain. The Sisters baptized the child "Mary Catherine Merci."

The Gift

At the sound of the newborn's wail Margarite felt a strange sensation, as though her breasts were swelling and tingling, followed by wetness that soaked her undershirt. At first she didn't understand what might have happened, but gradually the dawn of a miracle entered her mind. By the Grace of God, in His infinite wisdom, manna from Heaven had been provided for the child. The milk that flowed from Margarite was a thing of wonder. That God should manifest his love in such a way had at first confused the Sisters, but when they realized it was a gift to save one of his children they accepted it, and in great wonderment watched as Sister Magarite, who would never give birth, was granted the opportunity to enjoy motherhood. As Sister Margarite gave nourishment to their foundling, they glowed with happiness and gratitude for God's mercy in providing a miracle to save their child.

CHAPTER III

For Merci, growing up with the Friends of Jesus was normal, normal in the way that all lives are lived with some hardships and some happiness. The loving arms of Sister Margarite were always there to hold and comfort her whenever she was hurt or sick or hungry. In her childhood she would never realize how very young Sister Margarite was and never aware of her comforter's physical pain.

The Friends were a cohesive bunch, all coming from different backgrounds and harboring their own demons they hoped the mission they had undertaken, (that of giving aid to others), would resolve.

Margarite was born club-footed to parents living in poverty who had hoped for a stalwart son to work the farm with the two brothers already in their teens. She had suffered through her obvious inadequacies, but became unable to longer cope with the constant reminders of her failing to contribute to the family welfare and the improbability of her ever finding a husband to care for her. Seeing herself as merely a burden to be grudgingly tolerated, she decided to leave and make her own life, and chose the life of a nun. At the seminary she had been joined by other novices, misfits from a demanding society, and together they made plans. They would make their own way and shun the world that had caused their suffering.

Margarite knew how to farm, and limped her way through the seasons, pushing the plow behind the swarthy steer, digging, planting, and harvesting. Her broad face and kind eyes reflected love and satisfaction from her heart, and her understanding personality handled any problems that arose, mediating any dissention between the sisters, quickly resolving every problem with an impartial resolution. Her crippled feet were no hindrance to her leadership and her authority was never questioned. Not even by Sister Iris, who at times had let her own miserable past control her mind. A victim of taunting by cruel children because of an unfortunate facial deformity, she was often tempted to criticize others in retaliation, a subconscious need to "pay back" the world around her and elevate her own self-esteem by transferring her pain to others. In her great wisdom Margarite would gently correct Iris, put her loving arms around her and remind her how much God loved her and how He would want her to pass His love on to others. Usually it was a "quick fix", and not very long lasting but Margarite only sighed and saved some patience for the next episode.

Sister Delphia was the cook. Incest had scarred her but she had comforted herself with food. She was round and jolly and lighthearted. By casting out her devils when she ran off to the seminary, she joined the small group of friends and found a way to heal as she served others. The combination of jollity and cooking ability endeared her to all. Even Margarite basked in her praise of the vegetables and herbs (though sometimes she feared her enjoyment of praise might be a small sin).

Jolene kept the house clean, really clean. She had not revealed the tribulation that haunted her soul; she had kept it between herself and God. Sometimes Margarite had to stop Jolene from scrubbing the sanctuary and demand that she take time to rest. As leader, she wisely did not question the girl, but accepted her as she was. If Jolene ever wanted to reveal her reasons for adopting their way of life she would listen and understand, but for now, Jolene could work her way to contentment in the only way she knew how, and the sanctuary was VERY clean.

Marti wove. She gathered the wool from the sheep every spring and spent hours carding and spinning the soft fibers into yarn for sweaters and thread for weaving. Everyone knitted their own sweaters, caps, mittens and socks in their quiet time. They were so adept at the craft that candlelight was sufficient for the task. Marti wove her fine thread into homespun from which their frocks were made. In the two years since their arrival near Eagle Lake some of their clothing was beginning to wear, so there was a reckoning as to who needed the next item of clothing. As the sheep multiplied there was less care in the division of goods. The clothing was sometimes itchy, but warm, and in time one became accustomed to the scratchy fabric. Having little comparison, its rough texture was easily tolerated.

Sarah and Iris had been friends since childhood and worked together acting as one, willing and quiet and steadfast in the security they found in the Sisterhood. Their closeness was not questioned but accepted with grace and charity. They never protested doing any job presented to them and their work could never be criticized, so loyal and true was their calling.

The final member of the group was Catherine, the keeper of the farm animals. She laboriously hand cut the grasses in summer, storing the sun dried hay in the barn loft above the cattle and sheep stalls to be sure there would be plenty of feed during the long winter months. With the help of Rudy, (the collie so generously given them by the monks), she guarded the small herd from predators, bringing them into the barn at any sign of danger announced by the ever watchful dog. Each animal was carefully inspected each night to be sure they were healthy, brushed, fed and watered, as Catherine knew the Sisters very existence might depend on the milk and wool they provided as well as the healthy increase of the herd by their proper breeding. Joyfully, the cows had been bred before they made the journey to Maine and one had given birth to a healthy bull calf assuring future producing ability.

CHAPTER IV

1761

The Amitie le Christ welcomed any traveler, offering food and a night's lodging in the warm barn loft. Their kindness and compassion had become so appreciated they had no fear of harm from any trapper or native traveling through the area on their way to Quebec or up the St. Lawrence for passage on working boats that traversed the great river. Their prayers for protection from the Almighty were answered, and those who might have caused them harm feared and respected the Power that was their protectorate. Many visited the convent, some with gifts or lingering a day or so, lending help with a fence or chopping a pile of wood or some other helpful act.

But one gift was different. When Merci was just barely three years old two Penobscots arrived late one cold winter evening, pulling the chain that hung by the sanctuary door to ring the brass bell within. They were bearing not a gift of furs or corn or offer of work, but like themselves, bundled in fur and doeskin, they carried a small wriggling bundle of life. A tearful mother held the bundle forward, and as the hooded rabbit fur wrap fell back, a dark eyed child about two years old emerged. With thick black hair and shining white teeth he raised his small fist from the fur that was restraining him and looked about at the surprised faces of the Sister before him.

"Pezhik Onindj,"* the mother said. "You take Pezhik Onindj" and as soon as she had thrust the baby in Sister

Margarite's arms the couple quickly left, traveling swiftly into the woods and disappearing into the night on their snowshoes. Bewildered as to why the young couple would tearfully give up so precious a child she sat down on the nearest bench in the chapel, and Merci, upon hearing the sound of voices, left her warm bed and ran to Margarite's side.

"Oh, Sister!" the precocious Merci exclaimed. "Look at his dark eyes, and his hair stands on end like *le porce`pic*. Let me hold him, *sil vous plaie*!

Laughing, they unwrapped the child who was indeed a boy, but sadly, they discovered the reason he had become a foundling. One small hand was perfect, but one small wrist ended with no hand at all. They both felt tears welling in their eyes.

* Pezhik Onindj—pronounced "Pez-ik Ninch"

"Never mind, Merci. He has come to us to be loved and cared for. He would not have survived rigorous native life. His *me`re* and *pe`re* knew we would care for him and protect him. Run and fetch a small pan of goat's milk. He will soon be hungry. They have brought him now because he is weaned, and look at his strong teeth! Bring a bit of mashed potato along with the milk. Soon he will eat whatever we have, but we must be careful at first. He is not used to our food."

"Pezhik Onindj." Margarite mulled the words over in her mind. Since they had been in Maine she had learned a lot of the Algonquin language, but she had been taken off guard. "Pezhik Onindj"—"one hand." We will call you "Thomas", little one, and we will baptize you "Thomas un Main" as those are the words your mother last spoke to you."

Merci became his constant little surrogate mother, and his every smile, and every new achievement filled her with glee. His first stuttering words caused such an uproar the sisters had to all gather and listen to his new vocabulary as though the event had never happened in another family. The Sisters' hearts warmed at the miracle that had come to be amongst them and they all doted on the child. He grew as much on their love as the food he was given. Pezhik Onindj had become Thomas, another beloved child of all the Sisters who would never bear children of their own.

The many days of sunshine, the long winter snows, all found the children of Amitie le Christ happily roaming about the compound, learning chores and learning to be a family. When they were seven and eight years old they decided to build a slide. They had plenty of time for play after they had studied and performed all the duties assigned to them. The Sisters were determined "their children" would become responsible members of the convent and also learn the skill that would enable them to care for themselves later on. On this particular day they had found a board that had bark on one side but was fairly smooth, except for the marks from the cross cutting saw on the other. It, and several that were not needed for their project had been neatly stacked in the barn behind the animal cribs. Dragging it out, they happily walked in line with the long board carried proudly on their shoulders, thinking that Sister Margarite would think them so clever at entertaining themselves. Checking the apple trees to find one with the right height to give the board the proper slant for a good slide they propped it against the limb, then made sure the bottom end was securely wedged into the ground. Standing back and admiring their work they decided to give it a try, thinking that it would be almost as much fun as snow sliding in winter.

"Here, Merci, I will give you a boost up the tree," and Thomas held his wrist with his good hand as a cradle for her to step on for a lift. Up she went to the limb, and grasping the tree with one arm she put her feet over the end of the board and sat down. Whoosh! Away she slid down the board—but her shrieks were not of delight but of pain.

"Merci! What is wrong? What is wrong?"

"My derriere! Oh, Thomas!" And as tears rolled down her face she clutched her bottom.

"No, no, you cannot see. *Non, non,*" and she ran to the sanctuary to find Sister Margarite with Thomas close behind.

Sobbing, she tried to tell the Sister who could see no visible signs of injury.

"I am to blame, Sister, I am to blame. She has hurt her derriere!"

"What have you done, Thomas?" Expecting the worst, she demanded, "What have you done to Merci?"

Then Thomas began to cry. "I made the slide, so it is my fault. The board was too rough and I think it has given her splinters."

"Splinters? Come, Merci, and you, Thomas, do away with the slide *si'l vous plait.*"

Taking Merci to the Sister's sleeping room, she sat on the bed, placed Merci face down on her lap and pulled down her bloomers. There they were, about twenty bloody little splinters. Reaching for her sewing basket she withdrew a needle and one by one she removed the embedded slivers of wood from the yelping, crying child.

"Wait here," she commanded, and Sister Margarite went to the wine cupboard, brought back a bottle of elderberry wine usually saved for communion and splashed it on the bare bottom, pulled the bloomers up and sent her on her way.

As soon as the child left the room Margarite threw her hands in the air, then folded her arms across her stomach and rocked with laughter. What would those two think up next! At least there was no permanent damage from this adventure. Oh, her children were such joy. Even when they got into trouble they were her heart's delight!

Thomas was eight before he questioned Merci as to why everyone had two hands and he, only one.

"Because you are special, Thomas. You are so clever God gave you only one because it is all you need." She would be required to reiterate this many times over the years, but gradually he seemed content and accepted himself the same as they. No small boy was ever so loved as Thomas un Main, and it surprised Merci when early one morning as they sat by the stream that ran beside the compound watching the sun burst through the fringed boughs of the evergreens on its daily journey across the sky, that Thomas suddenly implored, "Merci, my name is Thomas un Main, my birth name was Pezhik Onindj. Must I be "One Hand" always? Can I be "Lone Wolf"? If I am Indian, I want to be a real Indian, not a one hand Indian."

Taken aback because of the realization that her beloved companion had been carrying the pain of his deformity within, she put her arm around his slim shoulders.

"Yes, you can be "Lone Wolf", but it will be just between us. I cannot change your Christian name and the Sisters will always call you "Thomas" and perhaps I, too, will call you Thomas in their presence. I will call you "Lone Wolf" when we are together, for you are brave like a wolf, though you are not alone. To the people of your heritage you will be Pezhik Onindj. They were so sad to leave you here, but they loved you so very much that they brought you here so you would not fall prey to savage men. Many other children have been captured as slaves and you might have been sacrificed if they had captured you. You will be safe here with us."

"But Merci, I cannot always be here, I will need to find my life in the forest when I am grown."

"Yes, Lone Wolf, if it is your desire when you are grown you will be free to leave, but save that decision until the day when you will be able to protect yourself."

"But, Merci, I will never want to leave you. I will always want you with me."

"That is what you think now, but when you become a tall Indian brave you will think differently. I love you like a brother, and I will always keep you close to my heart."

Thomas thought for a few moments before softly saying, "When I am a tall Indian brave I want to marry you, Merci."

"Oh, Thomas Lone Wolf, my little love, you will change your mind when you grow up and I will probably become a Sister and never marry."

"Is it my missing hand that will keep you from loving me?"

"To me you are more than whole and always will be. But never mind. Let us go and tend the rabbits and gather the eggs from the hens before morning vespers!"

Merci and Thomas studied their French, English and Latin, and all the mathematics and geography the Sisters could teach from their limited library. Their well-rounded education would serve them well in future years but it seemed drudgery at the time. Sister Margarite gathered all the knowledge she could from visiting natives in order to prepare Thomas for the day when he might take his place in a world that would not appreciate his ability or education. She was saddened knowing the child they were raising with such care would never be accepted in a society that considered natives to be inferior, and his deformity would make life even more difficult. All she and the Sisters could do was raise him with love and assure him he would always have a home with them. His value increased daily as he learned farming and carpentry and with the leather glove they had fitted to his wrist he had proved to be far from handicapped. Thomas un Main, their child, would always be theirs.

CHAPTER V

Next to fishing in the stream with Thomas, Merci's favorite pastime was feeding and petting the rabbits. The Sisters had originally trapped them for food by laying snares near their burrows and keeping them in hutches. Rabbit stew became a favorite of all and the skins were pieced and made into warm hats and jackets for winter. Merci was thrilled, (frequently, due to the does being such rapid multipliers), when a litter arrived and she could hold and stroke the tiny wiggling newborns. She grieved that they would quickly grow to adulthood and that their demise would be in stew warming her stomach and that she would be wearing their fur when the snows of winter arrived. Margarite assured her that it was the cycle of life and that the rabbits' job was to take care of her as intended by their loving God. It was hard to accept but she refrained from naming them or becoming attached to any of them. "Someday", she thought, "I will have a rabbit for my very own, and I will name it, and I will never eat it. Someday."

There were many things about life that didn't settle easily. She loved honey, but wondered about stealing the food that bees had so laboriously laid up for winter. She knew how hurt and angry the Sisters were when a deer or raccoon raided their vegetable garden so it was hard to justify stealing from the bees. Of course they had built the bee gums and provided storage for the altered nectar and they always left plenty to last the bees through the winter. Sister Catherine explained that the bees just didn't know when to stop gathering from the flowers and if they didn't take a share it would only be wasted. It was their duty to clean out the bee gum, for if they didn't, the bees would not have a clean vault for next year's harvest. Oh, the balance of life could be so confusing!

CHAPTER VI

With the help of Sister Margarite, Merci embarked on a special project. Thomas was old enough to play bagataway. No one had considered the feelings of the small boy sitting on the sidelines of the clearing where they played during recreation time, but Merci had seen the sad brown eyes. How guilty she felt running past the lonely little boy hugging his knees as she and the Sisters ran and laughed as they played. When the day ended she and Margarite wandered into the woods with a hatchet and emerged with a small ash sapling, trimmed of leaves and branches and scraped to a shine. Finding the bag of doeskin they cut strips and braided a sturdy loop, incorporating a limber willow stick from the near-by stream into the braid. Cutting more narrow strips they wove them into a basket. Wetting some stripping, they secured the basket solidly to the end of the stick, knowing that as the leather dried the attachment would become all the more secure. Finally, Merci wrapped the holding end for ten inches to provide a secure grip.

After several days, (when she knew the leather would be dry), Merci called Thomas to accompany her to the barn where the prize awaited.

"Thomas, we have something for you. Here is your very own bagataway stick. See? It has a shorter length so you can easily balance it with one hand!"

In amazement, Thomas reached for the stick. With wonder he looked it all over, then burst into a grateful smile. "Oh, Merci, you have given Lone Wolf his life! I love you *bon ami!*"

"Come. Lone Wolf, I have my bagataway ball in my pocket. We will practice. You are such a fast runner you will be the best in the field!"

Merci and Thomas practiced for an hour before it was time for supper. Merci was amazed by his agility and the quickness of his ability in learning to catch and pass. "Just wait until the next day of La Crosse, Lone Wolf. We will show everyone what a talent you are!

Chapter VII

With the arrival of spring a trader journeying from Quebec was not an unusual event, but the goods he brought were unusual indeed. Along with much appreciated tea, sewing needles and ironware, trotting behind the trader's heavily loaded wooden wagon were two small horses of less than a year old, a black and a white. When the Sisters saw them they collectively ran to their stockpile of honey, rabbit pelts, woolen goods and smoked meat. With flushed faces they quickly counted the supplies, deciding what they absolutely needed or could replace before the following winter. Gathering their bounty they presented their goods to the trader.

"We wish to trade for the ponies," Sister Margarite negotiated. "We feel these items far exceed their value. The riding ponies are very young and must be trained to be of any value, and if you are traveling far they will be exposed to many dangers on the trail. These small horses could become prey to mountain lions or a pack of wolves. If you lost them on a long journey, why, then you would have nothing. These goods we offer are much more easily transported and protected."

BoJean Fargue thought over the proposal, rubbing his whiskers and turning aside. Certainly the value was there, but the animals were of striking beauty. On the other hand, the Sisters' analysis of the dangers was true, and after all, their hospitality had made his stop pleasant on several of his trips. There was always plenty of food and a warm bed in the barn loft. Somewhat reluctantly he made the trade, put the small horses in the barn and prepared to leave the following morning. He hoped the Sisters could manage the animals. They were small now, but he had seen the sire of the black colt and knew that one day he would become a large powerful riding horse. The filly was much smaller but would breed in a few years. The large amount of rabbit pelts alone would have been acceptable in the trade so he left on his journey the following morning with a full stomach, boiled eggs for his lunch and a light heart. What a Blessing the Sisters were to a hungry traveler! All the traders knew them and respected their lifestyle in gratitude for their kindness.

BoJean Farque would never reveal the truth of the matter, that the horses had been sent to the convent by a wealthy merchant who wished to remain anonymous. He had planned to sell them on his trip and now he had done it early on his route. Whistling happily he continued on his trading route, richer, happier and content that the secret origin of the two horses was safe. Yes, the Friends of Jesus were truly a Blessing.

When Merci and Thomas arose they felt a mystery in the air. The previous day they had been gathering firewood from the near-by forest, limbs that had been wrested from the trees during the winter storms. When they returned with their drag loaded with firewood they had found only some leftover stew in the kitchen. Being tired, they had crawled into their loft beds in their sleeping quarters above the connected storage shed where they slept soundly until the sound of the departing wagon of the trader leaving on his journey to the South awakened them. They hadn't seen him arrive but being accustomed to visits from trappers and traders, they recognized the sound of an unfamiliar departing wagon. They didn't really like having their happy lives shared with strangers. The Sisters had read to them about the "Good Samaritan" and explained that they must be their brother's keeper, but it never set just right with them. They were too young to realize that they had been taken in and given a home by the Sisters when they could have been cast aside. The pair would eventually figure it out, but for now, the Sisters only smiled about the foibles of "their children."

During breakfast the bustling about of Sarah and Jolene deemed unusual, and Sister Margarite had a bright twinkle in her eye. Merci and Thomas exchanged "what's going on?" glances, then ate their eggs and muffin and were about to leave to stack the wood they had gathered the day before when Margarite proclaimed, "There will be no wood gathering today. The day will be a Holiday for all. The only task for you children will be to go to the barn and make sure all is well since the trader left."

With that, she turned her back to them, saying, "Run along, you two, if you wish to have the day for play."

Wondering why they were the only ones assigned a task if it were truly to be a Holiday, they resignedly left the table and slowly walked towards the barn. The Sisters gathered by the door of the kitchen, giggling with anticipation as they watched Merci and Thomas as they dragged along towards the barn, then reaching the barn doors, pushing up the locking bar and pulling the doors open.

Squeals of delight from the barn drew the Sisters to the building where the children were hugging and stroking the small animals. Tears streamed down Margarite's face and welled in the eyes of the others. No matter what sacrifices they would be forced to make to replace the traded goods, the moment was worth it all.

"Oh, Sisters, this one is white as wheat bread and her mane like the white caps from the wind on the lake. She is *Petit Bon Mer Pain*—Oh, is she mine? Tell me, is she mine?"

Sternly, Margarite answered. "Yes, Merci. She is your early Christmas gift. You must brush and care for her every day and teach her to be a good riding horse. It will not be easy, and you must do all your other chores as well. But you may spend today getting to know Mer Pain, and she will get to know you. Thomas, have you a name for yours?"

My horse is *Chevalier Noir*. He will be strong and powerful like a black knight. Oh, thank you Sisters. I will train him to be a good horse and we will ride like the wind. We will be your protectors always, like the knights of old, and Merci, I will help you care for and train Mer Pain and I will always take care of you both."

Margarite was surprised by his words. Sometimes it was as though he were the older of the two children. She wondered if his deformity had caused him to mature beyond his years, even though he seemed unhindered physically. Oh, to know the mysteries of life! For now, she and the other Sisters would just enjoy the day, their adopted children and the bounty of all that God had provided.

CHAPTER VIII

As Merci and Thomas continued their happy lives, their play changed from romping about the fields where the daisies and paintbrushes tickled their bare legs and the stubble of cut grasses crunched under their toughened feet in the summertime, (except when Sister Catherine admonished them for trampling and flattening the hay, making it difficult to harvest), to caring for their growing riding ponies who had grown nearly large enough to ride. They fed the chickens, gathered the eggs, washed and bagged the feathers of every chicken they ate until there was enough to make either a pillow or even a feather bed.

The bagataway game they had learned while visiting the children at the Indian village on the other side of Eagle Lake proved to be a wonderful diversion from daily chores. It had become a weekly event at the commune, and finally even reticent Jolene entered the game. They had never seen her smile until the day she "scored", catching the ball from Iris, slipping past Thomas, (not easy), and slinging it into their woven grass goal net. Thomas had become quite formidable on the field so it was quite an accomplishment. In the excitement of the moment they all dissolved into laughter and threw themselves into a pile on the ground. Even Sister Margarite, the scorekeeper, joined the quivering heap and they laughed until someone cried out "Vespers" and they all ran for the chapel.

So was Merci's life complete, loving and secure until "that day."

"That day," life changed for Merci. They had a visiting traveler arrive at the Amitie le Christ. After he had consumed a meal of corn bread, potatoes, squash and baked apples during which time he had watched Merci constantly from the corner of his eye, he requested a meeting with Sister Margarite, followed by a meeting of all the Sisters. Then Merci was called to the chapel. She wondered if she had unintentionally done something wrong.

Timidly, Merci entered the small chapel. Kneeling in the isle between the evenly spaced benches, she humbly crossed herself and then arose and continued to the front of the chapel where she lit a tallow candle, silently asking forgiveness for whatever transgression she had unknowingly committed and then waited. The rustle of soft clothing and a warm hand on her shoulders told her to turn and face a solemn Sister Margarite. Falling on her knees before her surrogate mother, Merci cried, "I implore you to forgive me, Sister, whatever my sin. I beg you to forgive me!"

"Merci, Merci, you have done nothing wrong. It is only that I have a wonderful opportunity for you, *Cherie*. It is time for you to find your way in life. This small convent is for those who have lived out in the world and for many reasons have chosen this life. You have never experienced the world beyond this conclave. When you have seen more of the world and if events convince you to live here with us, we will rejoice in your choosing, but now, my dearest child, you must go. Mr. Renault will be taking you to a wonderful home in Massachusetts where you will be able to work for fine ladies dressed in China silk. You will learn to serve and wait on them and have opportunities to study from many books and you will see and learn about wondrous things. You will even have real tea from England and the Orient to drink, and from dainty teacups made of porcelain. Oh! What marvelous things you will learn! You may even find the love of a fine young man and perhaps raise a family. Oh, Merci, you will be so happy!"

Bewildered, Merci was quiet. She didn't want to leave the only home she had ever known and she certainly had no desire for a fine young man! Oh, she had listened to the readings and recitations from the Holy Bible, and males seemed to be a lot more trouble than they were worth, and they seemed to like wars and fighting. She certainly knew nothing about babies nor did she have any desire for them. As tears began to glisten in her eyes Sister Margarite put her arms about her shoulders, saying, "Come, we must pack your things. Sister Marti has some lovely soft blankets and a finely spun frock for you to wear. I, myself have a newly finished sweater and boggin as well as a hooded shawl of boiled wool that will keep you warm and dry in the coldest of weather. Do not be afraid, my child, you are even going to see the ocean! You are going to a wonderful place by the sea!"

Holding back her own tears caused a lump to form in Sister Margarite's throat until she could hardly speak, but she knew how Thomas felt about Merci and soon his stirrings of manhood might cause trouble. This opportunity for Merci would keep them apart and prevent any accidental pairing at their tender age. Oh, Thomas would be lonely for a little while but he would adjust, she was sure, and soon forget about his emotional attachment to Merci. Yes, this was the best solution for them both.

CHAPTER IX

Jacques Renault had planned to stay for a meal and then quickly move on in his journey to the East Coast but when he saw Merci he knew he could turn the discovery to his advantage. A good windfall would be in his pocket in exchange for a young indentured servant, especially such an attractive young lady as Merci. He wisely did not reveal to the Sisters any hint of monetary exchange, knowing they would never "sell" their beloved protégé. Rather, he offered an opportunity (in false heartfelt good will), with a promise of safe passage to a wonderful life. His smooth manners and expressions of compassion for a girl not old enough to decide if the convent life was meant for her completely beguiled the Sisters, and they would have felt guilty if they had not given her the "freedom" to experience the opportunity afforded her by acquiescing to his suggestion.

And so, with her clothes, blankets and belongings, a fifteen-year old girl was off to her new life, but not before being informed that on the coast her name would be Mercy, with the English spelling. Sister Margarite prayed that her Merci would be granted mercy in her new English controlled life.

Would her new home be wonderful? Merci doubted it, but she had left without a whimper lest she disappoint the Sisters. They truly believed in the vision painted by Mr. Renault, but even her name had been taken from her, so how could she cope with it all? Life had become unfair so suddenly it was almost more than she could stand.

As the wagon joggled and rattled along the tree crowded trail Merci thought about the life she was leaving behind. The quiet prayer hours, the bountiful meals steaming on the table on cold winter days while the wind howled outside, the sweet smell of fresh fir branches in her mattress, their aromatic vapors surrounding her with the freshness of a forest glade, all seemed to linger in her thoughts. Would her bed in her new home smell as fresh as the one she had always known? And what about leisure time, would there be games to play? What fun it had been playing bagataway,— and Thomas. What a thrill it had been to watch his beautiful stride and strong attack of the game!

Her heart was breaking. Everything had happened so quickly. How could she be happy without her dear little friend? He looked so forlorn. She had only a few minutes to say good-by to him and Mer Pain. His eyes sparkled with moisture as he promised to care for Mer Pain until she returned. Merci's only consolation was those words of promise and the faith that some day she would return.

She noticed the slowness of the turning of the leaves. Beginning with just a tinge of color, adding more as the weeks had worn on. The turning had been seemingly reluctant in its changing, a gradual ripening being held back by sunny days. Some trees gave the appearance of having "hunkered down," digging in their roots, refusing to turn from their summertime green, waiting for frost or snow or freezing rain to destroy them in their attempt to cling to summer. She had heard it was warmer near the ocean and wondered if the leaves were turning to red and gold there, also.

Camping by the river for the night Jacques Renault built a fire and advised Mercy to make her bed near its sputtering warmth but she declined. "Mr. Renault, I would prefer *dorm a vous* the wagon," she declared in her broken English, and she quickly spread her blankets in the wagon between the sacks of produce and supplies.

"Jest as well." Jacques decided. The child was too young and skinny to afford him a comfortable fireside frolic. He preferred plumper entertainment like his wife, and he didn't want to deliver Mercy damaged and traumatized. Picking his teeth with a small stick he had whittled from a near-by bush he laughed and folded his blanket over his stocky body and went to sleep.

Mercy's dark eyes held their gaze on Mr. Renault until she saw his mouth open and loud snoring assured her he was sleeping. She wasn't sure what she was afraid of or why she didn't trust him. The Sisters had never mentioned any reason for caution, but there was something uncomfortable about her position and something about him that was very distasteful. She thought perhaps the Sisters had been too trusting. Why hadn't Sister Margarite seen him as she did?—Probably because someone as pure as she was incapable of seeing evil in anyone. Mercy decided that life outside the Friends of Jesus compound was very scary. She was fortunate to have studied English, and though broken with French she didn't like being laughed at every time she attempted to carry on a conversation by this male she deemed untrustworthy. From now on, she decided, she would speak only when spoken to and then with as few words as possible.

She wondered how long it would be before they reached their destination. One thing for sure, tomorrow she would place her feather pillow under her hips on the wagon seat. She was sore and rattled from the wagon's bouncing on the rough trail. At least Mr. Renault seemed to know where he was going and she hoped her suspicions proved untrue. Surely God would take care of her and provide the life Margarite had envisioned.

When she finally drifted off to sleep she dreamed she was under swamp water, face up with the grasses brushing over her and tangling in her hair. There was no way to escape and struggling was useless, so there she remained, waiting for the inevitable cessation of her life. Waking in a sweat as wet as though the dream carried its manifestation into her waking, she wondered if it was a premonition of an event to come or perhaps the revelation of a past life that had ended tragically. She did recall the calmness with which she had faced the dying dream ordeal.

The following day arrived with brilliant sunshine and blue skies. After a breakfast of stale biscuits and water they again mounted the cart and resumed their journey eastward, following the trail beside the St. Croix River. Mercy sat as far away from Mr. Renault as she could without falling off the wagon and kept her mind busy so she would not have to think about her distaste for the man. Her mind drifted back to the only home she had ever known. It had been such fun to live with the diverse group of women, all with their own special talents and problems, but all enjoying charitable Christian love no matter what their idiosyncrasies, living together in self-sufficiency. Whenever traders stopped by for an overnight stay in the barn loft they usually made wonderful swaps. Either knitted goods or woven wool blankets were traded for metal tools or cooking pots and when she was small the Sisters had traded a box of homemade soap for a small cloth bodied doll with carved wooden hands and head and lambs wool hair. She had loved it so much she slept with it on the pillow beside her every night. Only recently had she moved it to the chair beside her bed. Jolene thought she was being spoiled but Margarite assured her that a child needed a toy to love that she might learn what love was. Now she realized how expensive the doll had been. Watching the rendering of fat and then adding just the right amount of wood ash, stirring the pot over the hot fire in the yard near the garden and seeing the sweat run down Delphia's cheeks, convinced Merci that she had truly been loved unconditionally. Now she must be careful to fulfill the Sisters' dreams of a good life. She could not bear to think of letting anything she did be less than what they had expected of her. Perhaps she was only fifteen years old, but she would hold to the principles she had been taught and would forever fight for the dreams of the Friends of Jesus.

PART II

CHAPTER I

When the news of the firing on colonists in Boston by the British Army reached Maine the incident had been greatly modified and exaggerated into a so-called "massacre," when in reality it had been a small skirmish. Outraged by a new tax on imported lead, tea, paper, paint and glass (called "The Townsend Acts"), a group of colonists had gathered outside the Boston Customs House and the British mistakenly fired on the crowd. The situation gave impetus to the growing secret anti-British organization of the American colonists and was a catalyst for the formation of their emerging army. No action would be taken for several years, but preparations for the future had been instigated by this seemingly unjustified act.

When a people suffer oppression small skirmishes assume the importance of large battles. Thus, throughout the colonial world supplies were being stockpiled, arms were being made ready and hearts were being primed for a strike when the time came that the people could stand no more. At the convent Amitie le Christ no one was touched by the events of 1770 or the unrest that followed. Theirs was a world apart and the Sisters had no inkling that Merci would soon be affected by all the problems of a world for which she was unprepared.

CHAPTER II

1775

The journey towards the coast took a roundabout route. Once Mercy and Mr. Renault reached the headwaters of the St. Croix River they followed the trail beside it on to Calais. There Mr. Renault traded goods and sold his horse and wagon. Gaining passage on a fore and aft rigged brigantine whose small crew allowed room for passengers and goods, they followed the coastline, stopping at Machias, where several traders making the same trip traded dried venison for salted cod and boxes of blueberry jam and honey.

It was exciting, watching the ocean that she had read so much about, and when they embarked once more and continued toward their destination Mercy stood on the deck in the brilliant sunlight. Pulling her hood back from her head and letting it fall against her back making a warm thickness about her shoulders, her thick amber hair was blown by the ocean wind, glowing in the sunshine like fresh taffy that turns lighter in streaks as it is buttered and pulled. Short tendrils curled about her face framing her smooth white skin as she looked to windward. Dark eyes below perfectly arched brows gazed at the rough sea with its white caps being tossed by the wind.

"It's magnificent," she thought, so much larger and more powerful than she had ever imagined. But it was not Thomas, it was not the Sisters, it was not Petit le Bon Mer Pain. It was not home.

Approaching Monhegan Island the captain opted not to stop there, saying that the people there were so self sufficient that they seldom dealt with traders. They traveled on through calm seas to the small port of Meduncook with its sandy harbor where the water was so clear one could see the ocean floor in places. As they dropped anchor the captain pointed to a small island to starboard.

"That's Garrison Island," he said. "The small fort there is quite sound and in the past saved many from the attacks of Indians. It can be easily reached at low tide by a road over a rocky ledge that extends from the mainland to the island itself. However, when the tide is high it can only be reached by boat. One cannot pass over the ledge in a large fishing boat or ship lest the bottom be scraped and opened to the sea. Oh, a dory or small craft might make it over at high tide, but very carefully, of course. It is only twenty years since the last Indian attack. Most of the Meduncook residents fled to the garrison for safety when the savages came, all except poor James Bradford. He believed his family was safe from the Indians, having previously saved Chief Moxie from drowning in a fall through the ice. Unfortunately, he, his wife and several children were killed and scalped except for one daughter who had hid under a bed but crawled out to grab the baby and run for the garrison. She took a tomahawk in the back but thanks to it being low tide, she was able to reach safety. She survived the horrible wound, even raised a large family, so I heard, somewhere in Vermont."

Garrison Island

Merci listened attentively to everything the captain had to say. It was hard to believe that Indians would do such a thing. The natives at home were all friendly and would never think of doing harm. And Thomas, he was an Indian and his weapons were for hunting, not for hurting. Oh, how she missed him! She would have this great learning experience since it was the will of the Sisters, then she would return home to Eagle Lake.

The stop at Meduncook was very pleasant, sunny and breezy, gulls calling, the air mingling sea smells with fir and balsam, the busy docks alive with fishermen putting in and out with their little fishing boats, small white sails puffed with the fragrant winds. They took on some dried cod and some fresh clams and lobster which they stored in a small pound in the hold. They would trade or sell the seafood at the next stop or let the crew feast if they found no buyer. The captain was good to his crew and therefore they were a happy and friendly bunch. They had eyed Merci in a way that made her nervous, but the captain had given them a little talk so it went no further. All in all, the trip thus far had not been unpleasant, except for the distrust Merci held for Mr. Renault.

They circled back and the stop at Thomaston was the last stop for Merci. She had not been informed that her journey was over, but she realized it when her bag of clothes and goods were unloaded on the dock. Mr. Renault left her there bewildered and alone. He couldn't risk her protests when she discovered she was sold as a bonded servant, in the event she understood such a position. She had no idea of the deal being made at the large house in the town center.

A smiling Jacques Renault returned and advised Mercy that a carriage would soon come for her, and he quickly re-boarded the ship as it prepared to set sail. A happy man, he had sold Mercy into a five-year bondage as an indentured servant and the music of the coins jingling in his pocket was very pleasant. It had been, for him, a very profitable trip.

CHAPTER III

Mother Clarke was pleased. She had needed more help at the big house, it was too much for poor Allie Tuttle to keep clean and Rachel, her cook, could also use a little help. A girl educated in a convent would be a fine addition to the household workers. She assumed the girl would be well trained in servitude, probably either very overweight or pitifully ugly. A child left at a convent would be expected to have some imperfection, but having been assured the girl was young, hardworking and English speaking had convinced her to pay the rather exorbitant price Mr. Renault had demanded. An opportunity to acquire an indentured servant in Maine did not arrive very often.

Calling her son, she instructed him to drive the carriage to the dock.

"Jeremiah, we have acquired a new servant. Please go to the dock for her. She is young and may not be comfortable at first, so be kind to her. She may be reclusive so do all you can to reassure her that she will be treated well."

"Very well, Mother, I will do my best. By the way, the goods that came on the brigantine today must be logged in and accounted for. They are safely stored in the barn and I will attend to their sorting and cataloguing when I return."

"That is fine, Jeremiah. There is no rush with business matters. The trading post has done well this year and your carefully kept books have helped make wise dealings. You could run our businesses by yourself if needed. Come kiss me good-by and be on your way."

Jeremiah harnessed up the horse to the smallest carriage assuming a girl from a nunnery would (rightly so) have few possessions. The bay trotted through town, happy to leave the confines of the stable for an outing. He was a spirited animal but Jeremiah was a good driver and kept him under control.

Approaching the dock he was surprised to see no one about, only a small forlorn form sitting on a small bag of goods. Tying the horse to a piling that protruded above the planks of the wharf he approached the small figure.

"Miss, are you the girl I am to take to my mother?"

"I do not know Monsieur. Mr. Renault told to wait here until someone comes for me, so I can only assume it is I you are looking for."

"I'm sure it is you that I seek. Are you from the Friends of Jesus convent?"

"*Oui, Monsieur.*"

"Then come along. Here, let me carry that for you," and picking up the bag he returned to the carriage with the frightened girl following.

"Up you go," he smilingly offered and quickly put his hands on her waist and boosted her into the carriage.

Noticing tears sprinkling on her cheeks, he consoled. "Now, don't cry. Everything will be all right. This must all be so new to you. You will find my mother is kind and loving and very good to her help. By the way, my name is Jeremiah. What is yours?"

"Merci", I mean, "Mercy", I assume you will wish it pronounced in English."

"I have no preference, but I am sure most everyone will call you "Mercy," and so, I, too, will call you "Mercy."

"Thank you, Monsieur, I mean, "Sir." Forgive my poor English. I have had little practice but I will work hard to improve."

"I'm sure you will, Mercy, I'm sure you will."

Jeremiah was amazed. Never had he seen such large wide-set eyes in such a small face. Her slight build had rendered her light as a feather when he had lifted her into the carriage. The taffy hair fighting its way for its freedom from her closely tied bonnet lost wisps to the breeze of the carriage motion as the bay trotted through the streets.

Timidly, Mercy offered, "I have a horse. Her name is Mer Pain. I will see her again next year when I go home."

MerPain

Jeremiah

"Poor girl," Jeremiah thought. She doesn't seem to understand she is under bond for five years. He wondered what circumstances had brought her to Thomaston without knowledge of her indentured position. He decided not to press or reveal any of the facts at the time. If she didn't know she was an indentured servant perhaps she was not as bright as his mother had been made to believe. Her wide-eyed beauty would make up for a lot. There was something appealing about the slight body in the simple woolen frock with a matching bonnet that in their simplicity were a perfect background for her innocent looks and polite demeanor. He hoped she would prove to be a good worker. He hated to see his mother cheated in her dealings. Her good heart sometimes allowed her being taken advantage of.

Upon their arrival at the house, Mother Clarke welcomed Mercy, showed her the sleeping quarters she would be sharing with Allie Tuttle and the facilities for bathing and private care. It was all too much to digest in one day. She was given supper in the kitchen with Rachel (the cook) and after being advised to get a good night's sleep she bathed, (at last!) and donning her night clothes, she fell fast asleep. She would learn of her duties in the morning, but the relief of the long arduous journey being over had not stemmed her exhaustion.

As Mercy lay in the clean bed provided for her she mulled over the day, and thought about the wonderful house she was now to call her home for awhile. "Clarke House," they called it, and it had real glass windows, not the oiled cloth coverings used at the convent. The oiled cloth kept out the flies and let in light, but real glass allowed one to see the world outside, which oiled cloth did not.

The kitchen where she had eaten such a wonderful meal of biscuits and stew had a black iron sink that had been greased to prevent its rusting. She recognized the process as Thomas had always greased their precious iron plow and the knives and tools they used at the convent. Water could be poured directly into the sink and by pulling a plug the liquid drained out a pipe that led to a rock filled pit in the yard in back of the house. It was unlike the wooden box sink Mercy was accustomed to using, that held basins to be emptied outside. The water pail sat to the left of the sink with a dipper hanging on a hook above. The Sisters had used a carved out gourd for a dipper but this one was of gleaming copper. The cook explained these workings to an amazed Mercy, and then showed her the oven built into the chimney for baking bread and cakes while the stew-pot boiled and simmered over the fire in the fireplace. No pan bread here. Everything was so amazingly convenient it would be an astonishing and exciting revelation she would take home next year.

The following morning Mercy arose to the friendly chatter of Allie Tuttle. She was anxious to show Mercy about as Mother Clarke had given Allie the job of helping the new servant learn her way around the huge house. The servant's quarters were on the third floor, spacious, comfortable and clean. Rachel went to her own home across town every night, returning each morning with her huge shopping basket filled with foodstuffs for the day. She shopped at the Clarkes' own store and thoroughly enjoyed the freedom to choose whatever she wished for the day's meals.

The two men servants who tended the grounds, gardens and barn slept in their quarters over the stables and did not have much contact with the house servants. This arrangement suited Mercy just fine, having grown up with a family of all women, except for Thomas. To her, men were transient travelers and traders, and after her nervous trip to the coast, she had little use for them. The friendly monk who stopped at the convent was not considered part of the male society in her mind. So jovial and kind, always telling stories about Quebec and Rivie`re du Loup, and funny tales that kept everyone laughing and in a happy mood. When he brought the message last year from the Bishop that the Sisters' dedication and hard work had earned the Amitie` le Christ accepted status as a true convent of the church they had celebrated with elderberry wine that was usually saved for communion and with much feasting. They had roasted a young rooster, (he had wanted to be the cock of the walk, the center of attention, and he got his wish) served with new potatoes, green beans, peas and turnips, and corn bread cakes with plenty of fresh butter. Fre`re Alfred had eaten and drank until he couldn't stand so the Sisters covered him with a blanket and let him sleep in his chair until morning. When they sounded the gong calling everyone to morning prayers, the rotund Fre`re jumped up and laughingly joined them in their praise to God. So Mercy's contact with males had been limited and she was in no hurry to change her thoughts on the matter.

The third floor also housed the children's rooms when they were growing up. They were unused now except when the grandchildren arrived for visits. Rosemary, Bridgette and Jeremiah, with Jeremiah the youngest, had enjoyed their separate rooms as they outgrew the nursery, and the play room still contained rocking horses, dolls, blocks and books, small wagons and doll beds with their little coverlets in place and a small silver tea service on a child sized table and little chairs. The toys amazed Mercy and she thought of her own doll. She had meant to bring it with her but in the rush to depart it had been left behind. She hoped someone found it and was saving it for her. There was also a linen room on the third floor where neatly folded sheets, towels and blankets filled shelves along the walls. One of the chimneys passed through the linen room where a fireplace allowed sad irons to be heated. It was quite a trek from the laundry in the back of the house on the main floor. The sheets and clothing billowed in the ocean breeze on the lines and when they dried they were carried up the servants' stairs to the third floor to be pressed and put away. The clothing was ironed in the laundry room and hung on racks until they were delivered to the second floor bedrooms.

The family quarters on the second floor were quite astonishing. Never had Mercy imagined such luxurious furniture and bedding. Beds and dressers of carved mahogany held the belongings of the elder Clarkes. The bed was glowing with a satin comforter that was so soft and thick it was like a huge mushroom, and ruffled pillows were piled at the head. Each room had a large closet and Allie gave Mercy a peek at the wardrobe of the lady of the house. Dresses with panniers made of fine silk in lovely pastels, fur trimmed shawls, plumed bonnets. Her everyday dresses were of the finest woven fabrics in rich colors with pearl buttons and bobbin lace collars and cuffs.

The master suite also had a dressing room and sitting room. The sitting room was an inviting respite with flowered tapestries, soft chairs, footstools, and cupboards filled with books and memorabilia.

Jeremiah's room was "off limits", but Allie pushed the door just a crack so that Mercy could see a bed with striped blankets, polished boots in a corner and on a large desk, huge ledger books with one open where from her vantage point she could just barely see the many neat entries meticulously written with the quill by the inkwell in the corner of the massive desk.

The main floor was more formal. The huge entry room housed dark red fabric covered furniture, polished mahogany stands on which sat large ferns, their fronds dripping gracefully from each pot, the pots themselves of Chinese porcelain. Large figurines of knights and their ladies graced the corners of the room while oriental rugs were carefully placed over polished oak floors.

The dining room also had an oriental look with gleaming black lacquered table, chairs and two sideboards. Massive china cabinets were filled with delicate English bone china sets and pewter tea services stood ready for use. Silver flatware filled the drawers below the glass-fronted cabinets and linen tablecloths and embroidered napkins were neatly stacked in the sideboard storage spaces. Silver candlesticks sat on the marble topped sideboards and a matching candelabra graced the top of the table that could easily seat twelve couples.

As soon as Mercy saw the library she knew it was her favorite room in the whole house. Shelf upon shelf was filled with every kind of book in English and French, even some in Latin. She hoped she would be allowed to read and study if she had leisure time. She was beginning to realize she might not just be a visitor there and her wonderful new life was going to be that of a servant, and though she had not been advised of the particulars she feared she was not going to enjoy a lot of freedom.

The happiest room in the house was next to the kitchen. The family ate their regular meals there in the casual atmosphere of flowery fabric at a round cherry table. Comfortable lounge chairs invited relaxation and conversation. The room was warm and inviting and although as neat and clean as the rest of the house, it had a "lived in" feeling. Allie informed Mercy that they were to eat in the kitchen with Rachel and after each meal they were to take meals to the hired help housed in the barn. To Mercy's relief, Allie informed her that she would retain that chore as it had always been her duty.

There were three sets of stairs in the mansion. The grand staircase at the front receiving room was double sided. From the center back of the room a staircase arose on each side of the room like the wings of a butterfly. It took Mercy's breath away the first time she saw it. She had never imagined anything so grand. The ornately carved dark mahogany spindles and smooth banisters, the oak steps edged in the same mahogany as the rail and both staircases reaching the landing of the hallway above. Another set of stairs led to the back of the rooms on the second floor. It was smaller and led directly to the hallway outside the master suite. Mercy noticed that as she approached the stairs and took a few upward steps there was a distinctively pleasant odor like no other part of the house and as she climbed further and reached the halfway landing she placed her hand on the smooth round sphere that marked the beginning of the second set of stairs. Sensing the aroma intensifying the further she climbed she realized it was a mingling of flower scented powders and perfumes, bouquet of cedar emanating from the closets, all from the dressing room of the lady of the house. The pleasant fragrances reminded her of the all the times she had put her nose to apple blossoms and wood flowers. She decided not to venture up that stairway any more often than she could help. It was too painful a reminder of home. Besides, it was Mother Clarke's private domain and she felt like an intruder. Turning, she walked back down the stairs and entered the kitchen. Allie had shown her the whole house and from now on she would use the third set of stairs, those that led from the kitchen, past the landings that exited to each floor, and up to her own room on the third floor. If she planned to live here it would be best if she kept her place. Mercy was learning very quickly. Allie was fun to be with. She was not well educated but she had a kind heart and Mercy was grateful to have her as her newly found friend. Perhaps this experience wasn't going to be so bad, she could accept it for a year or so, and then she would go home.

CHAPTER IV

Back at the Amitie le Christ an unexpected stillness settled over the convent. The flurry of activity when the Sisters were readying Merci for her trip followed by settling back into their regular routines was an explanation at first. Sister Margarite noticed the gradual solemnity creeping into the atmosphere. No one went about their work joyfully as before. Their joy was gone, and they were not sure where or how to find it. There was always one Sister or another in the chapel, and when they emerged with reddened eyes their pain was obvious. The sound of silence had settled over the Friends of Jesus, and the Sisters found themselves speaking in whispers. Even prayers that were usually spoken aloud were offered in soft murmers. It was as though a great tragedy had struck and a time of mourning had begun. Their elation over Merci's great good fortune had been short lived and somehow had not been what they had anticipated, and though they constantly rationalized their complicity in her leaving, they found their thanks to God for her great opportunity morphing into prayers for her safety, and eventually prayers for forgiveness if they had contributed in any wrongdoing. Never had they felt such confusion and pain as the cold fear that had crept into their hearts. The unknown sin they harbored created the hush as each Sister dealt with her feelings individually, none daring to voice the fear they felt, and Thomas suffered most of all.

CHAPTER V

While the war for independence escalated from the beginning dissatisfaction with British rule to threats, the Declaration of Independence was signed and finally full-scale war erupted. At the convent Amitie le Christ a boy was growing up. His feelings for his childhood companion had changed from that of brother to something different. The girl who had been his sister was no longer a sister. She was simply, or not so simply, "Merci". The suddenness of her leaving had shocked and confused him. In a day he changed from a carefree boy to the person he would be. It took time for him to sort out the deluge of changed feelings that crowded his mind. He had discovered the injustices of life were beyond his control, but time changed everything, and he planned to gain as much control over his life as he could.

As Merci and Mr. Renault left the Friends of Jesus convent Thomas had stood for a long time after they were out of sight, looking steadfastly at the opening in the forest glade where the marked trail to places beyond looked dark and ominous. The incredulity of events left him speechless and motionless. Now, beyond tears, the shock of his shattered life rendered him helpless. Rudy sat beside the devastated boy, remaining quietly by his side, there for consolation when it could be accepted.

Finally, Thomas slowly walked to his room next to the one that had belonged to Merci. Looking through the doorway at the emptiness left behind he spied something under her bed. Entering, he reached down and retrieved

Merci's doll, the doll she had always cherished and cared for, keeping it on the chair near her bedside when she had outgrown playing with it. Straightening its clothing, realizing she surely had not meant to leave something so dear to her heart, he clutched it to his chest and walked slowly to his room. He felt it was a sign she would return, and then, with the doll close to his face he realized he could smell a familiar odor. It was the scent of Merci. Inhaling the familiar aroma of his dearest friend the tears finally escaped his eyes and he sat on the floor with legs crossed, tilted his head back and moaned as the salted drops ran down his face and onto his chest where he held the only part of Merci that he could still touch.

Rudy crept forward on his haunches, inching forward until he rested his head on Thomas' knees, rolling sad eyes up at him in commiseration.

Through Thomas' head raced all the days they had spent together in such happiness—bagataway, picking apples and berries, brushing and petting Mer Pain and Chevalier Noir, leading them about the yard and watering them in the stream. In winter they had slid down the small hill beyond the barn on grass mats, sliding, sliding until they reached the frozen stream and slid along between the rocky banks. They even gave Rudy rides and away down the hill they went, Rudy's ears laid back from the rush of air as they flew down the grade. They would come in from the cold to cups of hot cider and then after supper the three of them slept by the fireplace as the Sisters felt it best they sleep there rather than their unheated rooms above the shed. They had loved having Rudy enjoy the winter rest and only being a companion and watchdog for his people, but when the first green sprigs of grass peeked through the snow he became anxious to resume his patrol of the pastured animals.

These and all the other adventures they had shared raced through his mind until at last he slept, with Rudy warm against him in his instinctive way of giving comfort. "That day" changed Thomas forever from the carefree boy he had been.

In the days that followed Thomas began to think of himself more and more as "Lone Wolf." Taking the box of deer hair he had saved from the tanning of hides and setting it on the stool by his bed, he then carefully selected from his scraps of deer hide enough of the pieces to make a bagataway ball. The French word for bagataway was "La Crosse," but in his mind it would always be the original native "bagataway." Making several frustrating tries before he was able to design a pattern that would create a round ball the right size, it took several days of concentration before he was ready to put it together. Piercing the edges of the carefully measured and cut swirls of leather, he laced it together with stout hairs from the tails of Chavelier Noir and Mer Pain. Leaving an opening on one side he began filling it with the deer hair, packing it firmly in the opening. Reaching under his pillow he retrieved the doll Merci had left behind and with his knife cut a small amount of wool hair from the doll's head and placed it in the center before completing the fill, then laced the opening closed.

BAGATAWAY BALL

Cut the two pieces of leather.
Match the notches, large end "A" to "A" of second piece and "B" to "B".
Sew edges together with horsehair in cross-stitch, always placing stitches
from the outside to the inside of the edge, leaving a space for stuffing. Fill
with tightly packed deer hair, placing an inchworm, flea or other "medicine"
in the center. Sew closed.

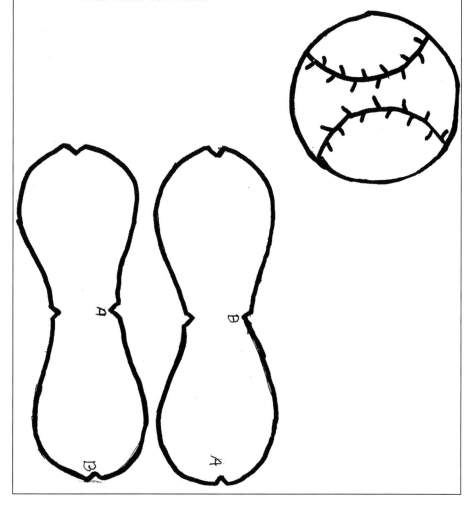

While Thomas was spending the first days following Merci's departure in seclusion, Margarite, Jolene and Catherine all tried to lure him from his room above the shed with food and kind words to no avail.

"Thomas, look what we have made for you, corn biscuits and fresh butter. Come, come and eat!"

"Thomas, come to vespers! It will make you feel better! You should be happy your friend has gone to a wonderful place. Come and pray for her and thank God for her good fortune!"

"Thomas, we need your help, come and help us with the clearing of a new garden space!"

All efforts were fruitless. The only movement he made was to feed and water Mer Pain and Chevalier Noir. After a week, he emerged. Leading the two horses he walked in the direction he had last seen Merci, then stopped at the edge of the woods. He stroked Chevalier Noir, then Mer Pain. Finally laying his head against the soft hair of the white filly tears again rolled down his cheeks. "I will get her back," he vowed. "I will grow strong and I will find her and bring her back where she belongs, that I promise. I promise myself, I promise Merci, and I promise God. As soon as I am grown I swear I will bring her back!"

Drying his tears lest the Sisters suspect he had cried like a child, he led the horses back to the barn and brushed them until they glowed. "Mer Pain, I fear you will be grown when she returns to us, but do not be afraid. I will take care of you until that day!"

When Thomas finally ended his hunger strike and emerged from his self-imposed prison he ate ravenously and went about his chores as usual. The Sisters were glad he had "returned to normal," but little did they know of his secret plans. Upon finishing his day's work he went to the forest and selected a large stout cedar tree and felled it with his ax. Cedar was easy to carve into a canoe and it would be light to portage. He wondered, as he worked, if he could paddle his canoe to find Merci. For now he would have to wait until he was older and stronger, then he would bring her back home.

The Sisters were pleased that Thomas no longer mourned the absence of his friend. They assumed he had recovered from his loss as he ate his meals heartily, worked diligently on the fields and gardens and kept the buildings and fences in repair without complaint. Having no experience raising children it did not occur to them that Thomas was much more mature than boys his age, that he had been forced to grow up from circumstance. They often heard his whistle, imitating every birdcall, even the sound of the wind in the trees and the rush of the water's small waves that lapped on the shore of the lake. Sometimes he whistled sweet melodies until he gave the appearance of complete happiness. They were completely unaware of his plan, that he was just biding time. The commune was so isolated in the woods they were only vaguely aware of the war and threats of war that were to the north, south and west of their convent in the forest and they never feared for their safety as God was watching over them. After all, they had been given Thomas to raise and to help them as he grew into manhood. They delighted in making him clothes for Sunday devotions, and were proud that it was necessary to make new ones each year to accommodate his growth. They even purchased fine leather boots from a trader but they were too large at the time, so he saved them in his room for the day they would fit as he grew. The Sisters were coming to realize that their little boy was becoming a man.

CHAPTER VI

Thomas was faithful in all his work, doing his chores and also the chores that Merci had done when she was there. Never complaining, he kept the wood box filled and fresh water from the spring was always available for the Sister's use. As winter of the second year of Merci's departure approached he decided it was time to hunt game for smoking to fill the larder for the oncoming snows when he could not always hunt fresh meat.

Packing his blankets, bow and arrows and of course his hunting knife at his side, he mounted Chevalier Noir. Followed closely by Mer Pain he informed the Sisters that he might be away for several days. He could shoot his arrows with a special hook he had fashioned that he could attach to his leather covered wrist, but he preferred closer contact with his prey. He was expert at wielding his knife and the method had proven sure with no escape for any animal he chose.

Tying his horses to a tree at the base of a cliff where their scent would not be easily carried on the wind, he climbed the ridge and near the top spied a tree with a strong low limb. By the tracks that led across the ridge toward a spring he knew many deer used the trail daily. With a leap he grasped the limb with his good hand and swung himself up into the foliage and waited. Soon a large buck wandered up the trail. Broad, with a great rack of horns, the size of the animal caused Thomas Pezhik Onindj to hesitate a moment. He would have to be accurate in his leap or be torn by the sharp points of the animal's antlers.

As the buck crossed under the branch he made his move. With knife drawn he leaped to the deer's back, holding onto the horns with his wrist and with the other hand drew the blade across the animal's throat. It dropped like a stone and Pezhik Onindj stood by his prey in triumph. Hearing a rustle, he turned and saw a wide-eyed doe with a fawn that had not yet outgrown its spots. He had killed the mate of one and the sire of another, but knew it was the way of nature. They would survive and the fawn would eventually leave its mother and she would find another mate. It was just life in the wilderness. After gutting the deer he hung it from the tree and went to the base of the cliff and retrieved the horses. He built a fire and stood in the flickering light from the flames, and raising his hand to the sky, he prayed.

"Holy Mary and Great Spirit, I, Lone Wolf, Thomas Pezhik Onindj am broken in many ways. I am torn between my native birth and the ways of the kind Sisters that have cared for me. I have only one good hand and my heart is broken with loneliness. My soul is crushed by my helplessness. My prayer is divided between the Powers that guide my life. Oh, help me grow in wisdom and stature and lead Lone Wolf in the path you have planned. My heart has been taken from me. I beg, Oh, Holy Ones, only for the return of my heart."

The following day, the victorious hunter was happily received by the Sisters at the convent, the large amount of meat meant they would not have to sacrifice any of their domestic animals for food for some time. They thought that perhaps Thomas was leaning toward the priesthood because of his devotion to duty, not knowing of the nights he spent in the woods seeking his heritage there.

Thomas was well aware of the war raging in the colonies and close by across the Canadian border. He talked to every trader and trapper that came by the convent, knowing the innocence of the Sisters. He wanted to be sure they were protected from harm. Somewhere along the way as time went by, he had changed from being protected and cared for by the Sisters to being their protector. Being poorly equipped to hold and fire a musket he did not feel compelled to aid in a fight he considered unnecessary. In the time of his forefathers the land had been free to all inhabitants to roam and hunt and protect. When the white man came to the continent the fighting for control of the land began. He would have no part in any determination of land ownership but would continue to care for the corner of the world to which he had been born, and someday he would bring Merci back to the place where she belonged.

As time passed Thomas seemed more and more content with life without Merci. Sister Margarite became convinced that she had done a good thing, that giving Merci the opportunity to experience life outside the convent was the course she was meant to follow—and Thomas, he seemed quiet, as though perhaps he had left childhood and was growing into adulthood. Perhaps he had been forced to mature beyond his years, perhaps it was simply time for him to grow up.

She was amused when he began to collect stones. She discovered his pile of smooth stones in the woods just beyond the cleared fields. There was no reason to question his new form of entertainment. He was prompt at vespers and his chores were always completed without protest. If he wanted to collect stones and pile them in the woods she saw no reason to interfere.

Thomas loved his stones. When he had a few hours following completion of his duties he wandered the woodland hills beyond the compound when the nearby woods had given up all the smooth stones they possessed.

He took two leather sacks and tied them to Chevalier Noir's back and two smaller ones for Mer Pain, searching the hills, riverbanks and lakeshore for exactly what he wanted. The pile grew larger and higher and one day when the pile had reached a height taller than he, a flat, dark, gray slate rock tumbled from the top and split open. The rock contained sheets of a hard, clear substance. With his knife he placed the tip of the blade on the edge of the substance and it split off in a clear sheet. Holding it to the light he became excited. He could see shadows and light and even the shape of the balsam firs through the crystalline sheets. It was tough and hard and could be cut with his sharp knife if he placed it on a hard surface.

Quickly, he clambered over the pile, searching for more of the dark rocks, and finding streaks of the substance on the edges of some of the stones he carefully struck them with another rock and retrieved the sheets until he had a considerable amount. These sheets he carefully placed in the pack on the back of his horse and took them to his room, hiding them under the bed. Whenever he had time he worked on frames to hold the translucent sheets. They were small, so he cut frames of fragrant cedar, carefully drilling holes and attaching them together with wooden pegs. By spring of the second year he had six windows ready for the house he planned to build. He had taken a small piece of the translucent material to Sister Margarite and she explained.

"It is called "mica", Thomas, and it is formed in stone. Sometimes it is in very small amounts and is interspersed throughout a rock, making it sparkle in the sunlight, sometimes it is in larger pieces such as this. You are fortunate to have found such a nice specimen, you should save it among your collections."

Nodding, Thomas did not reveal his use of the "mica". Perhaps he would find more. Now that his windows were complete perhaps he would surprise the Sisters at Christmas with a framed cross for the sanctuary. Yes, he could make a fine cross of framed squares that would glow in the candlelight. It would be fitting for all the care they had given him. He could not work on his house when the great snows came, and he would have time to collect the mica sheets in the summer and have the gift made by Christmas day.

All these things, these thoughts, these plans, worked to develop the mind of a boy into that of a man. Forced to overcome his disability through perseverance he had discarded disappointment and bitterness in favor of planning, expectation, anticipation and loving-kindness.

1777

Thomas had already laid the base for his house. It was a log cabin, and he planned to veneer the outside with the stones he had gathered. As soon as it was weather tight he began to work on the interior. The cabin consisted of two rooms, one with a large stone hearth with an oven built over the fireplace for baking, and a sleeping room. Instead of the usual dirt floor he had split logs and placed them flat side up, and shaved the tightly fitted flooring to an amazing smoothness. Building furniture, he had made a table whose top was built in the same manner as the flooring. Chairs had slotted and joined backs and seats woven from rawhide, and wall cupboards waited for dishes and cookware. The bedroom held a carved bed with a woven rawhide sleeping base and storage shelves on the wall. A carefully pieced leather mattress cover awaited a filling of goose down, rugs of wolf and bear fur rested on the floor by the bed. He planned to finish the house when the fall harvest was in and he would have more time.

CHAPTER VII

Thomaston

As days went by Mercy decided the work she loved best was bread making. The white flour that she had seen little of at the Friends of Jesus was in a flour barrel, a really large flour barrel. Rachel had shown her how to measure the flour, add the sugar, warm milk, butter and starter in the correct proportions. It was the rising that surprised Mercy. She thought it was a miracle the way it grew and grew until it was rounded over the top of the bowl. The fact that the rising occurred from a small amount of dough left over from previous bread mixing was equally mysterious. Rachel's fat fist would punch it down, then it was to set until it rose again. The first time she was allowed to punch it down she realized it took strength. She had to stand on tiptoe and lean her body into it, but when the cook said, "That's enough," she was elated.

Jeremiah had stepped into the kitchen and as he looked at the flushed girl with flour on her nose he had to laugh. She, in turn, began to laugh, then Rachel. At that moment she realized she could accept her new life in Thomaston.

Jeremiah was somewhat confused. Surely he was not becoming attracted to this simple girl from the Maine wilderness, yet her open honesty appealed to him. She had asked permission to borrow books from the library and he had taken her there to choose. He had never known a girl to be delighted with history and reference books. He kept his surprise at her choices hidden and told her she could exchange them at will.

"Oh," she replied, "but we must tell your mother. I would be dismayed if she found me in the library and was unaware of your permission."

"Of course, Mercy, I will tell her myself. I assure you that my mother will be pleased that you wish to better yourself."

He immediately regretted his last words, lest Mercy feel he thought she needed bettering. It was strange that he felt awkward as a schoolboy in her presence. This girl evoked strange emotions to which he was unaccustomed. His family, the town's wealthiest, owning both the trading post and the market with an apothecary, had put him in the position of being the town's most eligible bachelor. With both sisters married and with children of their own, he found himself being constantly pursued. He did not have any intention of marrying young as they had, but some of the girls in town were relentless. His blond curls and quiet manner seemed to attract every single girl in town. Young ladies in their ruffled silks and parasols constantly cast flirtatious glances his way and he received invitations weekly to parties, picnics and the like, from which he usually excused himself as needing to work on his accounting for the family business. Their obvious pursuit discouraged any advances he might have made. He was not so confident as to believe his attraction did not include the family fortune.

But Mercy was different. She seemed to love every chore she was given and no trace of guile ever revealed itself in her words or manner. It was her innocence, her sincerity, her dedication to her work and her willingness, nay, her ambition to learn that intrigued him. It was her soft eyes, her taffy hair,—her very simplicity that was stirring his heart. He decided he must see less of Mercy to prevent any crossing of the line with the household help. What would his father think if he saw any such attraction on his son's part to a bonded servant? His father was away much of the time, even making trips to England in the past for tea and spices, but lately with all the trouble stirred up in Boston he was home more, making shorter trips to Boston, Waldoboro, Biddeford, Pownalborough and Georgeana for goods to supply the post and market. He enjoyed journeying about Maine dealing with farmers for potatoes, squash, smoked hams and bacon, jams, jellies and honey, as well as with fishermen up and down the coast for smoked alewives and salted cod. Fresh meats and fish he purchased locally creating good will and friendly customers for his stores. He found dry goods in Falmouth and met ships as they unloaded iron nails, rope, plows and brass fastened horse harnesses, always in great demand. Herbs and medicines came in on the ships, also, and he always bought generous supplies to keep up with the demands of medical needs in the community. Sometimes he traded pelts brought down from the wilderness, sometimes he bought things outright, but always, always, he kept his eye on the profit margin.

Thus the Clarkes became wealthy, and Jeremiah kept the records. He knew every aspect of merchandizing but he did not possess the "dickering" personality of his father. He was more like his mother, unassuming, modest and exceptionally kindhearted—but the arrival of the small French servant had given him a jolt.

Chapter VIII

At the end of the day after Allie and Mercy had washed the windows on the inside (the male hired hands would wash the outsides standing on ladders), they returned to their room to find new clothing, three dresses each on their beds. To Mercy's surprise they were all alike, pale blue with wide white collars, white aprons and small white caps with narrow string ties. They were of fine broadcloth but Mercy questioned their all being the same.

"It is the custom," Allie said. "I'm sure Rachel has new frocks also. The other rich people in town dress their help in like clothing and now that you are here Mother Clarke must have decided it would be proper to follow suit. Everyone will know we belong to the Clarkes because we wear her chosen color for us all. You will see when we go to church. We will be going next Sunday and you will see the groups in like clothing sitting at the back."

"Belong?" She "belonged" to the Clarkes? She didn't object to the dresses being the same as her friends, and she appreciated the lovely smooth fabric and detail, but "belonging" to anyone struck a strange chord in her mind.—And she certainly would take note on Sunday as Allie suggested. She hadn't attended services since arriving in Thomaston but had said her prayers faithfully. She wondered what their church would be like. Probably not at all like the church to which she was accustomed, but she was here to take advantage of all the coastal community had to offer, and she certainly planned to learn all she could.

When Sunday arrived they wore their new frocks for the first time, leaving off the aprons for Holy Day dress. The church was in walking distance, and although the Clarkes rode in their carriage the two slender girls happily strolled the half-mile to the church house. Upon arriving they made a trip to the small outhouse at the back of the church. They sat for a minute and then they heard voices.

"That new French maid at the Clarkes probably thinks she can catch Jeremiah. Have you seen her? They say she has big flirty eyes."

"That's what I heard, but a very skinny body."

"If she thinks she can get him into bed to sleep with her, fine, but he would never marry below his station."

This was followed by laughter, which ceased when Mercy and Allie opened the door and emerged from the facility.

Mercy could not control herself. Politely, while fluttering her eyelashes, she declared, "You may use the facilities now, Mademoiselles, we are *finis*."

Quietly they walked around the corner to the side of the church, then hugged each other and dissolved into giggles.

Sure enough, the hired help from each wealthy family sat at the back of the church in groups of like colored clothing. Merci preferred the back, anyway, and she certainly didn't want to be among those obnoxious girls they had overheard being such snippets.

As the service began Mercy thought again about their cruel words. She hadn't thought of pursuing Jeremiah, she was there to learn and no thought of attracting any male had entered her mind, and why did they discuss sleeping? They each had their own beds in different parts of the house and—Oh! They meant breeding! She knew about that. She did not want to breed at all. She came into season monthly but no desire to breed had been triggered. She decided the rich town girls didn't know much about real life. If she did plan to breed, Jeremiah would sire beautiful children. His nieces and nephews were adorable with their blue eyes and pale blond curls, but he was just her friend, and people were not like animals. They married before breeding so the children would have a mother and a father, whereas animals didn't seem to care much about the family stability. And she didn't feel she "belonged" to the Clarkes. She would have to think more on the situation. She belonged to the Friends of Jesus if she "belonged" to anyone, but mostly she felt she belonged to God.

The Reverend Joshua Franklin could preach for hours. He had never entertained a thought to the discomfort of his parishioners ensconced on the hard wooden benches. Surely he must reason that the more uncomfortable his congregation became the more likely it was that they would reflect on their sinful ways. His sermon on "Jesus Wept" lasted way over an hour. After a long dissertation on just who Jesus was, he then launched into an equally lengthy analysis of the word "wept." After explaining the source of the word he described the cause of his weeping in great detail. Then the reasoning was explained, why he was weeping, who caused the weeping, his physical posture while weeping, his clothing, whether he was barefoot or wearing sandals. On with his sermon he went, with what weeping is, how many tears were shed, how long he wept and how dry his eyes became and how they felt after the weeping, and every other minute detail that anyone who had ever wept would know.

Mercy would much rather have heard a sermon on "Love One Another." She might have received a Blessing from hearing when to love, who to love and how to demonstrate love. Then she wouldn't have been so depressed about weeping.—And she wouldn't have to feel guilty because Jesus' pain was caused by her misdeeds or mis-thoughts, and the droning on and on made her want to weep. Her stomach growled and her back hurt from sitting on the bench for so long. She wondered how many others felt as she did. There seemed to be so many interesting stories in the Bible with so many wonderful heroic followers of Christ. She would love to hear the words and stories told in an interesting way. She enjoyed the scriptures more by reading them herself when she had no hard bench to distract her.

With reports of the war to separate the colonies from England bandied about it made one wonder why preaching in church didn't talk about "studying war no more." It seemed men fabricated excuses to start wars. Teachings of loving peace seemed to be abandoned on one excuse or another. It was as though hours of exhortation on peace would be wasted as long as men chose to fight. Mercy would like to see more arbitration to avoid conflict. In her studies of history the results of war hardly seemed worth the lives that were lost. It was her observation that many based their opinions on religion by circumstance. If a doctrine was comfortable it was more easily accepted, but when circumstances changed, so changed their actions, followed by a change in attitude and that followed by acceptance and possibly a declaration that a true concept had been discovered.

As the sermon went on Mercy's thoughts continued to wander. Perhaps the way to pray was not bowing and closing the eyes. Perhaps it was more fitting to stand and look at the heavens with open eyes and an open heart, that God might see all one's faults and transgressions, the openness showing the willingness of the sinner to accept whatever understanding and forgiveness God might want to bestow on the repenting offender.

Then she thought about the silly girls that had been speaking against her when they were unaware of her presence. She had noticed their elegant clothing, the flounced dresses, their parasols and lace gloves. She thought they must be a sight in the small out house, trying to gather their skirts to keep from soiling them. They must look like mushrooms on a stem when they sat on their pots at home, unless they removed their clothing every time they had to void. She imagined they whined and cried if they pricked their fingers while sewing their dainty embroidery, when they could be studying or reading about heroes of the past instead. She assumed they wasted their time and she could envision them languishing for several days a month with the curse while she felt better completing her duties as usual. She supposed their curse days were much worse than hers from their lack of exercise. They should realize that the monthly indisposition was merely a weak practice session for what would lie ahead if they ever gave birth. She had assisted with animals and could see the suffering needed to bring life into the world.

It was possible their very softness might make childbirth easier, but she was positive their wailing would be loud and long to impress those concerned with their situation that they might appreciate the suffering they endured. How pitiful that suffering could be exaggerated into a useful commodity as though there wasn't enough real pain in the world. Mercy wondered if her thoughts were embedded in jealousy or hate. She would try to convert her feelings to pity and tolerance. After all, she had to consider the condition of her own soul.

Still, she was glad she didn't have to empty and wash their pots every morning. She didn't mind the chore at Clarke House, where all the jars had lids to retain the odor and protect privacy. She never removed the lid until the last minute, then she didn't breathe and she didn't look as she emptied the contents down the hole in the outside toilet. Washing the vessels clean in the brook that bubbled towards the river completed the job. It was a duty she had rather not perform. She never wanted anyone to empty her pot. She preferred to keep her private functions private. All in all, it wasn't so bad. Most of her work seemed like fun and one couldn't have everything perfect. That was for Heaven.

All these things filled her mind as the minister droned on and on. She missed the short and earnest morning prayers at the Amitie le Christ. One could read the Bible by oneself and with careful study decipher the meaning in the passages. Here, no one crossed themselves, either coming into the church or leaving. She didn't want to offend anyone or make a scene so she crossed herself in her mind.

Mercy tried to interest Allie in learning from the books, but she was a simple girl and could hardly read at all, and was not interested in learning more. Mercy had heard her called "Tattle Tuttle," by some passing rough looking young boys and was upset over the crudity. Allie explained that her disgrace was her own fault, as she had told on one of the stable boys who stole a pie that had been cooling on the windowsill, and that was the reason she had been branded a tattler. Mercy explained to Allie that it had been her duty to tell even though bad people sometimes do more bad things to cover up the first offence, then she reassured Allie that they would always be friends no matter what anyone tried to do to spoil that friendship.

Days went by and winter arrived. Christmas at Clarke House was a very big to-do. Greenery decorated the halls, colorful bows were tied everywhere and lit candles burned in every nook and on every mantel. An enormous feast was being prepared for Christmas Day. Mercy helped Rachel with the preparation of the food. Together they made pumpkin and mince pies, squash, roast pig, mounds of mashed potatoes flavored with their freshly churned butter, (Mercy had happily churned, singing as she pushed and pulled the churn stem up and down, and delighted in the amount of butter she had made available for cooking). She learned how to make cookies, cutting the shapes of animals and trees, hearts and flowers, then grinding the sugar to a fine powder to make icing. Rachel showed her how to color the icing red with elderberry juice, yellow from wild snapdragon boilings, and brown from adding cocoa. She had a wonderful time decorating the cookies with fanciful designs with the palette of colors they had created. They baked fruitcakes and biscuits, gravy and spiced pudding made of breadcrumbs, eggs and currants. It was a most wonderful Christmas. Neighbors dropped in and the whole Clarke family arrived early Christmas morning, with much merriment and gift giving.

Mercy was delighted with the visitors' enjoyment of the food and sweets she had helped prepare, especially the children's pleasure eating the decorated cookies, and as the day ended she helped Rachel wash the dishes late into the evening to keep things in order for the next day.

"Oh, Rachel," she bubbled, "wasn't it a wonderful day, a wonderful Christmas. Everyone was so happy. I miss my own home, but I will be with them next Christmas, and it will be wonderful, too!"

"Oh, Mercy, don't you know you will be here four more years? You were bonded for five and this is only your first year. I'm surprised you are not aware of your position."

"Five years? A bonded servant? Mr. Renault promised the Sisters he was bringing me to learn wonderful things, and I have, but no mention was made of a bond. Am I a slave? Tell me, was I sold as a slave?"

Tears rolled down her cheeks and she began to shake.

Rachel put her big arms about the sobbing girl. "Oh, Mercy, you were sold as an indentured servant. Mr. Renault has been paid, but in five years you will be free."

"I know the Sisters received no payment for me. They thought it was a great opportunity. We were all deceived. Oh, what shall I do?"

"You will work here for five years and then you may leave. Until then, child, make the best of it. This is a fine family and they are good to their servants. You are fortunate Mr. Renault didn't sell you to a brothel or a shipmaster that might have misused you. Come, Mercy, dry your tears, you will be safe here. You are very fortunate to be with us, so do not reveal this to Mother Clarke. She would be very hurt to know that her bond purchase was that of a stolen girl. You must be grateful for her loving-kindness as you would find no better mistress than Prudence Clarke."

"I know, I know, and I must not let the Sisters find out that I was sold. They would die of remorse. I will serve my time and then I will go home."

And so, Mercy received the news of her bond on December twenty-fifth, 1775, a Christmas gift she had not expected.

CHAPTER IX

1776

The garrison at both Thomaston and St. George were becoming well supplied. Muskets and ammunition were being stored in magazines at both stockades. Preserved food, blankets, bandages and firewood were all neatly stored in preparation for any attack that might come. With the events in and around Boston, all the coastal towns were on the alert. The garrison at St. George had a large stable of horses under the charge of Osmond Buckington, a large rough bull of a man who frequented the alehouse in Thomaston whenever he could. His service was not a result of loyalty to the cause as he was completely lacking in scruples. He enjoyed the prestige of the job and the availability of the goods stored there. His pilfering had gone unnoticed as he was careful not to take enough to be obvious. His cruelty to animals had also gone unnoticed, being only the lesser of his evils. His feelings that he had the right to control women, children and animals was deeply ingrained into his being and so automatic was his abuse that he, himself, was completely unaware that he ever planned his methods.

Osmond always wore a slouch tassel cap covering his nearly bald head even while eating. He had no manners and felt no compunction to follow any rule of etiquette and he was decidedly the meanest man in town. He was just born mean. From the time he cut his first tooth and discovered he could cause pain by biting his mother's nipple until he was old enough to torture snakes and dogs, he continued in his joy to cause pain. He caught his first small snake at age six, and thrilled when it hissed and thrust its slender tongue in fright as he prodded it with sharp sticks and pelted it with small stones until it bravely and mercifully died. And the dog—he was twenty when he caught Sam Carter's dog sucking eggs in the hen pen. He knew better than to kill the dog, but he devised a scheme worse that death to "cure" the dog of egg sucking. Tying a rope tightly about the poor creature's neck he threw the other end of the rope over the limb of a near-by apple tree and raised the squirming dog off the ground by its neck and held him there until just before he was asphyxiated, then let him drop to the ground. As soon as the dog revived enough to try to stagger away Osmond would repeat the procedure. After the fourth such torturous "near-hanging" he released the animal. The poor creature skulked away into the brush, unmarked physically but forever doomed to live spiritless. It was never known if the dog had learned to leave eggs alone, but he certainly knew never to go near Osmond's place again.

Buck was also verbally abusive to other males he considered of lesser stature than himself, being confident that he could behave in any manner he chose and go unpunished. Many cheered him on or supported him in his brutal actions because they lacked the bravery to carry out such actions themselves. They often lacked the intelligence to realize that the abused person may not have been simply too weak to retaliate, but were perhaps too intellectual to resort to physical violence and preferred to take the verbal abuse knowing that their day would come eventually. Osmond Buck was in a class by himself.

His practice of throwing stones was not left behind in childhood. Every squirrel, toad or singing bird was a target. He was proud of his accuracy and everyone knew to be aware that a stone could fly their way or a bird could drop from a tree as he meandered through town. Everyone found him distasteful but it did not effect any change in his actions. His coarse laughter announced his success if he had stoned a bird, and his presence was merely accepted as a discomfort they must endure. He was the keeper of the livestock at the garrison, and being unaware of the perks he enjoyed, no one else was clamoring for the job.

Little Bird

Who has thrown a stone at you,
        my pretty little singing bird?
Who has stilled your happy song,
        sweetest I have ever heard?
Here you lie as though you're sleeping,
        here am I beside you weeping,
Sweet bluebird with golden breast,
        now your fluttering heart is still,
Never again to sing your song,
        never an early morning trill.
As you reveled in the dawn,
        cruel one that did the deed,
Cursed soul who had no need
        to crush your heart that once was free,
And now you sleep eternally.
        I pray for vengeance on the one
Who dastardly has stopped your song,
        he had no need
To take your life from here on earth
        where it belonged.
Most hateful cruelty ever heard,
        to kill a poor defenseless bird.

Chapter X

War

Mercy was surprised to learn that Allie had a beau. His name was Lorenzo Plunkett. They had spied each other at the market as Lorenzo was delivering freshly caught fish and had instantly fallen in love, but before they made plans to marry he had felt the call to join the militia. Allie had confided her feelings for Lorenzo to Mercy and together they hoped the war would end quickly so he could return to the shores of Maine that he loved and the girl with whom he wished to spend the rest of his life. Allie's feelings for the stocky fisherman with eyes as blue as the ocean were so strong it caused Mercy to hate the war that was keeping them apart.

Word came that he had survived the bloody battle at Bunker Hill, (Breed's Hill), but had been mortally wounded in a later skirmish. His mouth and chin had been shot off and he had bled to death before anything could be done. Allie grieved, knowing she would never again be able to trace his beautiful full lips with her fingertip, never have a cottage by the sea and never be in his arms to fulfill their desires.

Mercy consoled her as best she could and held her in her arms throughout the night that the news arrived.

War, she thought, as she held the stricken girl. Some men would return physically unscathed but so mentally injured they would be totally useless as human beings, while some would return maimed and crippled and still be the best of men. Often those who marched off with a cocky attitude and ready to fight returned as mere shadows of their former selves while the meekest among them returned as heroes, and some, like Lorenzo, would not return at all. The graveyard would become filled with gravestones and memorials honoring the lost ones. Mercy wondered, "Is a graveyard a place of the dead with the solemn stones placed as a remembrance that in that spot lies someone who once lived, or are the stones a proclamation that though the ones beneath the sod are lost to us, yet they live, their souls content in another dimension unknown to those still in possession of their earthly life?" Perhaps the stones were originally placed to be visible reminders of the brevity of a lifetime, and thus that brief span of time should be used wisely. Sister Margarite had told her that a lifetime looks long from the early end, but so very short when one looks back from the closure end. She wondered if she would live long enough to experience that observation. She had come to accept her own position, the work was not difficult, the Clarke family was kind and she did not want for anything. And she and Jeremiah had become such good friends. She wondered what the next three years would bring. With so many young men dying in battle she was force to realize the fragility of life, and was determined to make the most of her time. But poor Allie, would she ever find another love or would she now be doomed to be a spinster? Mercy thought probably that would be the case. For herself, being unmarried would not be crushing, she could become a Sister and be happy at the Friends of Jesus, but for Allie, it meant a life of servitude and probably she had dreamed of sturdy children raised near the ocean.

Mercy held the girl more tightly and grieved not for Lorenzo, but for Allie.

Chapter XI

In the months that followed Allie continued in her duties and just as she seemed to brighten up a bit she suddenly fell into a great depression. Mercy tried to cheer her in every way she could to no avail. Finally late one night she cried and her problem burst forth in all its horror. Osmond Buck had violated her. He had grabbed her as she was returning from taking the evening meal to the hired hands and dragged her behind the haystack where he perpetrated his crime.

"Oh, Mercy," she cried. "He even said I should be happy Lorenzo is dead, because now a real man had used my body. Oh, Mercy, I cannot stand it!"

Mercy thought the situation through. If they reported it, probably nothing would be done. His drinking friends were probably all on his side, and if word got around her reputation would be ruined. The "Tattle Tuttle" label would return and Allie was already so injured from being teased and from the loss of Lorenzo. They decided to keep the event secret and again, Mercy would try to console her friend. She also decided to take precautions against future attacks, keeping a sharp knife in the pocket of her apron at all times, and even sleeping with it under her pillow at night. She also walked with Allie to deliver the evening meals to the hired hands from that day on.

Mercy decided to go to Mother Clarke with a request.

"Please, Madam, Allie is still despondent over the loss of Lorenzo. I make a request that I teach her to knit that she might rest her tortured mind. If you have worn out sweaters, socks or mittens that have holes and tears, I could unravel them and teach her to make new items. You see, I have already whittled needles from a hickory bush."

"Why, Mercy," Mother Clarke replied. "Of course you may, and there is a sack of old sweaters in the laundry room closet you are welcome to use. Come, I will show you."

"What an enterprising girl," Mother Clark thought. Sometimes she felt guilty thinking of Mercy as an indentured servant. She had become a valued addition to the household help but also a unique person to be respected. "Sometimes she seems like one of us," was a thought that ran through her mind.

It was with great delight Mercy viewed the many colored items and in the evening she washed them all and hung them to dry on the lines in the back yard. Darkness was falling and she heard stealthy footsteps behind her. Whirling about, she faced Osmond Buck.

Brandishing her knife, Mercy cried out, "If you come any closer I will strip you of your manhood before I kill you, you fat bastard, and no one will believe I did the deed. The knife will not be found and the constable will believe you came here for help after a fight and died at my feet. Who would suspect that I would let a man bleed to death? I am very strong from lifting the soup kettle from the fire and carrying water from the spring. But hard work has been to my advantage, for I am strong and you are fat and lazy. I can easily overpower you. Do not attack me or ever touch Allie again or you will pay dearly for the folly of your ways!"

Surprised, Buck backed off and left the yard. Mercy was relieved and shaken but she was glad she had stood her ground. The fear in Buck's face gave her confidence that it would not happen again. Probably no one had dared face up to him before and she hoped the confrontation might save some other poor soul the trauma that Allie had endured.

Osmond Buckington had been surprised, indeed. Stumbling back towards town he made a vow. "Someday, little French missy, I'll catch you alone. Maybe not right away, but someday I'll take my pleasure with you. That's a promise I make to meself and to you."

Mercy returned to her room trembling, but secure and confident. Climbing up the back steps from the kitchen and reaching their bedroom on the third floor she was shocked to find Allie holding her stomach with her arms crossed tightly over her cramped body. She had gushed blood like a spring freshet and Mercy knew she would surely die if the flow were not staunched. Grabbing Allie's skirts she applied all the pressure she could. Helping her from her cot, she decided she should lie flat on the floor with her knees bent, while she continued the pressure. Whether she fainted or slept, neither girl knew, but upon waking several hours later the hemorrhage had subsided, though Allie was too weak to walk.

Allie was unable to work the following day or attend the evening meal so Mercy brought her a bowl of soup, explaining to Rachel that Allie was having an especially difficult time with her curse. By morning she was able to appear, pale and wan at breakfast, but was excused from her chores for the day. Mercy gladly worked quickly, taking Allie's responsibilities along with her own, as well as washing her friend's soiled garments and hanging them on the drying line. No questions were asked when she took the extra rags from the personal needs bag.

Mercy's thoughts were directed to protecting Allie and herself from future horrors and she vowed vengeance on Buck for his treatment of Allie and all she had been through. At least God had been merciful and cast out the filth from her womb. A small blessing after all she had suffered.

The knitting lessons went well and Allie slowly regained her strength. She was amazed as Mercy carefully unraveled all the old sweaters, caps, mittens and socks, making piles of yarn on their bedroom floor. There was a whole rainbow of colors of salvageable yarn, and Allie was delighted to help with the winding of each separate color into balls. They felt rich with their newfound hoard and Allie even managed a giggle of delight. After learning to knit and pearl Mercy discovered she had to teach the girl to count. Following a few weeks of practice in both the counting and the knitting, Allie finally made a boggin complete with tassel and she was euphoric. They made mittens and scarves and Mercy was making a striped sweater for Jeremiah, all to be given at Christmas, so they happily hid them away in their room awaiting the holiday season.

Mercy had requested a few buttons from Mother Clarke and she handed Mercy a large jar filled with all kinds of buttons, telling her to use all she wanted as they had been saved from old discarded clothing.

What fun Mercy had sorting the buttons! She made piles of buttons on the floor of their room, sorting them by size and color. There were black glass buttons, cobalt blue buttons the color of the ocean at mid-day, mother of pearl buttons made of oyster shells, buttons with two holes for sewing to shirts, or four holes to be sewn on with a cross of threads, some with carved edges, some square, some round, metal buttons with military design stamped on them, gold or silver, some plain, some with eagles or anchors engraved on the rounded surfaces. There were large ornate buttons for coats for fine ladies, tiny pearl buttons for baby dresses, and chunky buttons for buttoning galluses onto canvas trousers. She was thrilled with the myriad of colors, shapes and intriguing designs. Mercy chose plain black for the sweater she was knitting for Jeremiah, and seven gray shanked buttons to save for future use. Much as she enjoyed her evening with the buttons, she didn't want to waste time in the future sorting them again so she happily strung and tied each set of buttons on an odd strand of yarn, keeping the sets together. She had saved out a large amount of gray yarn for another sweater, but she would finish the striped one first and then see how much time she had before Christmas.

CHAPTER XII

There had been constant worry in Thomaston and the surrounding area that spring. One after another, young men were leaving to join the militia. There was a tendency in some households to remain loyal to the crown. Whether it was true loyalty was under suspicion, as those too timid to put their lives on the line for liberty sometimes found it easier to declare their support for English rule, while some feared the repercussions they would face if the colonists lost the war. In the face of all the many pros and cons, Jeremiah was diligent in his efforts to insure that his books were up to date and that the trading post and market supplies were complete.

By April 30th he announced his intent to join the militia. His father was proud, his mother was wounded but bravely stood by him, and Mercy had made a discovery. Life at Clarke house would not be the same if he left and she realized she cared more for him than she had admitted even to herself. Throughout the winter they had grown close, laughing and throwing snowballs at each other. She was thrilled that he had worn the sweater she had knitted especially for him. His parents had not noticed their affection for each other or if they did, they had not objected. They realized that she was bright, hardworking and kind, and being of liberal minds they did not wish to control their son. Since Mercy and Jeremiah had taken no noticeable actions on their feelings there had been no need to intercede if they had even thought of doing so. They were close to accepting Mercy as part of their family when their son made the announcement of his eminent enlistment. Any plans anyone had even vaguely entertained were now on hold.

Mercy hadn't seen Jeremiah for several days. She assumed that he had gone fishing. Spring had arrived. Today had been a glorious day, so typical of Maine to suddenly burst forth after a long winter. It had been particularly long and harsh with snow arriving early in November, blanketing the hills and valleys. The sleeping pastures cuddled under the comforter of white until late March, the rivers bursting free of their icy prisons and rushing over rocks, fighting their way to the sea. Now it was late April and the fields had begun their greening in the warm sun as the melting snow provided nourishment following the icy drought. The sudden warmth of the sun was urgently drawing the sprouting leaves of bulbs from the softening earth as though they could hardly wait to bust into dazzling color. The first crocus had already splashed their blooms, some unable to wait until the last snow melted. The end of winter and the arrival of spring were further announced by the peeping and chattering of small, brilliantly plumed birds, fluttering and chasing their paler females pretending it to be only a game with no wish to mate. Even the blue jay had returned to his perch on the old apple tree as though he was a new arrival when in reality he had wintered near-by. The other birds didn't like him because of his disposition or perhaps they were jealous of his beautiful blue feathers. Humans weren't so obvious in their actions. Usually good looks were sought after and admired and many undesirable personality flaws were overlooked and easily forgotten in the presence of loveliness. Perhaps the birds' way was better, at least, it was more honest.

Later that evening as the sun was setting behind the trees and the evening air was fresh and moist, Mercy sat on the back steps and was enjoying the smells and sounds of the season when Jeremiah approached. He had a small cloth sack in his hand and he quietly sat down beside her.

"Mercy, I have something for you. I hope you will like it. Here, put your hand in the sack. It's a surprise."

"Jeremiah, you are playing a trick on me—"

"No, no. Do as I say. You will not be tricked."

Slowly she reached into the bag. She felt something soft and warm. She jumped.

"Jeremiah! It moved!"

"It's all right, Mercy, I promise."

Cautiously she slipped her hand into the cloth sack again and put her hand about a soft warm—rabbit!"

Extracting it from the bag she held it to her cheek, exclaiming, "Oh, my God, Oh, my God," as it snuggled against her neck.

"Oh, Jeremiah! It's the most wonderful gift I've ever had!"

"Come. Mercy, I have built a hutch so he will be safe from predators. He will be yours to keep and care for, so you will always think of me. You see, I have a selfish streak in my heart."

"I'll name him "Pierre", and he will be my darling pet. Oh, Jeremiah, I can never thank you enough!"

"Mercy, you mean more to me that anything or anyone in the world. It will not matter where I go or what I do, you will always be in my heart. Do not ask why I tell you this. Just trust that you will always be my truest love."

"Jeremiah, you are scaring me. Oh, surely you are not leaving now, surely not!"

"I can only say, Mercy, that you are the love of my heart."

Mercy turned to place the rabbit in the hutch and when she had fastened the door latch and turned he had disappeared into the quickly darkening evening shadows.

One thing for sure, she was never going to eat Pierre.

Chapter XIII

Jeremiah sailed at dawn on a small brig that had pulled into Thomaston. Several other young men joined him in the trip south. They would pass Boston round the waters of Cape Cod and pull into New Bedford where two hundred men along with arms and supplies would board for the trip to Philadelphia. There they would be assigned to various regiments. Some of the men considered the venture an escape from the boredom they found in farming but were soon put in their place when seasickness visited them— suddenly, violently and seemingly everlasting. The old sailors found it a source of jovial chiding, knowing that by the time they reached New Bedford they would have their sea legs and be in good shape to pass the joking along to the new recruits that would board there. They might be a little bleary and wobbly but they would have a new respect for the sea and perhaps view their mission in a more serious light.

Being one of the lucky ones, having spent enough time fishing along the coast of Maine in small crafts to season his stomach against such turmoil, Jeremiah spent his days on the windward side of the ship to avoid the acrid smell brought forth from the ill ones on the lee. With wind blowing his pale curls back from his face and his gaze mesmerized on the horizon, he envisioned all he had left behind in the rising and falling of the dark ocean. How he longed to be back with Mercy, sitting on the pier with their legs dangling above the brackish water where the St. George met the sea. He closed his eyes and could feel her warm hand in his. If things were different they would be planning their lives, even planning a family, the house he would build for her overlooking the blue harbor where the gulls and puffins played—but that would have to wait. The British rule had become unbearable, the taxes unacceptable, and every time a compromise had been made a new tax or law would suddenly start the whole mess all over again. There was nothing to be done except what was planned, and he intended to do his part, not out of bravado but from careful contemplation. The colonists must be freed from the British who considered the colonists inferior and unable to manage their own affairs. The tax burden to support the British troops placed in their midst was ridiculous. Who ever heard of men paying the salaries of their jailers, and even buying their own jails? The situation was laughable, but things were going to change. Supplies for the fight for freedom had been stockpiled in Lexington and Concord as well as many other barns and hidden buildings throughout New England. Now that the British had destroyed them the colonists' anger and fervor had assisted them in assembling even more hidden supplies with which to further their cause.

Jeremiah mulled the situation over in his mind. It seemed unfair that by the time his feelings for Mercy had reached the point of declaration he found that he could not ask her to marry him, not until the situation with the Crown was settled. To marry while the country was at war would be unfair. If he were killed and she was with child he would be condemning her to a life of hardship, and he cared too much for her to allow that to happen. He had sworn his duty to the emerging country and would do everything in his power to carry out that duty. He hoped he could survive the war and then he could be with Mercy and raise a family under a new flag in a country free from oppression.

Remembering the day Mercy had arrived in Thomaston, Jeremiah was suddenly struck by the realization that fate was often manifested in sudden encounters. A timid fifteen year-old girl in brown homespun had been left sitting on the dock, lonely and frightened but with a completely unaffected manner. He had seen a disheveled man at Clarke House and his mother giving him money, and the disreputable man had walked away jingling his money in his pocket. When his mother had requested Jeremiah to find her new indentured servant on the dock he had not expected the wide-eyed beauty he found there. Realizing she was a bonded servant, a purchase, if you will, the thought gave him a twinge. He didn't know the girl or the circumstances, but something about indenture smacked of slavery. He knew his mother would be kind to her as that was her nature, and perhaps the life of a bonded servant would be a better life than she had previously experienced.

Later that evening he had asked his mother the circumstances of the contract purchase and she replied. "Mr. Renault explained that she is from a convent in the North and this is a great opportunity for her. Do not trouble yourself, Jeremiah. She is probably quite simple, but I will do the best I can for the poor creature. The child can hardly speak English but I hope she will be able to learn. She will be an excellent helper if she is willing to work. I will make sure she is not ridiculed or abused."

Jeremiah had contemplated, "Perhaps she is not simple. Being unable to speak proper English is not criteria for intelligence." She certainly did not seem simple in the brief conversation in which they had engaged on the trip from the dock to Clarke House. He planned to make a point of finding out, and he did. As time went by he had found her to be the most intelligent girl he had ever met, and her sweet manners and enthusiasm to learn had completely won him over. Mercy was so special he hoped she would accept his proposal of marriage when he returned from the fight and they would raise their children in a new free country.

CHAPTER XIV

Upon discovering that Jeremiah had left to join the militia, Mercy walked to the shore where the Georges River reached its destination and joined the ocean it had sought on its journey from the inland hills and valleys of the Waldo tract.

Watching the morning mists
Rolling, rolling, rolling in,
That great white wall advancing
Over still water,
Hiding all, covering all,
With its damp softness.

What lies beyond that great blanket?
What secrets are hidden there?
Are there ships beyond this bank of cloud?
Do they proudly sail with sheets unfurled,
Or does it storm beyond this mysterious covering
With wind tossed vessels fighting to hold their course?

Here am I safely sheltered with comforts rare
While dangers plague my heart's love
In a far off place beyond my knowing.

With moist eyes Mercy returned to Clarke House, began her day's work and kept her thoughts to herself. She would not reveal to anyone her feelings for Jeremiah, or the feelings he had revealed to her, but each night she tenderly removed Pierre from his little hutch and held him close to her heart until the stars came out.

Chapter XV

Mother Prudence Clarke reflected on her life. She and Albert had both been raised in poverty and had been given nothing to help them establish their lives. With hard work Albert had slowly built up his businesses with shrewd dealings and careful planning, and had gradually built a small fortune, a large house and a highly respected position in the community. In his private moments he had always expressed his appreciation for all she had done. As their trading post was being built, and later the market, she had raised vegetables, made jams and jellies, and the eggs they sold were from her pens and all the while raising three small children. Their closeness, (not evident to any onlookers), was private; their mutual love and respect, solid, satisfying and lasting.

Lately, however, she had been entertaining the suspicion that perhaps the acquisition of Mercy had not been completely on the up and up. The girl's seeming happiness in learning new methods of cooking and cleaning did not follow the grudging pattern of work obtained from indentured servants she had encountered in the past. Her talents were many and the beautiful gifts she and Allie had presented to the family at Christmas were uncharacteristic of a servant. Even the grandchildren had received colorful mittens, complete with small poms and tassels on the backs. Their joy was surpassed only by the delight Mercy and Allie had exhibited over their acceptance. Prudence herself had given the girls and Rachel gifts but had not expected such fine handmade items in return, and all made from discarded wool. The girl had obviously been taught well at the convent from which she came. She hoped the convent benefited much from the price she had paid for the bond. She had been very generous knowing the money was going to a worthy cause.

Having come from poverty, she appreciated Mercy's industrious nature. She and Albert had worked hard in their early years together and Clarke House had not been built until after she had turned thirty, having raised the children the first few years in the log cabin they had built when they married. Now even the large house was paid for and the lifestyle they enjoyed was a luxury she had not expected.

She did wonder about the friendship her youngest child entertained with the French girl. Of course, there was no assurance that she was, indeed, French. Mercy's English had become excellent, but so was Jeremiah's French. The girl's innocence was touching, the way her eyes widened at any discovery, be it a new recipe, needlepoint, (which Prudence had taught her when Mercy had shown an interest), or even a new fruit or vegetable. Perhaps when the girl's bond was paid she would offer to pay her way back to the convent, unless, of course, the girl decided to marry or work on as a paid servant. Surely, although she tried not to be prejudiced, Jeremiah had no intentions toward the girl. She hoped she would not interfere if that were the case. There were plenty of attractive girls from proper families in town, but Jeremiah had shown no interest in courting any of them. He had preferred to work on his books, that is, until Mercy had come to live at Clarke House. At least her presence there had seemed to spark his interest in the opposite gender.

But—Mercy had seemed a little overly friendly with Jeremiah. She wondered if the interest Mercy showed in books had been a pretext to gain his companionship, although she did take a genuine interest in learning. Jeremiah would miss her when she returned to the convent, (assuming that would be Mercy's choice). The situation had been reasonably secure, but then her son had taken the notion to join the militia. She didn't understand her husband's easy acceptance of their son's leaving, but men always seemed to accept wars. She didn't believe in wars, she felt there must be a better way to settle things. She only hoped Jeremiah would return safely. The sooner the better for his well-being, but on the other hand, if he didn't return until Mercy's bond was paid, the girl would be a nun by then, happily serving others and teaching all she had learned to other poor abandoned girls. Usually things worked out for the best.

CHAPTER XVI

Albert Clarke was puzzled. He feared the luxurious lifestyle they had attained might have gradually changed his wife's thinking. The responsibilities of running the large house had required that she not only be in charge of the hired help due to his constant travel about Massachusetts dealing for goods, but it was also necessary that she supervise their enterprises in Thomaston. Jeremiah had become quite the manager so she was relieved of many responsibilities concerning their businesses. They had been so poor and worked so hard she deserved to feel a little aloof at times. Perhaps the stability of even one's marriage depends not on the privacy of the bedroom but on the kindness of the heart, the giving of oneself, the demonstration of love that one person shows to another in all the ways that love can be manifested. The constant passion of their youth had been replaced by a caring love but their occasional encounters were as passionate as the first time. That was the wonderful thing about their love. Sometimes he could not believe his good fortune in finding a wife like Prudence. She was "Mother Clarke" in the daytime but she was his Prudence at night.

His concern was with her attitude towards Mercy. If she could only realize the girl was a lot like Prudence herself, hardworking and loving. She had certainly been kind to poor simple Allie, and Allie had become a better worker because of Mercy's care and teaching. Allie obviously was much brighter than they had thought and only needed a kindhearted soul to teach her. There was a lot one could learn from not being too close to the household doings, and one thing he saw was the change in Jeremiah. His only passion had been for the perfecting of his bookkeeping and learning to manage the family businesses. But now there was a new sparkle in his son's eyes and he was sure Mercy had given it to him. If it were true he hoped Prudence would come around and accept the girl. He hoped she had not drawn too rigid a line between themselves and those who worked for the family.

There was another more important worry he carried in his mind. The battle for independence had taken shape and now his only son had decided that his duty lay with the cause for freedom. They had been stockpiling supplies at the garrison on the hill overlooking the mouth of the St. George River. Shelves had been filled with bandages, spirits for disinfecting wounds and preparing the wounded for surgery, tincture of opium, warm clothing, cured hams, root vegetables, water buckets and eating utensils.

Mercy had helped, searching the moist meadows near the marshes for the pointed green leaves of woundwort to be sure there was plenty to staunch the flow of blood and ease the pain of the wounded. Scissors, knives, saws and probes had been washed and stored in clean, ironed cloths. Pillows, sheets and warm blankets were packed in wooden chests, cots were stacked and a heavy table with buckets beneath for receiving medical refuse was provided for surgical use.

Albert felt they were doing their part in the fight for freedom, but Jeremiah had not felt the same, and now he was on his way South. He had thought Prudence would have put up more of a fight to keep her baby at home, but she had bravely stood beside Albert and waved him off to the fray. He hoped her fears that he was becoming too fond of Mercy had not influenced her willingness for him to leave.

He prayed his son would return unharmed. Surely he would be granted a position behind the front lines in comparable safety due to his education and experience, perhaps in logistics. At least that was his hope. He would rather his son had escaped the war than escape the clutches of a girl he considered would make a great wife for any man.

He wondered, too, if Jeremiah had perhaps been raised with too many of the comforts of the well-to-do and perhaps did not have his feet planted squarely on the ground. Mercy had come into their lives as a poor servant girl but she was certainly well educated. If he were twenty years old and had not met Prudence he would certainly be interested. Yes, she would make a good wife for his son, but he knew enough to stay out of the matchmaking business. Children had to choose their own spouses, good or bad, and his girls had chosen well. He had to trust Jeremiah to do the same.

Contemplating the family history he thought of his father, a trapper and a trader, roaming the wilderness and setting traps on far off streams and rivers, a robust man who left his wife and children for long periods while he hunted the northwest regions. His mother had been of Norwegian blood, the blond strain showing up in their children and grandchildren. Albert had always been fair in his dealing for furs with the hardy hunters who came to the post with their pelts; mink and rabbit, raccoon and well prepared doeskin, (some soft enough for baby clothing, some tough enough for buckskin breeches and jackets), bearskin for rugs and heavy outerwear that would keep out any Canadian blast of snow and ice in winter. Sometimes they brought mukluks and moccasins they had bartered for with natives across the border, even fur lined leather mittens, with the thumb and forefinger separate from the body of the mitt to enable a hunter to pull the trigger of his musket or draw the string of a bow.

There was no denying the competence of the natives. They had lived in the northern climes for generations, knew the ways of all the animals and herbal cures and had all the skills to survive the winter's blast. In summer their lightweight canoes were easily ported around falls and rapids, their sinewy bodies glowing in the sun as they paddled the lakes and streams. The white man's abilities paled in the shadow of their ingenuity.

He had always traded fairly with them and never had any trouble. They had welcomed the white man thinking he would take care of the land as they had, not realizing the difference in cultures. The Europeans had brought them diseases they had never before suffered, and many had died, sometimes whole villages, from simple infections for which they had no cure. It was no wonder that their frustration sometimes erupted into violence, as with the Bradford family in Meduncook. He tried to keep his mind clear with his dealings, always being fair but having no illusions that his honest dealings were any guarantee of a trusting friendship. They were natives and he was an encroaching white man, and their sudden eruptions into savagery were understandable. There were white men in the town hanging out in the tavern he would trust less than any natives. He had lived long enough to know that savagery was not confined to any one race of people.

Prudence feared the natives because she didn't understand them. She had been born in England as most of the population in Thomaston. The German immigrants had settled in Waldoboro, Warren and Breman, along with Scots and a few Swedes and Norwegians, although vastly outnumbered by the British. Many of them were still loyal to the Crown, hoping that Britain would eventually become fair in their taxation and control. He doubted that would happen. Trying to control an expanding country thousands of miles away across a vast ocean was a difficult endeavor. Too many unscrupulous treasure seekers and land grabbers gladly "volunteered" to assist in the management of the colonies. Their hearts were in their pockets without any understanding of the needs of the growing colonies in the new land. He feared the struggle for independence would be very costly. Many young men would be lost, and he hoped his son would not be in that number.

PART III

The greening fields of springtime
        will soon be washed in blood,
As those who fall for freedom
        give up the lives they led,
That those remaining might enjoy
        a better way to live,
With their defeat of tyranny,
        giving all that they could give.

And when a new flag we may raise
        above our troubled land,
We must remember every man
        who made his final stand,
And gave his life for liberty.
        So let the church bells toll,
For men who bled and died for all,
        to make our country whole.

CHAPTER I

As the British army advanced toward Lexington and Concord, the two lights that shone from the tower of the old North Church in Boston proclaimed that the troops were coming by sea. Paul Revere and William Dawes began their rides to warn the countryside of the impending arrival of the English regiments. Their cries of "The Redcoats are coming, the Redcoats are coming" rang out through the villages and the colonists that had been preparing for the fight on a minute's notice readied themselves and their arms. Seven hundred British soldiers had anticipated marching through the colonists in Lexington easily, but only succeeded in killing eight men. Marching on to Concord they found three hundred and fifty Minutemen waiting, and although they killed nearly a hundred, the British suffered two hundred and fifty dead or wounded. Revere and Dawes had been captured just outside Lexington by a patrol but Doctor Samuel Prescott had completed the mission of warning the colonists.

The carefully stored arms the Patriots had hidden in Concord were destroyed but it had not discouraged or disheartened the Patriot's cause. Since the unfortunate killing of men at the Customs House in Boston back in 1770, the event had been glamorized and exaggerated far beyond the actual skirmish. Albeit the unjust taxation had prompted the small angry group of men to pelt the British guards with snowballs and ice, an inadvertent misunderstanding or misheard order to "fire" had resulted in the unfortunate fiasco. With the five casualties, (including

Crispus Attucks, a negro in the group), the event was soon named "The Boston Massacre", and inflamed passions that had been held in check for nearly five years burst forth.

Now the whole suppressed energy stored in the hearts and minds of many oppressed colonists erupted into complete dedication to the cause of freedom from England. Some remained loyal to the British crown, some were timid souls unable to commit themselves to the fray, some feared reprisal on relatives still living in England, and some wished to continue the comfortable positions they held under English rule, and therefore did not join the fight. They declared neutrality as with the family of Colonel Joshua Worthington.

The situation seemed to be tolerated by the freedom fighters. After all, they fought for freedom of choice for all and they knew that eventually all of the colonists would join them or leave when victory was won. Until then, they planned to use some of the loyalists to advantage. Thus was planned the assignment to be awarded to one Jeremiah Clarke from Maine.

CHAPTER II

The Wilderness

As battles raged on many fronts a new plan was formed. If the colonial army could rout the British from Canada the western front would be secure, and from there they would gradually push the Redcoats eastward back to the sea where their ships could take them back to England. If they could capture Quebec and Montreal they could form a line that would advance the plan. The man chosen to storm Quebec was Benedict Arnold and his highly disciplined troops. Arnold's wife had recently died leaving his three sons without a mother, but his sister "Hannah" lovingly cared for them as though they were her own. His grief at the loss of his beloved wife transformed his thinking. He could do nothing to bring Peggy back, but he could help bring freedom to his country. Hannah also took charge of his business affairs, allowing him the personal freedom to serve the cause. His meeting with George Washington went surprisingly well. They decided together to invade Canada from the Maine wilderness and from the Champlain region simultaneously. If the Brits took the majority of their troops to either Montreal or Quebec, they were sure to capture at least one major city. This control would prevent an attack from the northwest.

Washington liked the young officer immediately. He was bright and eager, and held an air of authority that was the essence of a good leader. Upon review of his men, he found them as well disciplined as his own, and felt confident he had found the right man for the mission.

Plans were made for bateaux to be built in Gardinerstown, Maine, enough to hold fourteen hundred men, with supplies and equipment for the trip by rivers, lakes and overland to surprise the English forces at Quebec. Daniel Morgan and his buckskin-clad men from Virginia joined the force for the clandestine mission. The combined force boarded seven sloops and schooners at Newburyport and reached Fort Western in Augusta on September 23.

The mission was held back because the bateaux were smaller than ordered, necessitating twenty more to be quickly built. They were poorly made of green lumber and soon leaked, spoiling much of their supplies. The progress upriver was slowed by the driving rain, snow and cold of late autumn.

The planned assault on Canada was fraught with problems from the beginning. Schuyler, commander of the troops marching north from Champlain became ill and Montgomery took command, planning to join Arnold's regiment for the assault on Quebec City. His army took Montreal, routing Governor Carleton who fled before them to Quebec. Arnold was late arriving because of the hardships he and his men had endured in the Maine wilderness. The arduous trip had taken its toll. With supplies lost because of leaking boats, the men were cold and hungry and their clothes torn and ragged from carrying the bateaux over portages. They hunted game whenever possible, they ate the tallow candles, some boiled their shoes for the nourishment from the leather. Arnold had them make moccasins from leather obtained from farmers and trappers they encountered as the men could not march on frozen feet. The trip was later compared to that of Hannibal crossing the Alps.

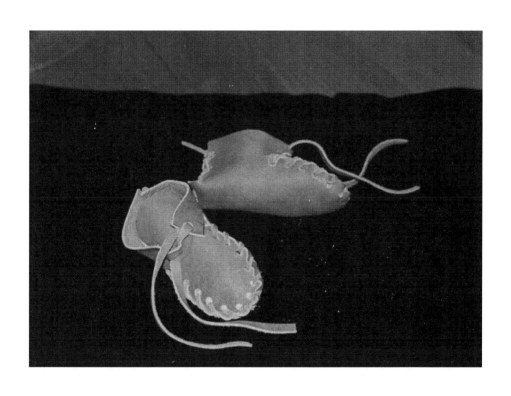

WILDERNESS MOCCASINS

(1) Overlap "B" edges and
secure with leather strip.
Fold flap "D" up and secure.
(2) Attach "A" to "A" and
"C" to "C". Lace curved
edges together.
(3) Make a leather tie
joining slots "E" to "E".
Tie can be long and
wrapped around ankle
and tied

A

moccasin tongue

C

A

slots "E"   slots "E"

C   C

Sole and sides
of moccasin

B   D   B

The city of Quebec proved to be a natural fortress. Sitting proudly on a three hundred foot bluff overlooking the mighty Saint Lawrence River, it was practically impenetrable. Montgomery did not arrive to join forces, being fatally wounded in a meeting with the British on his journey north, and Arnold's men were unable to take the city. Arnold himself was wounded as he led his men in the attempt. He had to be content blockading the city.

Then pestilence struck. Smallpox raged in the city and soon reached Arnold's men. Being weak from the hardships of the battle with the elements in the wilderness they were easy prey for illness. Many men inoculated themselves by rubbing fluid from the pustules of the sick into self-inflicted wounds, thereby giving themselves lighter cases of the disease. By February the snow was five feet deep, and pneumonia, influenza and frostbite plagued the troops.

Arnold's own merchant ship, the "Peggy" was anchored in the harbor and they filled it with explosives to use to ram any British ship attempting to cross the blockade. Leaving David Wooster in command Arnold rode south. He was sure all would be lost under the new command and as he had foreseen, the Patriots were overwhelmed and his schooner was blown up two hundred yards from the harbor entrance. Thomas, (who had taken over the command from Wooster when he died of the smallpox) and the Patriots were forced to retreat May third.

There were many problems within the military and congressional organizations. The Continental Congress insisted on being in control, but they were not schooled in military tactics. There was much promotional favoritism, with young protégés of certain congressmen given commands and promotions far above their qualifications, learning and experience. There were some who readily slandered superior officers and their unfair practices were well received by their mentors in power. Such was the case with Benedict Arnold. His leg wound was serious, and while he recuperated junior officers were given undeserved promotions due to their wealth and influence. One case in particular was the promotion of General Horatio Gates who was given command of the Patriot forces in Canada.

CHAPTER III

1776 would prove to be a time of great turmoil. After the first hurrah of patriotism recruitment had slowed. The Declaration of Independence had been signed on July 4th but one fourth of the Americans were still loyal to the Crown. The British general Sir William Howe drove Washington back to White Plains, New York and then across to Delaware. The American general struck back with victories at Trenton and Princeton, New Jersey, and then camped his men at Morristown. Back in early '75 King George had sent General Howe, Henry Clinton and John Burgoyne with a large force of regulars to the colonies to "scare" the rebels into submission, but the ploy hadn't worked. Upon taking command in Boston and the resulting retreat of the colonial forces from Massachusetts the British had become very confident of their ultimate victory. They ignored the western front where Benedict Arnold's "Foot Guards", (with the Blessing of the Reverend Jonathan Edwards), had been organizing to take Fort Ticonderoga on Lake Champlain. Arnold reported to Washington that it would be advantageous to the war effort. Given four hundred men he had ridden west, recruiting on the way, and with help from Ethan Allen and his Green Mountain Boys from Vermont they took the fort in ten minutes.

Arnold reported to Washington that a great number of cannons were available from Ticonderoga (previously named "Carrillon" under the French for the sound of the waterfall as Lake George tumbled into Lake Champlain).

If the cannon could be moved to Boston, he reported, they could retake the city from British control.

Benedict was not happy with Ethan Allen or his men. They plundered and pillaged and had become roaring drunk on confiscated rum, and his appeal to Allen for discipline went unheeded. Allen himself was a hard drinking man and saw no problem with his men doing the same.

In spite of his unhappiness with the Vermonters, Arnold was elated over the fifty-seven usable cannon that could be transported to Dorchester Heights overlooking Boston. He was sure Washington's artillery commander, Henry Knox, would find a way to accomplish just that.

CHAPTER IV

Benedict Arnold

Benedict Arnold contemplated that religion was a strange institution. The church of his mother required a religious experience to be the basis for membership, but who was to judge such an experience? Did the dawning of salvation have to come to a sinner in church, and any awakening to God's will that called to the heart and mind that occurred on a lone journey to the ocean or to a mountaintop be discarded as false? And who could be sure an awakening accompanied by tears of guilt during church was more sincere, or perhaps not sincere at all, though seemingly acceptable as long as one declared a changed life? What about a personal relationship with God through the Christ? Benedict could not accept the treatment his father had received from the church. The death of his mother, brother and sister had driven him to drink. As far as he was concerned, if the church had done its part and the parishioners had put their arms around him in his time of trouble his drinking might not have occurred. How easily his father had been blamed when perhaps the shortcomings of the congregation had assisted in his downfall.

Benedict's own relationship with God was profound. He believed in Divine Providence and that it was a loving God that guided his actions. He would never allow his men to pillage the countryside as did Ethan Allen and his Green Mountain Boys. Their heavy drinking was legend while Benedict made sure the ration of rum for each man in his regiment was limited to that ration, and he adhered to that small ration himself. One drink to warm a man after a hard day was one thing, but drunkenness was not to be tolerated. Too much drink festered arrogance and often made a man less honest and with a vainglorious view of himself. Allen had claimed sole victory at Ticonderoga and with great speed he informed the Continental Congress of his achievement, claiming all the glory for himself. Aside from the fact that he had not done it by himself, the battle had only lasted minutes and it was difficult to imagine that Allen's need for glory was so great that he would falsify his part in the small skirmish. Benedict swore to himself that he would not let such a thing happen again and he would refuse to go into battle with such a bunch of undisciplined louts, though he blamed the drink more than he blamed the men themselves.

There was also a lot about General Gates that bothered him. He had once been his friend but the friendship had ended. The man's ambition to be an important hero was quite disgusting. The way he pandered to the congressional "powers that be" was like a thorn under Arnold's skin that could not be easily dislodged. Gates never led his men. He always remained out of harm's way behind the skirmish line until a battle was won, then he would suddenly re-appear in a crisp clean uniform with a gleaming sword at his side as though he had actually been involved in the fight. He was always safely beyond any chance of injury and had been very little involved in actual battle planning. Whether he was scheming, lucky or treacherous was difficult to determine. He couldn't even sit a horse well, possessing a large cumbersome posterior and legs that flattened against the horse's sides because of their lack of muscle tone. His slight potbelly did keep him solidly on his steed, and Benedict had to admit his gold embellished uniform was impressive. Of course Arnold's own uniform might have been as resplendent as Gates' if it were not so worn and with mended tears from his battle wounds. His emergence from battle in such a state did not distinguish him from a foot soldier.

Benedict's ambivalence went much deeper than whose uniform was more effulgent. Losing acclaim for his bravery as well as the pain and suffering from his battle wounds bothered him, but more important was the compassion he felt for his battle weary soldiers. The war was proving to be long and exhausting and the men seemed to be wavering in their loyalty to the cause. He was beginning to doubt there were enough dedicated troops and available supplies to actually win freedom from England.

Life was much simpler when he was growing up. When he was a child and then a teen his only thoughts were of his next adventure. He had always striven to run faster, jump higher, and even throw rocks farther than any of his friends. His mother, Hannah, had seen to his being restricted in his wild physical pursuits enough to accomplish his studies and he was quite attentive. His interest in knowledge went beyond just being inquisitive, it spanned every aspect of learning because his ambition was to out-do any of his compatriots. It was a driving force from within that was beyond his control. Knowing his family heritage of wealth, honor and leadership had been won, lost, and then partially regained by his father marrying a rich widow, he, as a teen, decided his aim in life would be to restore the family fortune to the full glory it had held when his ancestors owned most of Rhode Island. 'Not that he didn't love Connecticut. He had grown up in Norwich and with his father's shipping business he never lacked comforts and after studies he had time to develop his athletic prowess; marksmanship, swordsmanship, and equestrian skills. He had caused quite a stir by clambering onto the huge waterwheel that turned the grist mill on the Thames River and rode it all the way around. The townspeople had reported that adventure to his parents with many a "Fie, Fie" on him. Actually all his cronies had been taking wagers as to whether such a ride could be accomplished and several had tried and failed with many a lump, bruise and splinter to show for the effort. He, however, had hung on for the complete revolution and only received a few splinters, (which he kept hidden and removed later in secret, lest his heroic image be tarnished). These devilish pranks of his teen years would prove to be only the beginning of his ambition, and as he led his friends in challenges as a youth, so he would lead as an adult. Never holding back, he led his men and fought by their sides, rewarding him with the title, "The Fighting General", one who never asked more of his men than he did of himself. His men had the utmost respect for his abilities and trusted his judgment. His way of making them feel that the regiment was theirs together was by his constant presence among their ranks, sharing the fighting, the cold, the miseries of war and never eating any food better than was available for his men. He shared the whole effort for the cause at the same economic level as the troops he commanded. He was, indeed, most beloved and respected.

Not until after the battle at Ticonderoga, did he at last achieve victory. Though he had been successful, he was still uncertain. Having abandoned the strict religion of his mother he still, nonetheless, believed in a Supreme God. He had never reconciled his feeling over the loss of his siblings in the innocence of their childhood, and often felt guilty that his own strong constitution had saved him from a similar fate. In the privacy of his quarters he spent many a nighttime hour seeking guidance from the Almighty as the candle burned down. He hoped his prayers would be answered by God and not be used as just a confirmation of his own desires. He had heard too many declare that God had spoken directly to them and had given them permission to enact their own selfish decisions. More and more he had become suspicious of such confident hypocrites who insisted that they had a direct contact with God but always seemed to absolve themselves from any wrongdoing as well as relieving themselves from any responsibility toward kindness, tolerance and love of their fellow man.

His early campaigns had not been so difficult. Though more physically demanding, and plagued by the problems of fatigue, dysentery and pestilence, the confusion and indecisiveness were not present. Having to share authority had been more difficult than any hardships he had heretofore endured. In his younger years he had never thought of himself as particularly brave, his boyish antics of bravado had been more explorations of his ability and a method of seeking acceptance from his boyhood chums. War was a different ball of wax. The time he and his friends had been caught trying to pilfer a couple small barrels of tar to use for a bonfire had taught him a lesson in caution. Usually the "good people" who claimed their sons were innocent of any wrongdoing had to find a "ringleader" to blame. Since that incident he had made his plans more exacting. The odd result of his handwork seemed to be the interference of usurpers taking credit for his achievements. In his pursuit of respect to restore the family name after the loss of his father who, sadly, had drunk himself to death following the demise of his family, (except for Benedict and Hannah), and the hypocritical snubbing by the self righteous church members that had once been their friends, he had since reevaluated his relationship with God. He could not accept that God had destroyed his family as a warning that he should "live pure" lest the wrath of God destroy him, also. He came to accept the frailties of life as just that, and believed in a loving all-powerful Deity from whom he could seek leadership and guidance, though his prayers did not explain why he had to deal with General Gates.

CHAPTER V

Colonel Henry Knox, Washington's youthful artillery commander, contemplated the house he would build some day. The land that Lucy's grandfather had given them as a wedding present was in Maine, the northern part of Massachusetts. He imagined the winters might be harsh, not like George's Mount Vernon with its fast melting snows, but the summers would be delightful. Besides, they could always travel south for the winter, visiting George and Martha and also Thomas Jefferson at Monticello. Virginia might have a more temperate climate but it lacked the fresh breeze off the ocean and the definitive seasonal changes. Maine would be beautiful the year round with the maples, oaks and poplars changing their green to brilliant color in fall, the green of pine, hemlock, spruce and fir against a snowy white backdrop in winter, followed by the bursting forth of spring with its rivulets, dancing brooks and sparkling lakes. The joy of spring would turn golden in July and August with harvests of hay, corn, squashes and all the fruit trees sporting their colorful globes just waiting to be cooked into pies and jams. Root cellars would be filled with potatoes, turnip, beets and cabbages. Yes, it would be a great place to retire, there on a hill overlooking the river meeting the ocean.

By the time he could retire the children would be grown. Oh, how he wished they had all lived! His darling Lucy had followed him through all his campaigns and had endured hard living conditions at the military camps, but nothing had been as hard to bear as the loss of several children in their infancy. He and Lucy were both of robust health but the children had all been born frail and only a few survived. He hoped by the time they built their final home there would be grandchildren about the house.

These thoughts comforted him when he saw so many young men dying on the battlefield. He hoped their dying might not be in vain and that the next generation of children would grow up without oppression in a free country because of their sacrifice.

The good news was that a man had been found for the mission he and George had planned. Together, the friends had decided that a way needed to be found to infiltrate the British army without arousing suspicion. They needed someone intelligent, dedicated and single. Their plan to place an informant in Philadelphia could be carried out if the right man were found and now word had come that the very man they sought had arrived with a new contingent of recruits.

Having already secured property in Philadelphia, a building that could be quickly converted into a large dry goods store, the news that their man had been located was cause for celebration. Orders for a young man named "Jeremiah Clarke" were swiftly drawn up and a meeting was put in place. The sooner the plan was implemented the better. If they had known in advance that the British army was going to arrive in Boston Harbor there would have been no need for the alarm to be sounded. They could have fortified the city before the arrival of the troops and Revere and Dawes would not have needed to make their wild ride. Their capture at Lexington and their mission completed by Dr. Prescott would have been unnecessary. But the British came and made Boston theirs. Washington wished to get his new man set up in Philadelphia as soon as possible. Knox, himself, had just returned from a difficult mission. Armed with the information from Benedict Arnold that there were many cannon at Ticonderoga, he had been successful in retrieving them in spite of adverse weather conditions. He had planned to transport the cannon on horse drawn sledges over frozen ground. It should have been easy, but the weather had turned warm and the trail became mud. More horses had to be found to pull the heavy mud bogged sledges and the trip had taken much longer than anticipated. He prayed for cold weather, and getting none, he was satisfied with the extra men, horses and oxen he had procured.

Arriving in Massachusetts he soon had the cannon placed strategically on Dorchester Heights, and with the bombardment the city of Boston was once again under colonial control. Knox had promised himself that he would accomplish his mission and his success had been heralded. His greatest satisfaction was that he had not disappointed his friend George.

General Washington had hoped Henry could deliver the cannon but had feared it would be impossible in the mild weather, and he planned to reward him with a generalship. The victory provided both men with satisfaction and further strengthened their bond of friendship.

CHAPTER VI

Henry Knox was given the task of advising the new recruit of the plans for subversive activity in Philadelphia. Jeremiah had not been unwilling to be a regular foot soldier, but each volunteer had been asked to fill out a questionnaire. Many could not read or write and Jeremiah had helped them list their qualifications. Most had little, so the task did not have a chance to become tedious. The regimental captain had allowed him to assist any man unable to complete his own papers, and he had been watched closely as he wrote in his neat manuscript. He noted that the captain had set his own papers aside and had made notations on the form. He hoped the notations were complimentary and nothing that would hinder his selection to fight for the cause in which he so strongly believed. Never would he have believed he would be selected to obtain any information he could by mixing with the neutralists and loyalists for General Washington. When Colonel Knox called for Corporal Clarke, he explained the mission to Jeremiah. The young soldier was surprised to find the colonel so young, although he had the bearing of a much older man. He sensed that perhaps the man had been given much responsibility, and probably had carried out many a hard mission for the commander of the armies.

"We need your help, Son. We have called you up because your trustworthiness cannot be questioned. Your experience in the managing of a store is the talent we require, and your ability will make you beyond suspicion. You must go to Philadelphia and set up a dry goods store. You will mix with the locals and become a trusted confidant and express your sympathy to the British control of the colonies, and your distaste for the revolution in which we are embroiled. Your loyalty to the Crown must never be doubted. You will be safe, as there are many loyalists there, and many a wife and family of British officers reside there."

"But Sir, how will casual talk in a dry goods store help us obtain freedom? Am I to spy?"

"In a sense, yes, Jeremiah. If you can find an opportunity to make yourself trusted the information will be available to you easily. By taking part in the events and social affairs of the English sympathizers you will be able to mingle with servants, daughters of soldiers, wives of soldiers and even children often hear and repeat things that would help our cause. Your position must not be discovered, you must live, eat, sleep and if necessary, marry to carry out your assignment."

"Marry? But I have a true love. How can I marry?"

"Jeremiah, in the cause of liberty men give up their lives every day. You can serve with far less danger than in the field of battle. What say you to this mission, "Yea" or "Nay?"

"Of course I say "Yea", Sir. Forgive me for a moment of immaturity. I can do this mission and I will give it my all. Do not doubt my fidelity for a moment."

"There will be no contact with you for three months. We have supplied you with adequate funds to set up the store with more goods than it will hold as well as enough to convince the public that you are a gentleman of means. You may furnish quarters on the floor above the store. Be sure that you do not contact your family, friends or even any command center. You will be completely on your own. It is the only way your safety will be assured. This is no easy assignment. You were chosen because of your ability, intelligence and fealty. In three months you will have made your place in the hearts and minds of the loyalists and hopefully by then you will have found a way to access troop movements. General Washington and myself are counting on you. We have instigated this endeavor and I trust that between us we can obtain the desired results. On December first you will find a man in Tolliver's Tavern with a Bob-White feather in his cap. He will be pretending to be a drunkard. Touch him and he will fall from his chair. You are to help him back to his seat and slip any information you have into his pocket during the assistance. From then on you will find him at the tavern on a regular monthly basis and find a way to make contact. Offer to assist him to his lodgings or whatever is necessary. Do you understand?"

"Yes, Sir. I will not fail you. I promise you that."

"Do not give any indication in the messages as to your identity. If our courier is caught there must be no reference from whence the information was obtained. Am I clear?"

"Yes, Sir. Very clear."

"Here is your stipend. You will find it extremely generous, but to arrange the necessary conditions we could do no less." Placing a hand on Jeremiah's shoulder he said, "I'm sorry, Jeremiah. I realize your heart is with someone from your home, but this assignment is more important than any personal feelings. If you have a chance to marry to become close to a source of information it is your duty to do so. You understand, don't you, my boy? By the way, it would do you great service if you pretend to be less bright than you are. It would make you more acceptable and beyond suspicion, do you think you can manage that?"

"Of course, Sir. I stand ready to go forward."

Saluting, he turned and left Knox. Returning to his quarters he packed his bags and prepared for his journey to Philadelphia and whatever fate awaited him there. He wondered what his mother would think. Of course he couldn't tell her anything about a secret assignment, and what she didn't know wouldn't hurt her, but he remembered that when he was a child she always seemed to know what he was doing. Whether from God, from witchcraft, or from woman's intuition, the results were the same. Thinking she had eyes in the back of her head, he had finally realized that it was because she watched him closely and listened attentively, always catching him in any act of mischief. He could not inform her of his mission, or even the circumstances if he were forced to marry. And Mercy, there was no way he could contact her and explain the assignment. Their love would be a sacrifice for the cause of freedom, and there was nothing he could do about it. If he had known what his assignment would entail he might have deserted before beginning his active military career.

That night as he lay on his cot, Jeremiah's mind began to race. He had envisioned battles he would fight, bravery he would execute, marching on to victory waving a flag. Never had he imagined an assignment such as this. Just before he dropped off to sleep a courier brought him a note. He was to return to command headquarters at seven in the morning. He wondered what more would be asked of him. There seemed to be little he could do no matter what the request, so he resigned himself to whatever fate lay in store and slept soundly until reveille the next morning. Quickly washing, shaving, and smoothing his clothing, paying strict attention to his appearance to be sure to present the proper impression, he reported as instructed. To his surprise the meeting included General Washington himself.

"Henry Knox was the first to speak. "Corporal Clarke, the general wishes to be sure we have the right man for the operation we are planning."

Washington sat at a desk and thoughtfully looked over the young man that had entered. He wished to be assured that the man from the outer reaches of Massachusetts, in far away Maine, would be capable of carrying off the charade. He had expected a bumpkin and had prepared himself to continue the search for a proper prospect. Though his friend had assured him that the man was well educated, spoke fluent French (albeit with a decided accent) as well as proper English, he had not expected the obvious good grooming and fair countenance. Jeremiah was surprised, also, with the gracious manner with which he was received. It was an honor he had not expected and he fought not to tremble, trying to keep his composure as a soldier.

He was somewhat taken aback when the Commander of the armies spoke words that changed a possibility to a definite probability.

"We have chosen your path. It has been brought to our attention that a Colonel Joshua Worthington of his Majesty's army has a wife and daughter living in Philadelphia. Worthington is closely associated with Cornwallis and Clinton as well as Howe. The fact that Worthington considers the Patriots as just so much rabble that can be easily squashed has led him in the past to host many parties and social occasions. He is known as a gracious and generous host to those loyal to British rule. This is the realm into which you must infiltrate. Though the captain is with his regiment we are sure he occasionally visits his family."

Jeremiah knew they did not understand the difficulty of the assignment, an assignment to which he had sworn to adhere.

Knox entered into the conversation at that point.

"Woo Worthington's daughter, marry her, and send reports of any information you can glean from the contact."

The words hit like a hammer. The wooing he could have handled, but the marrying seemed a little beyond the call of duty.

"Corporal Clarke," Knox continued, "Wooing in just frivolity, marrying the girl will, to Worthington, seal your loyalty to England. This must be done if we are to be successful."

"With all due respect, Sir. I have a true love and planned to marry if I live through this revolution. What you ask will be the death of my life."

"My dear corporal. Many have already given their lives and many more will also die, while you, although this plan is not your choice, will live. That is, you will live as long as you are faithful to your British wife and perform your duty to your country with caution. In the information we were given last night after our initial meeting, it seems the daughter is very glib. You can do much for your country's cause and your life will be spared in the bargain. Have we chosen the right man for this assignment?"

"Yes, Sir."

After a silence Washington again entered the discussion. He sat back in his chair behind the desk for a moment, and then he leaned forward, looking intently into the eyes of the corporal who was processing his future and rearranging his thinking to the mission at hand.

"Another problem we discussed is the manner in which messages can be sent to us. Too many messages have been discovered hidden in quill pens, messages written in code or written in invisible ink. Their discovery has courted disaster. We must devise a method that cannot be easily decoded or pose a threat to the bearer. To lose a messenger is a serious loss and must be avoided if at all possible."

"Sir," Jeremiah returned. "If I may be so bold, I believe I can offer a solution. I could formulate a plan that could not be detected, a way of writing a message that would pose no threat to anyone. Since I worked at a garrison as well as ordering supplies for my father's store, I could make a code within the orders for supplies. As I will be opening a store in Philadelphia, no one would be the wiser. Supplies must be ordered regularly to run the business and a messenger carrying an order for dry goods would not be suspect, especially if the goods were actually delivered after your reading of the message. If you give me another day I'm sure I can deliver the code into your hands for approval.

"I hope you realize how much we will be relying on your ability to extract the information we need."

"Yes, Sir, I do. My heart is devoted to this assignment and my life dedicated to freeing our new nation. I will memorize the code and the only copy of the key will be in your hands. God grant us the victory we desire. My part will be very small compared to those who die daily for our cause. My life belongs to my country."

With that, Jeremiah Clarke snapped to attention and saluted his commander. He had, in one day become a Tory, and he had a job to do. The code would be in Washington's hands on the morrow, and Jeremiah would be on his way to Philadelphia.

The Code

Direction of Troop Movement

Wool = North   Howe's Troops = horseradish
Silk = East   Clinton's Troops = stick candy
Cotton = South   Burgoyne's Troops = bees wax
Shoe Leather = West

Code I
1 barrel of flour =10 barrels of powder
Brooms = cannon
Oz. tea = muskets
1 knife = 100 men

Code II
1 barrel of oats = 10 barrels of powder
Horseshoes = cannon
Sewing needles = muskets
1 fork = 100 men

Code III
1 pound nails = 10 barrels of powder
Knitting needles = cannon
Spools of thread = muskets
1 spoon = 100 men

Code IV
1 Cake of soap = 10 barrels of powder
Jugs of molasses = cannon
Rations of rum = muskets
1 tin of snuff = 100 men

Jeremiah studied the code over and over, then committed to memory a simple formula to be sure he would not err.

Powder = flour, oats, nails and soap
Cannon = brooms, horseshoes, knitting needles and
    jugs of molasses
Muskets = oz. tea, sewing needles, spools of thread and
    rations of rum
Per 100 men = knives, forks, spoons and tins of snuff

The code words indicating the directions of troop movements was easy, as the words depicted goods from the designated areas, and logic dictated the amounts. When he was sure the whole code was securely committed to his memory he took it to Colonel Knox who put it in Washington's hands. Now he was sure they had chosen their man wisely.

Chapter VII

Abigail Worthington. The bevy of giggling girls in the corner centered around the daughter of Colonel Joshua Worthington of His Majesty's Royal Army. Their silliness did not bother Jeremiah, and he took little notice beyond hoping the object of his mission was not one of them. If his life was to be sacrificed for his country he had hoped the daughter of Captain Worthington would be intelligent and pleasant even if she were plain. It was not to be. The China silk dresses and upswept curls did nothing to erase the ridiculous impression Abigail Worthington presented. Slightly plump with a white boson bursting over her bodice in a supposed appealing display of femininity, her giggling kept the soft tissue in a constant jiggle. It was all Jeremiah could do to keep a calm countenance. Now he could see how difficult this assignment was going to be.

The reception flowed with French wine smuggled into England and shipped on to America, tables overflowed with jellied beef, potatoes in rich gravy, steak and kidney pies, carrots in sugared sauce, oysters, sea urchins, pheasant and freshly baked breads. The desserts were small pastries with dried fruit fillings, strudels and apple dumplings, sweet cream and several blends of English tea.

Partaking of the delicacies gave Jeremiah a chance to plan. He had felt fortunate in being invited to the affair, but once there he discovered many of the neutralists and loyalist shop owners were present, and there was nothing special about his inclusion. However, it was just the opportunity he had been waiting for. The store was half stocked, (with space waiting for future 'special' orders), and it was time to proceed with his assignment. He ate slowly and carefully, attempting to prolong the agony of meeting the Colonel's daughter as long as possible.

Finally, he felt he could put off the inevitable no longer. Approaching the group of girls he introduced himself.

"Excuse me, my name is Jeremiah Clarke and I am new in town. I recently came from Maine and have been setting up a dry goods store and grocery in town. Having so recently arrived I could use some advice as I plan to settle here in Philadelphia permanently. Perhaps you could tell me some of the needs and wants of the people of this fair city. Are you Miss Worthington? This is such a lovely social affair I would like to thank the Worthington family for allowing me to attend."

"No, my name is Elizabeth Stuart. I am her friend," and pointing to the plump girl sitting on the love seat, "this is Abigail."

The pale Abigail wiggled in her seat as Jeremiah reached down and raised the soft hand to his lips, kissing the soft knuckles, rather, the dents where her knuckles were hidden.

"I'm so pleased to meet you, Abigail. This is an exceptional party and I appreciate the hospitality."

Elizabeth withdrew, wondering at the cordiality with which Jeremiah had greeted Abigail. Usually men considered Abigail too silly to spend their time making polite conversation. She decided Maine men must be so deprived of female companions they confused giddiness with femininity. If that were the case she had no interest in the handsome young man from the North. After all, being handsome wasn't all that important, she surmised.

Sitting beside Abigail, Jeremiah tried to think of something to further the conversation. The wiggling seemed to be some involuntary nervous reflex so he had difficulty deciding what course to take. If he offered to fetch her some tea she would probably spill it on her gown so he suggested that he bring her more solid refreshment to which she agreed.

Trying not to sweat he walked to the dessert table and found a plate of raspberry filled blintzes and brought her one on a small plate.

Giggling, Abigail took a bite and a crumb fell down onto her ample bosom and there it lodged in the cleavage. She continued eating until it was completely devoured, then wiped her mouth on her handkerchief and beamed up at the very self controlled Jeremiah. He didn't dare mention the crumb for fear he would be asked to retrieve it, or if she retrieved it herself and then ate it he might not be able to control his amusement. 'Better let sleeping crumbs lie, he decided. It would be a great snack for her later.

"Miss Abigail, would you like to take a carriage ride tomorrow? I have little knowledge of the town and would appreciate a guided tour. I would see that you were back home by early afternoon."

"Why, Mr. Clarke, I would be delighted, (giggle, giggle). I will be ready at nine. Oh, I can hardly wait for tomorrow!"

With that she jumped up from her seat, the bosom crumb popping from its resting place and landing on the floor as she ran to the corner and burst into the group of girls gathered there. With much giggling, the news had been spread.

Jeremiah felt like a fish in a bowl but he told himself, "so far, so good." He rather wished Elizabeth had been Worthington's daughter, but perhaps she would not have been as glib and easily duped as the real Abigail. Drawing in a deep breath he searched out the hostess, expressed his appreciation for the evening and took his carriage back across town to his establishment. Sleep did not come easily as thoughts of his duty, of Mercy and home all crowded his mind. He went over the code several times until he finally drifted off into a fitful sleep.

CHAPTER VIII

Abigail Worthington was giddy with delight. No man of quality had ever paid her much attention. Oh, Rupert Brown had always fantasized that someday they would become sweethearts, but he was fat and had crooked teeth that had shown decay since he was eleven years old. His love of sweets was evident in his smile. Of course she had never really discouraged him because he was of a generous sort and shared his treats with her. She knew it was just a bribe or excuse to touch her. He'd try to tickle her under her arms to make her giggle, (as if she needed any help), and she didn't like that, but tolerated it somewhat because the sweets from his mother's bakery shop were quite tasty. She resented comments she had heard that they were "two of a kind." Rupert was fat but she considered herself merely pleasingly plump. In her opinion, girls should not be thin and witch-like. A little flesh smoothed out the body. No, Rupert would never have been acceptable as a contender for her affections. Besides, her father's position in the British army heightened her position as a desirable female, and there was no reason that she should settle for a less than attractive suitor. But Jeremiah Clarke had surprised her and everyone else. Her mother had spent hours curling her hair, having attractive gowns made that she hoped would conceal her daughters soft formless figure and had tried in vain to control her food portions.

The new grocer in town had not exactly impressed her family at first. They had heard of him and the general opinion was that he was rather "milk toast," but since they had a rather plain daughter they decided not to be too fussy. When the opportunity arose they decided to invite him to their party and they would become tolerant of his shortcomings if he became interested in Abigail. He was certainly more acceptable than Rupert Brown. Their diminished hopes of ever finding a suitable husband for their plump daughter was again aroused and if a liaison was accomplished it would be advantageous for them all. With all the current trouble in obtaining quality food and goods from the homeland, having a grocer in the family seemed a stroke of good fortune.

The eagerness with which Jeremiah Clarke pursued Abigail was never questioned. He appeared to be genuinely impatient. To onlookers he was merely an amorous young man caught up in the throws of hormonal anticipation. His avid pursuit became rather comical to elders who perhaps had forgotten their own younger days when love and copulation were synonymous. With clucking of tongues and winks of eyes, the romance blossomed and the day Jeremiah knelt before the flustered Abigail and asked for her hand in marriage, the giggling effusive reply was an answer to many dreams. Silly Abigail believed she was truly loved by her Prince Charming, her parents were relieved that she would not become a spinster, and Jeremiah, his dreams of possibly obtaining access to British stores and troop movements became a more promising reality.

"Yes, yes," she had exclaimed almost before the words of proposal had left his lips. "I just knew you loved me! I just knew it! I can hardly wait to tell everyone! It will be the most wonderful wedding! I must plan the food! I must order my dress! Oh, Oh, let's plan it as soon as possible! My friends will be so envious!" With that she rushed out, leaving Jeremiah on his knees. She had not realized there had been no declaration of love from Jeremiah. In her innocence and limited thinking capacity his importance in the wedding had immediately been minimized with deference to the food and clothing.

It was with great relief and gratitude he accepted the situation as a complete success. At least he had not been forced to lie.

The wedding was everything Abigail had ever dreamed. Her gown was of white silk with flounces and ribbons and rosettes, the food was abundant and the dancing went on until late in the night. When the "'til death do we part" came Jeremiah felt as though he might faint as every hope he held in his heart to be with Mercy was drained from his being. Before the ceremony he had contemplated his assignment. Having made the commitment to discover all possible information on the British invasion he had little time to reflect on what his own peril would be if his activities were discovered. In the first place, he had no ambition toward achieving personal glory, the only accomplishment he sought was that of aiding the cause of victory for the Patriots. His position in the Worthington household was secure. His rough quarters over the grocery were not fitting for his wife, her being used to the finer things in life and when the Worthingtons suggested that he move into their large mansion he feigned reluctance but finally agreed. It was as though Providence was smiling on him. Now he had an even better opportunity to accomplish the mission he had been assigned. He had heard rumors of "the fop that married the Colonel's daughter" and "the coward who preferred the grocery business to fighting."

Shouldering false name-calling did not affect Jeremiah. It was exactly the impression he desired. He usually managed to purposely spill some liquid or foodstuff on his waistcoat or upset a cup of punch at every social gathering. Everyone pretended to overlook the bumbling of the good affable grocer who gave more goods per pennyweight than anyone else in town. The Worthingtons were often embarrassed by his bumbling business practices but concealed their feelings well. After all, the young man had saved their plump daughter from certain spinsterhood. He knew he would have fought to the death for his country if it had been asked of him, and sometimes he wished he had chosen the battlefield over subterfuge. He was constantly reminded of his sacrifice by the presence of his giddy wife. The day of his marriage to Abigail had been the death knell for his life with Mercy, and his heart had broken as he forced the ring on her chubby finger. He had sweated until the salt ran into his eyes, masquerading his tears. Amid the laughter and backslapping that followed the ceremony and along with the jokes about loss of freedom and so forth, he raised his cup and toasted his bride, while in his heart he knew it was raised to freedom for his fledgling country. Though duty forced him to be bound in matrimony, his earlier sworn duty as a Patriot would always be foremost in his mind. A few more toasts, then a few more drinks and he had been carried, unconscious, to the wedding chamber. The only utterance anyone heard was that of "Mercy", and the jovial revelers had enjoyed the mild grocer's French word of thanks for the assistance they had given. Jeremiah had at least been spared from his connubial duty on his wedding night.

Counting the Cost

What is the price of liberty?
What sacrifice made?
Must it require a broken heart,
Must one be unafraid,
To live a life in love's contempt,
And yield to tortured lies?
Then complete this wild charade,
Of true love to deny.
When victory may come at last,
Will this pain still follow me,
As now I give my life, my love,
For the cause of liberty.

CHAPTER IX

Jeremiah's business in Philadelphia was booming. He became well respected as a humble merchant and showed no prejudice toward loyalists, neutralists or colonials, and he dealt fairly with all who came to his well—stocked general store. The surprising addition of apothecary goods and even the seemingly oversupply of many items kept customers eager to peruse the shelves for anything added to the current stock. The Worthingtons were amazed and pleased with their new son-in-law, and as the business prospered they became more and more appreciative of the New Englander in their midst. Their only complaint was the winter sweater he seemed inordinately fond of and had suggested that a brass buttoned jacket might be more fitting for his position, but Jeremiah maintained it was a special sweater worn in Maine and that he would not be comfortable in any other until the weather warmed. Little could they know that it was the only part of his true love and the only consolation he still possessed.

With eyes and ears open he discovered tidbits of information to pass on to General Washington. Since many couriers in the past had been captured he was extremely cautious, always using the code to protect the courier. He made rare visits to Tolliver's Tavern and usually purchased a small bottle of liquor for mixing with medicines for his apothecary, sometimes assisting the "drunken" courier, sometimes meeting him outside late at night when the tavern closed and the man had been escorted out to the alley behind the establishment. The few times the courier was apprehended he was released and the "grocery lists" were never suspected. There was no reason to hold a man who was openly carrying an order in his pocket for grocery store items. Sometimes it became amusing to Jeremiah that he had an abundance of certain items, so he put them safely out of sight in the upstairs room that had been his quarters before his marriage. Sometimes he held "specials" of overstocked items, but there was never any link to the actual reason for his excess of stock. Since he had put forth an image of being less than brilliant, the excess stock that had to be put on sale further demonstrated his lack of talent for proper ordering of supplies. The townspeople enjoyed the sales, thinking they were fortunate their grocer was inefficient in handling his business. It all worked to Jeremiah's advantage.

Abigail soon expressed a desire to have a home of her own and Jeremiah promised her that in two years time they would think about building her dream house. He was in no hurry to leave the Worthington household but he had no choice but to let her have the home she desired. He hoped that in two years the war would be ended, but if not, he would still be at her parents' home as much as he could manage. She seemed satisfied and it gave him peace and time to gather all the information he could. At any rate, he was stuck with her and they would need a home eventually, after the war ended. He had written his mother of his marriage and he could only envision the blow it must have given Mercy. There was nothing he could do about it. He could not explain, and it would have served no purpose if he could. He was married and he was doomed to live a life of misery even after the war. He tried not to think about his bleak future. It was too painful.

Mere luck presented him with the opportunity for which he had been waiting. There was a discussion at the dinner table of "Gentleman" Johnny Burgoyne. There were several officers present and there was much laughter throughout the conversation. It seemed that since Burgoyne's wife died he had been quite the rascal. Being fond of drinking, singing and general carousing he had taken the wife of his commissary for his mistress, and there seemed to be no trouble or objection over the situation. Evidently the husband was honored that his wife was so appreciated. The officers' joviality over the liaison was quite entertaining, but as the evening wore on and rum was consumed, lips began to loosen. Pretending disinterest and spending the evening pouring over the figures in his leather bound record book, he gleaned enough to piece together Burgoyne's plans for the near future. The men had joked that "Johnny Boy" would have to take time out from his paramour to march from Canada to Albany, and his mistress might be worn out from the trip. Another mentioned that she could rest at the fort at Lake Champlain (Ticonderoga), and then catch up and resume their romance and partying when they reached Saratoga. They laughed again when one officer stated that with over seven thousand men and six hundred and fifty Indians the shared wife of the commissary would be able to work her way through the troops. Changing subjects, they went on to say that the British could do as they very well pleased and advance whenever they felt like it. After that the revelry became dull.

Their overconfidence galled Jeremiah. They considered the Patriots ignorant ruffians and that it would be just a matter of time until the colonists lay down their arms. Jeremiah knew that capitulation was not in General Washington's vocabulary and the Whigs would fight as long as it took to gain freedom from King George. These Brits could eat, drink and laugh, but eventually they would be laughing all the way back across the Atlantic.

The evening had been productive and Jeremiah quietly said his good nights to the family after the reveling officers left. He hoped Abigail would not be pestering him for attention tonight. He was anxious to make out a new order for the store and send it on its way so General Washington could strategically dispatch forces to bring Burgoyne to his knees, and not with his mistress.

CHAPTER X

General Burgoyne

General Burgoyne did not like the way the war was going. When he left England he had been assured that the colonists were a rag tag bunch of common ill educated ruffians with no knowledge of real warfare. When he was captain of the 11th Dragoons and later as lieutenant colonel of the Coldstream Guards at Cherbourg and St. Malo, he knew what he was up against in those expeditions. Even when he was promoted to brigadier general leading the storming of Valencia de Alcantara in Portugal he had been sure of his troops and he knew his enemy. Here in the colonies things were different. The colonials were mostly poorly uniformed but they managed to be far more organized than he had expected. He was also very disappointed in Sir Guy Carleton and did not relish being placed second in command to someone for whom he had little respect. He had taken the time to return to England to visit his wife, Lady Charlotte. (She had been pleased to see him while he was unaware that the visit would be the last he would see of her, as she died shortly after his visit). As a soldier and parliamentarian, he would not shirk his duty, and bidding her farewell he returned to the colonies.

Burgoyne's orders were to march north to Canada and lead an expedition southward. It was believed that they could box in the colonials from the north and by sea and easily force the rebels to capitulate. As much as he would have preferred to remain in England with his family he accepted his duty and was glad to be part of the force to cut the colonies in two, demoralizing them into submission, abandoning their foolish craving for independence. The plan was to move south, capture Fort Ticonderoga and move down the Hudson Valley where they would meet the army of Sir William Howe coming from the South. With Colonel Barry St. Leger moving eastward through the Mohawk Valley to join forces they could easily defeat the ill supplied militia.

And so, it was, when he arrived in Canada the plan had become a reality. With 7,000 regulars and with the help of 650 Indians, they easily took Fort Ticonderoga. It was proof that careful planning and well-trained troops led to easy victory. Continuing the march they decided to pass through Bennington, Vermont. He was dumfounded. The small American force fought with such ferocity they were repelled. The failure of Howe and St. Leger to assist his advance infuriated him, but he continued on until he was surrounded and outnumbered at Saratoga where he was forced to surrender to General Horatio Gates. He was humiliated and angry that the two armies that were to aid him had not completed their missions, robbing him of victory. He wondered if they had been merely overly cautious, if they had been cowardly or perhaps been cut off by forces that had somehow learned of their tactics.

How could the rebels assemble such a vast force that they were able to take his well-trained army? Surely it was not mere luck that had caused his defeat. Somehow word must have reached them of their troop strength and battle plans. If only he knew how their strategy was discovered they could prevent such failures in the future. Not that his reputation could be saved. He could hardly wait until the war was over, and England succeeded in subduing the upstarts, then he would be released and return to his homeland to live a quiet life of service in parliament.

CHAPTER XI

General Gates

General Gates was satisfied. His battles had gone well. The men had rallied and managed to rout the British from Ticonderoga again. He had been fortunate to have a good fighting force even though he had been forced to work with what he considered inferior military commanders. Most were like that thorn, Benedict Arnold. He could wield a sword and rally the men all right, but he had not attended Yale and therefore should not ever have been appointed to Brigadier General in his opinion. Fortunately he had been able to court enough favors with the Continental Congress to secure a position of control and being possessed of a good tongue had been able to obtain credit for the victories in which he had been involved. Men needed a commander they could respect and revere. Oh, men like Arnold had their place. Ruffians enjoyed a good fighting general in their midst, but he was confident his own qualities expressed the brigadier position more effectively. He would be sure to tactfully present this position in his next meeting with the powers that be, and leave out any contribution Arnold had made to the victory. He planned to arrange a meeting as soon as possible.

CHAPTER XII

The Marquis de Lafayette
Spring, 1777

Marie Joseph Paul Yves Roch Gilbert Du Motier was bored with his life. He wasn't particularly fond of his first name as it seemed slightly effeminate to him, and he wasn't entranced with the prospect of spending a boring life without adventure at Chateau Chavaniac, Auvergne. Perhaps when he grew old he would like to retire there, but he was only nineteen years old and had attended the College du Plessis and was ready to move on. He had spent some time in the army and it had been unrewarding. He craved action. King Louis had denied him his request to go to America to help the colonists gain their freedom from English rule so he decided to go on his own. It was hard to believe the king did not grant his request when they had recently been at war on American soil with England themselves. Now was the time to declare themselves allies of the fledgling colonies. Fortunately, his wealth as the Marquis de Lafayette allowed him the freedom to buy his own ship and sail for America.

The disgruntled Frenchman, young, handsome and rich, sailed from France and arrived on the Carolina shores. His audience with King Louis to present his request for support in his endeavor had proved to be very disappointing. He had been sure that France would help the colonists gain their independence from English rule. Not only because of the recent war in which France itself had been involved with the English, but because England had not been just in its dealings with the new country across the ocean. From experience, the King should appreciate the difficulties involved in ruling a territory so far removed from the mother country. Adding to the logistical problems, the British seemed to believe the colonists were there for the Empire's profit, imposing taxes without any representation in parliament from those they controlled. When the colonists were required to house and feed the troops England had sent to "keep order" it seemed ludicrous to expect them to support their own jailers. Though his appeal to King Louis had been denied and his reasoning dismissed, he had taken matters into his own hands. He felt that once the king realized the importance of the colonists' freedom from England he would change his mind and assist them in their fight for liberty. For now, it would be only his ship and crew to offer their services.

Since he had undertaken this mission on his own, he immediately made plans to gain recognition from the Continental Congress and then seek their chosen military commander, General George Washington, and offer to serve at his pleasure.

Stepping onto American soil he felt a thrill of destiny. His heart told him he was doing the right thing. Perhaps even fame would accompany any achievements he might accomplish to help this new land become free of tyranny. He planned to do all he could to assist in its fight for freedom. If necessary, he would return to France later to plead the American cause, but for now, he was a free agent with his own ship and his own men, so there was nothing to deter him from his planned mission.

Approaching the shore, the Marquis de Lafayette was impressed by the sights, sounds and smells coming from the new land. As he stepped onto the pier from the small landing craft that had been rowed by a chosen few, he was amazed at the sight of gulls, ducks and geese gathered at the mouth of the river that emptied into the great ocean he had just crossed. The sea air was perfumed by profuse greenery and pungent spores of long leaf and loblolly pine, gum, cypress, oak and subtropical palmetto, all of which contributed to the sweetness of blooming spring wildflowers. He knew North Carolina was the first of the colonies to officially declare its independence, and that the militia called itself the "Sons of Liberty", but he had not expected a land of such beauty. No wonder England wished to control such a land! England's damp climate could hardly compete with this paradise, a land well worth fighting for.

Following his initial visit he quickly made plans to journey north and offer himself to assist in the revolution. He found no resistance to his proposal of aid and was not only welcomed by General Washington but was given an honorary commission as major general. The general took an immediate liking to the man. His professional acumen, good manners and self-discipline were traits he admired in his officers. They would become lifelong friends, along with artillery commander Henry Knox. Together, they made plans for the campaigns that would eventually result in victory by the Patriots.

The Marquis had not anticipated taking part in military action so soon, but Washington immediately sensed the ability of the young Frenchman and assigned him to take part in the Battle of Brandywine. The battle had raged through the creeks near Wilmington and he had been wounded, but not seriously. Healing, he had distinguished himself and had proven his ability to the extent that he was given a division of fighting colonials. His friendship and admiration of George Washington became solid following the Battle of Barren Hill and Monmouth Court House and he decided that if he ever had a son he would name him George Washington Lafayette. He had married the wealthy Adrienne d'Ayen of the Noailles family in France, as well as possessing great wealth of his own, but it had not been enough to hold him in France. His interest in helping the colonists gain their freedom had overwhelmed him. Now he felt he was fulfilling his destiny. Though his left arm was in a sling from his recent wound suffered at Brandywine Creek, he felt no pain. Tall and slim and strikingly handsome with pale brown curls about his cheeks, he looked more like an actor than a regimental officer. His former training had served him well and he was well liked by the men assigned him as well as his fellow officers. His association with General Washington and Colonel Knox had been both rewarding and fulfilling and he was sure France would soon support the American war effort.

To Washington, the Marquis de Lafayette was a bright encouragement in what was to be a dark winter.

CHAPTER XIII

As a young child struggles to reach the shores of adulthood and finally shakes off the traumas of childhood, so the struggling colonists would suffer, strive and fight their way to freedom. The changing times were becoming evident in the speech patterns of the newly declared independent country. The King's English was beginning to have subtle nuances. With the mixture of families from Holland, Spain and Germany the sounds of the languages were beginning to blend. Even native Indian terms had found their way into speech patterns. There was also a distinctive pattern forming in the South that was easily recognizable. The Scots had injected their influence, rolling their "Rs", and the Dutch "jan kees" had given a name to all the colonists west of the Atlantic. French settlers had scattered throughout the country and thus a country with a melding of speech and culture was being transformed from the individuals to the complete flavor of a new republic. Evidence of the struggle was the taking and retaking of forts and cities, as with Boston, Ticonderoga, Saratoga, Philadelphia and Savannah. Though it might seem that progress was not being accomplished, Washington saw a slow but steady advancement towards ultimate victory.

CHAPTER XIV

Jeremiah felt guilty. He could only send messages. He knew Washington's troops were suffering shortages of supplies while he was living a comfortable life in Philadelphia. There was no way he could send anything to help ease their hunger or pain without jeopardizing his own position. Knowing the food and medicine in his store was sorely needed was frustrating. The loyalists and neutralists in Philadelphia were not bad people, merely misguided. They honestly felt that England would eventually win the war and they would continue as before, therefore he could accept their indulgences, their wonderful food, and their gay parties.

He was constantly on guard lest he make a mistake that would cause suspicion. Not thinking, he had almost set a small bag of gunpowder on the counter at the store when someone requested flour. Of course, the meaning of the blunder would have been unnoticed as it would only have been evidence of the blundering fop he was portraying in his guise. He did not wish, however, to allow such a mistake to occur again.

In spite of Jeremiah's reports to Washington about Howe's movements and troop strength the colonial forces lost the Battle of Brandywine Creek and they were unable to hold Philadelphia. With the influx of British officers in what they considered a permanent achievement it was much easier to obtain information from loyalists who saw no reason to remain tight-lipped. The Brits were stopped at the Battles of Bennington, Bemis Heights and twice at

Freeman's farm, followed by Burgoyne being forced to lay down his arms at Saratoga. The best news was that France had been convinced by the Marquis de Lafayette to send aid although the official treaty would not be signed until the following year.

CHAPTER XV

Valley Forge

The autumn leaves had been at their peak of color. Maples glowed yellow and red and the birches small golden leaves fluttered in the breeze, all against a backdrop of evergreens pointing toward a pale blue sky. There had been no warning that the winter would be unbelievably harsh and cruel. When it arrived the winter at Valley Forge was fraught with misery. It was difficult for Washington and it was difficult for his men. His heart ached for his suffering troops and he was helpless in controlling the sickness and death that visited them, killing nearly a third of the ailing men under his direct command. Lack of proper food, medicine and clothing was a contributing factor, the weather was especially harsh and his army ill prepared for the combination of malnutrition, exceeding cold and the diseases that plagued the weakened men. They struggled against the physical threats of typhus and smallpox and contended with the mental struggle of fear, not knowing what sickness would assail their bodies. Some men, especially those from the northern regions seemed to fare better. Having been born and bred under similar weather conditions they not only took the freezing weather for granted, but seemed to have better coping mechanisms. Any scrap of paper or cloth they found went to either under the front of their jackets or lined their boots to keep out the cold. They even used birch bark for the same purpose. They were especially adept at trapping rabbits and small

Jean Edwards

game, using the skins for warmth as well as adding to the food supply. There was some suspicion as to the type of meat served, especially after the disappearance of the dogs and cats that had been part of the camp, and there were no rats even though the cats had disappeared.

General Washington had plenty of time to plan his strategy. The success he had achieved in defeating the British and driving them out of Boston was only the beginning, but spring seemed forever in arriving. Frostbite was crippling men, turning toes blue and gangrenous, and when men died their bodies were quickly stripped of clothing and boots, confiscated by those whose feet were bound only in rags. Congress had kept the lid clamped tight on the coffers, evidently not realizing how desperately the army needed not only necessities, but military paraphernalia as well. If they could get through the winter suffering the cold in their poor ragged tents Washington was determined to launch a powerful advance in the spring. Those who survived the winter would be well trained and toughened and the war would soon turn in favor of the colonial forces.

He thought about the many battles that must be fought before freedom would be gained. His officers were admirable, especially Knox, whom he had promoted to Brigadier General. He had been extremely impressive in bringing the cannon from Ticonderoga with inventive genius under adverse conditions, and he was only twenty-seven years old. His knowledge of artillery surpassed that of any older senior officer and his ability to accomplish any task assigned no matter what difficulties ensued made him invaluable. He would much rather be home at Mount Vernon with his beloved Martha, taste the chicken stew and apple pie she served on Sunday afternoon, followed by a fox hunt along the Potomac. Perhaps Martha would make her "Great Cake", to be eaten by friends following the hunt, along with steaming cups of hot mulled cider. But there would be plenty of time for that when the war was over. For now, he would have to be content planning future strategies of routing. He was determined to take back their cities from the (in their opinion) "Greatest Army on Earth". He was confident of an eventual win, but it would be costly. Oh, the magnificence of the British Army was not to be denied. Their perfection of marching in unison was exemplary, with their red coats blazing against the trees as they emerged onto a battlefield, muskets with their silver bayonets flashing in the sun and their black boots oiled and rubbed to a mirror shine. His own troops' attire was much less impressive, some uniforms were worn to rags, their boots and equipment ill-assorted, in most cases due to lack of funding by the congress, but he knew that after the first firings in phalanx and ranks began to break, his men would be unequalled in the skirmish.

Article copied from the Washington Post

Martha Washington celebrated Twelfth Night, their wedding anniversary by often baking her "Great Cake" suitably decorated. Here's the way her granddaughter Martha Parke Custis recorded the recipe (with ingredients, punctuation and spelling more appropriate to her time than to this.)

Take 40 eggs and divide the whites from the yolks & beat them to a froth then work 4 pounds of butter to a cream & put the whites of eggs to it a Spoon full at a time till it is well work'd then put 4 pounds of sugar finely powdered to it in the same manner then put in the Youlks of eggs & five pounds of flower & 5 pounds of fruit. 2 hours will bake it add to it half an ounce of mace & nutmeg half a pint of wine and some fresh brandy.

As the sun set behind the western hills, three friends gathered at Washington's Valley Forge headquarters. They were well aware of the ravages of disease and pestilence that had visited the troops camped at their base west of Philadelphia. Three thousand of the eleven thousand had succumbed, but those who survived were well trained and with grit and determination they would prepare to re-take Philadelphia.

Following the winter that had resulted in the loss of so many brave patriots, by April things were beginning to improve. The Marquis had sailed to France and returned with good news. The night was one for the gathering of friends, for making plans, for optimism.

Although the fare was conservative for men of such status, a dinner of venison, potatoes, biscuits and gravy had been prepared for the attending officers. The candles gave an unexpected ambiance to the affair. Three friends, three men dedicated to the cause of liberty. There was much discussion of tactics and battle plans following the meal as they warmed themselves by the stone fireplace, feeling fortunate to be able to enjoy their comradeship over such a fine meal.

A small bottle of wine that had been made available for the occasion was brought forth.

"My friend, Monsieur Knox," the Marquis de Lafayette voiced. "I understand it was your expertise that brought the cannon from Fort Ticonderoga to rescue Boston from the red infidels. We in France celebrate excellence in our women, our wine and most especially our heroes. Frenchmen glory in the defeat of self-appreciated British redcoats. I raise my glass to you."

Washington joined in the toast, and as the three glasses were tipped the Marquis exclaimed, "Wait, wait, do not think of ending the evening too soon. I have brought a token of esteem for General Knox, both for his promotion to Brigadier General and his amazing accomplishment of the cannon transport, that he will remember this night as we celebrate the return of Boston to its citizens."

Turning, the Marquis brought forth a box from the hallway. Opening the lid he lifted from the packing a beautiful inner box, which also had a lid. Inside, neatly placed in compartments were lidded tea and coffee jars, cups, silverware and at the back, a set of shaving supplies.

"In France we call it a "*necessaire*", and may you keep it with you to use on many successful campaigns. I also have a gift for you, General Washington. These three sets of epaulettes and sword knots are from my homeland, a set for you and anyone you might wish to grace with such a gift."

Washington and Knox again raised their glasses. "To the Marquis de Lafayette, our fellow soldier and generous friend. We give you thanks for these wonderful gifts and we will use them with thoughts of your generosity," came the toast from Washington.

The Marquis then informed his friends that his recent trip to France had resulted in convincing King Louis to send ships, goods and men to aid them.

Simultaneously the three emptied their glasses following the voicing in unison, "To France!"

The trip to France was productive in more than political ways. George Washington Lafayette was born Christmas eve, 1779.

The Necessaire

CHAPTER XVI

Sacrifice

When men must die that other men may live,
Their blood must never have been shed in vain.
As on the battlefield they gave all they could give,
For freedom's cause was stronger than their pain.

As through the night the battle rages on,
And though the flag might fall, it's raised again,
Until at last the calm comes with the dawn,
And stillness settles on the fallen men.

Men who didn't want to die, but fell,
And would have fallen twice to do the task,
Of purest cause they rang our freedom's bell,
We honor those who held our station fast.

Oh, hearts of bravest men we honor thee,
To you we owe our nation's victory.

Chapter XVII

Jeremiah had his suspicions concerning Benedict Arnold. His dashing presence at social affairs in Philadelphia, consorting and mingling with loyalists and neutralists and his interest in the opposite sex was more noticeably intense than he had been when courting Abigail. Of course he was a dashing general and he more or less could pick and choose. There was no denying his striking good looks, fine physique, albeit with a limp from his war wounds. He was obviously looking for a wife, and Jeremiah could understand that. Jeremiah's purpose had been clear to no one so he decided perhaps his thoughts were too critical. He certainly would not have wanted to walk in Arnold's shoes in the campaign through the wilderness to storm Quebec, though he would have done so had he been asked. Nor would he have wanted to suffer terrible wounds and have three horses shot out from under him. Arnold was wooing a girl that seemed to have no connections that would give information to the patriot cause so evidently he was only looking for company. If the man had been assigned to a mission similar to his own surely he would have been informed, lest conflicting attempts at espionage impair their efficiency. No, there was something else afoot. Perhaps the loss of his wife had changed Benedict in some way, causing him to seek fulfillment in other ways. Surely two would not be sent on the same mission, especially when one was a general with high visibility. Jeremiah had been very successful in his own commission with regular reports. Something was definitely out of line with Benedict Arnold. His reputation as a military tactician was legendary, but his difficulty in obtaining rank and glory had also been recorded. Jeremiah wondered if those problems had influenced the general's judgment to the point that perhaps he was seeking glory elsewhere. Time would tell, and Jeremiah decided it would be prudent to refrain from any contact with the illustrious General Arnold. Although the city of Philadelphia had changed hands there was always an openness that allowed the Whigs, the Tories and the neutralists to live their lives undisturbed, so social events often had many from each political belief in attendance, and it was not unusual for visiting military personnel to drop in. He was sure his own position was undisclosed beyond Washington, Knox, the Marquis and his courier. His caution heightened and he kept his distance from the famed soldier, but he remained watchful.

CHAPTER XVIII

Dearest Mother and Father,

I hope you can forgive me for not informing you of my activities before now, but my life has been exceedingly hectic since I came south and I have scarcely had a minute to take pen in hand. I have a grand dry goods and grocery store here in Philadelphia and thanks to your training I'm doing very well. There was a need for such an enterprise in the area and a generous backer helped me establish the business. Please do not be disappointed that I am now in a neutral position. Everything looks different as nearly all the population here are either from across the sea or direct descendants of immigrants, mostly English, and I could not find it in my heart to take aim against my brother.

A further change in my life may give you concern, but please be patient and tolerant. I have married the daughter of a Colonel Worthington, a fine English girl named Abigail, who, in spite of her father's affiliation with the English army, is neutral, as myself.

When the war is over we will visit you, as travel might be dangerous at this time. I will write again and inform you of our plans.

Please be kind to Mercy. I am very sorry if she is hurt by my actions, but life has led me in another direction.

With highest regards and deepest affection,
Jeremiah

Mother Clarke called Merci to the library, asking her to leave her duties and to come alone. She knew the news she had received would not set well with Mercy. It had not set well with Mother Clarke and she could only imagine the pain it would inflict on the girl she had come to care for. With Jeremiah away in Philadelphia she had felt closer to Mercy. It was a strange development as she had been somewhat prejudiced against the girl but had gradually accepted the idea that her son was sincere in his feelings for her. In two years the girl's debt would be paid, and she wondered what she could have been thinking, to acquire a servant under bond. She was ashamed of being so high minded when surely she could have found another girl like Allie, one that was rather simple and needing a home, working her way for a livelihood, one that would not be temptation for her son.

Now it was all gone, as the girl she had come to care for would never be Jeremiah's wife, as he had found another. It bothered her that she had not even had the chance to meet the girl or the family, but assumed that she must be a lovely girl from a family in good standing, perhaps even wealthy. The letter said she was the daughter of a British army officer. Obviously she had worried needlessly about her son going to war. Evidently he had found a place away from battle, setting up a new store. She was proud he had decided to set up his own business, though puzzled over his change of heart. He had gone off patriotic and now he had taken himself out of the fray and had started his own business. He knew all the connections to order supplies and he would be safe in a neutral position. She was somewhat surprised that he had married a British sympathizer, though she claimed neutrality. She must be a really special girl to take Jeremiah away from Mercy and away from his patriotic ambitions. Perhaps it was all for the best. Now Mercy would be free to return to the convent and not be at Clarke House when Jeremiah returned with his bride. There had been no mention of a trip to Maine before the war ended and travel would be safer when the situation was settled. By the news she had heard surely Mercy would be well on her way north by that time.

When Mercy stepped into the library she knew there was a problem. Mystery and tension hung in the air. Fearing that something terrible had happened to Jeremiah, her dark eyes widened in an effort to prevent tears from revealing her emotions.

Mother Clarke put her hand on Mercy's shoulder. "Mercy, there is something I must tell you about Jeremiah."

"Oh, No. Do not tell me that he is dead! Tell me that he is only wounded. Oh, Please, do not say that he is dead!"

"No, Mercy. He is not dead. I know you have feelings for my son, but he has found himself a wife."

"A wife? He has found a wife?"

"Yes, my dear, and we must wish him well. I'm sure she is a lovely girl."

Stunned, Mercy felt the room spin. How could he be married? How could it be? He said he would love me forever. Staggering, Mercy made her way through the house, out the back door and across the back yard grass to the rabbit hutch.

"Oh, Pierre, Oh, Pierre. You are all I have of him." As she held the rabbit close under her chin tears slowly spilled from her eyes and onto the soft fur of Pierre's back. The animal did not wiggle or move, as though he sensed the tragedy of the moment.

"He said he would love me forever. What did that mean?—Until he found someone he loved more? Oh, how could this be!"

Mercy sank to the ground, still holding Pierre. The days they had laughed together, their walks along the riverbank, working on the medical stores at the garrison, reading poetry together. All these things raced through her mind. Then she remembered Allie, who had lost Lorenzo. At least Mercy could imagine Jeremiah happy and alive, but he would not be hers to hold, to laugh with, to love. Love was not to be hers. When her debt was paid she would find a way to return to the safety of the convent. There, she would be spared this kind of pain.

Mother Clarke had done her duty. She had tried to be kind but it had been difficult with her own heart in turmoil. The letter from Jeremiah had left her feeling spurned and rejected. Her only son had made a new life in far away Pennsylvania and she had not only been excluded from his wedding, she had not been informed of it until after the fact. There was nothing to do but hold her head high and pretend she was happy with the situation. Town biddies would be buzzing with juicy gossip and speculation if she acted in the least perturbed. She was determined that no hint of her disappointment ever be revealed. Oh, why couldn't he have found a nice girl here in Maine, and not live so far away! Her anguish would be her secret, and she would make plans for the celebration of his marriage when the war was over and he returned. Perhaps then he would stay and things would be much as before. Of course the thing with Mercy was over, and she had not been entirely content with that prospect anyway. Perhaps all was going to work out for the best after all. One had to be optimistic in a case like this. Yes, she would smile and show the town that her son's happiness was also hers!

Albert Clarke was puzzled. His son had always been logical, loyal and their many private conversations about the status of the colonies had convinced him that Jeremiah would be the most fervent soldier in the militia. The turn of events seemed completely out of character. He strongly sensed that Jeremiah's change of heart was somehow less than honest. There was something afoot that his son was not saying, perhaps could not say. He felt the boy was safe, but perhaps he had gotten himself in trouble, particularly with the girl he married. Surely he would not have given his heart to another so quickly, but then a year or so was a long time for a young man. The letter did not vow any great love for his wife, and he had expressed concern for Mercy. Aside from the status of his marriage, Albert Clarke was suspicious, but he would keep his feelings hidden until he learned of any developments not mentioned in the letter. He was surprised at the ease with which Prudence accepted the situation, and was not about to upset her by voicing any concerns. Yes, he would hold his thoughts to himself and wait for enlightenment. Sooner or later Jeremiah would tell all, he was sure of that. He would send a letter of congratulations and offer any help he could give, but remain noncommittal.

CHAPTER XIX

As Philadelphia changed hands again there was much turmoil in the city. Fortunately for the inhabitants the Patriots rarely bothered the families of soldiers as the control of the city was once again returned to the colonial forces. The military men left the area feeling quite confident that their wives and children would be well treated, and Mrs. Worthington, along with her daughter, Abigail, was safe. Jeremiah wondered what the future would hold. It was 1778 and the war was beginning to turn in favor of the colonials. The Southern Campaign was taking shape and slowly, but surely, battle by battle, the tide was beginning to turn. The soldiers had even written a rousing song about the recent events and it became a popular tune throughout the regiments.

In old Philadelphia, where folks are much wealthier,
They partied and danced through the night.
So one might surmise there was great surprise,
When the British again lost the fight.

They lost their fair city, for Yankees are gritty,
Now they suffer remorse and lament.
They'll go back to England, it's where they belong.
And where they can learn to repent.

They never believed that we Yankees could win,
They clung to their red coats in vain.
We'll try to be kind, these Tories will find,
As we send them to Britain again.

Hi, Ho, all you doubters, you made a mistake,
The city we now will retake,
We'll not be abusing because of your losing,
Old Phillie is ours once again!

CHAPTER XX

Once Philadelphia had been recaptured the battles continued and gradually success was granted, first in small skirmishes and then in larger battles that showed the mettle of the undaunted troops that had suffered such a wicked winter. The signing of the treaty with France had heartened the troops as well as their commander. Truly, as John Paul Jones had declared in the battle off the coast of England, "I have not yet begun to fight," and then captured His Royal Majesty's ship, the "Serapis", the colonials were just beginning to fight in the land war.

Burgoyne's defeat at Saratoga boosted morale and with Spain and the Netherlands both joining the hostilities, victory now seemed to be possible. The French Fleet under Comte Jean d'Estaing was on its way across the Atlantic. The Patriots were enraged that Sir Henry Clinton had raided towns and commerce and every outrage gave impetus to their charge. When Clinton captured Savannah and Charleston the war changed course and was moved from the middle colonies to the South.

CHAPTER XXI

Benedict Arnold was angry. He had fought, he had led, and he had won battle after battle, yet he seemed to be unappreciated by his superiors. Following victories at Fort Ticonderoga with Ethan Allen and his Green Mountain Boys from Vermont and then the capture of Fort St. John on the northern end of Lake Champlain he had yet to be appreciated by the Continental Congress. His charge through the Maine wilderness in an attempt to capture Quebec and the hardships his men had endured had been much more difficult than he had imagined, much of the misery caused by lagging funds from the congress, giving him poor and insufficient equipment. By the time they reached the St. Lawrence River they were too exhausted to attack. Though General Richard Montgomery captured Montreal, the attack in a roaring blizzard failed, Montgomery had been killed and Arnold wounded in the knee. In spite of all the problems, Arnold had held his troops together and blockaded the city through the winter. He had been promoted to Brigadier General, but received no acclaim. When the siege of Quebec failed Arnold's men were forced to retreat back to Montreal. The British had hoped to capture New York City and control the Hudson River but the stubborn resistance of Arnold and his troops prevented that from happening by keeping them at Lake Champlain. When British General Guy Carleton took his large army to the northern end of the lake, Arnold and company had been waiting, hidden behind Valcour Island in crude ships they had quickly built and filled with soldiers. They had fought to a draw, but being unable to defeat Arnold's crude fleet humiliated General Carleton, and he returned to Canada, the north being saved.

Benedict had wanted to join George Washington but instead was sent to defend Newport, Rhode Island. He felt it was a lesser post than he deserved after the success he had exhibited under adverse conditions. Then he discovered that junior officers with influence in congress had been promoted to major general over him, and he was justifiably incensed. General Washington convinced him not to resign. Hearing that there were attacks on Danbury, Connecticut, he rallied some militia and forced the enemy to retreat. Congress then made him Major General but did not restore his seniority. Being persuaded to continue his military career he fought through New York and at the battle of Freeman's Farm he forced the British to a stalemate, but the British lost twice the men as the militia.

The report of the battle was sent to the congress, leaving out any mention of the bravery and contribution of Arnold and his men.

The British assaulted again but the militia stood firm due to the appearance of Arnold leading the charge, breaking the center of the British line. Arnold was shot again in the same leg as his previous wound, and his horse shot out from under him, the animal rolling onto the general. His men pulled him from under the horse and he continued the fight until ordered to the rear, but Burgoyne was defeated and surrendered at Saratoga.

Arnold's seniority was restored and he convalesced in Albany. Upon healing he joined Washington at Valley Forge. His visits to Philadelphia caused some consternation, and especially his association with some of the neutralists and loyalists. He wished to marry again and soon found a wife, a young English girl named Peggy, as was his first wife.

Being given command of West Point had not appeased Benedict Arnold. It was not an important post and he felt he deserved better for all he had given to his fledgling country. As days passed he became more and more convinced that the Continental Congress was no better than the British Parliament. They showed favoritism to those of wealth and privilege and though status and rank was not openly purchased as in England, nevertheless, the men from prominent families were being given positions above their qualifications. With much thought and spending many nights soul searching, he came to the conclusion that there was no way an army led by the unqualified could defeat the mighty army of King George. He foresaw the struggle for freedom going on for years and the men who had fought so valiantly under his command would eventually be killed, man by man over time, and the country would be run by a congress that was as tyrannical as British rule. He began reasoning continuously, even to the point of writing down his thoughts, but then holding the paper to a candle flame. These thoughts raced through his mind:

> I thought I could change the world if I tried hard enough,
> And if I put my heart and soul into the task.
> If I fought harder, led stronger, struggled longer,
> If I did all the things of which I was asked to do
> I would succeed.
> But fate has never smiled and I feel the presence of
> defeat.
> Perhaps the cause for which I have fought is doomed
> to fail,
> All around me, men stand discouraged.
> But there seems to be little more that can be done.

If I can return this torn land
Back to the country from which it was spawned,
A peaceful solution might be found
For this war that can never be won.
So many have followed me into battle
Those same will follow me now,
And when the land is peaceful again,
The respect I found from them in war
Will follow me in peace.
May those who passed me by in the conflict,
Recognize the sacrifices I have made
For my country, my men, and for peace.

After all the fighting and dying what would be left when all was said and done? If the colonial rebels won their independence the Continental Congress would be trying to control a shattered country. The southern states were slave states and even those who felt it was morally wrong would give in to pressure to accept slavery, while the northern Yankees would be trying to force their moral values on the South. The middle states could go either way. Even his friend, George Washington, with all his lofty principals would be in a shaky position, trying to appease and cajole the congress while forming a new country made up of citizens looking for a country with few fetters. The great puzzle called "war" was becoming difficult to solve. So many had died and so would many more if the fighting continued. He had lost faith in an unfair colonial government, and was becoming more and more convinced that the struggle would bear very little fruit.

He decided to make his move. He could at least save lives by assisting the inevitable. Quickly sketching the West Point fortifications, he signed the document and gave it to his courier to deliver to the British Command.

It was to be his last act on American soil. The courier was captured and Washington himself was soon advancing on West Point to arrest his once beloved friend.

Escaping quickly by horse Arnold was soon aboard an English ship, safe from capture but not from the scorn that would be attached to his name forever.

CHAPTER XXII

As we contemplate the power of Satan over the minds of men, we must consider the sins involved. If a man has given his all, led his men in battles to gain justice and liberty for his fellow man, and nearly given his life in the effort but is little appreciated because of an usurper, a grasping glory hog with friends in high places willing to further his unearned fame, and giving him the fame and glory that was earned by a true patriot, then how is the situation to be judged? Although both men might have craved the same glory, is it not understandable that the true hero might become disillusioned in time? The unearned disappointments could easily have become a factor in a change of view. With the closeness between Benedict Arnold and his men, living day in and day out enduring every hardship they suffered as his own, willingly offering his body in the defense of freedom to the point where he could hardly stand, and believing his troops were in as much pain and disappointment as himself, might he not look for an easier route than a long, tedious war? Pitifully, was it the fickle nature of man, more of Satan's control or simply the misguided thoughts of a tired and crippled man. How quickly the glory hogs seized the opportunity to capitalize on the mistakes of a disappointed man who had given up his health, his wealth, his youth and his energy for a cause he had come to believe could not be won.

CHAPTER XXIII

1780

George Washington was deeply troubled by the defection of Benedict Arnold. He realized the pain the young officer had suffered. He had considered him his friend and it pained him that Arnold had three horses shot out from under him in battle and that he was so physically injured. His shattered left leg had taken nearly a year to heal while he lay with it in a wooden box to immobilize it for months. It was difficult to imagine the agony of being wounded a second time in the same leg and having the horse roll onto it, crushing the bone nearly beyond repair. Amputation was considered but the valiant general had insisted he endure a long painful convalescence rather than lose the limb.

He had given Benedict a set of the epaulettes and sword knots the Marquis de Lafayette had presented him as a token of their friendship, he was so fond of the man. He thought about the value of the man in the many battles he had led, and how he had held his men to high standards of conduct. Along with Daniel Morgan and his buckskin clad Virginia militia, proper discipline had been strictly enforced. Washington's own code of civility and behavior had been given to the officers and passed along to their troops. He doubted any cooperation from Ethan Allen and the Green Mountain Boys; their hard drinking habits were merely a reflection of their leader's example. When Washington had asked Arnold if he would campaign again with Allen he had tersely replied, "I'd rather be shot."

Arnold's men, in spite of severe hardships had never pillaged or gone on drunken rampages. A man after his own heart, he had instilled proper behavior in his men, and now he was lost to the cause, a great and sorrowful loss.

As he sat at his campaign desk Washington contemplated the situation. No man had ever sat a horse like Benedict Arnold. His handsome countenance, rugged physique and courageous fighting and leadership ability could not be denied. He knew his own men served him out of respect, but Arnold's men served him out of love and admiration. How angry and disappointed they must feel in the betrayal! Washington was sure that Gates had kept himself safely behind the lines at the farmhouse at Freeman's Farm while Arnold led the charge and yet all the credit was given to Gates. The Congress had even struck a gold coin in his honor leaving Arnold completely without credit. He vowed that if he were ever in a position of congressional authority he would not tolerate discrimination such as he had witnessed in the case of promotions of the rich and influential over the deserving. It was an easy thing to be jealous of such a handsome, courageous man as Benedict, and wealth and privilege had won out. He hoped such favoritism would be purged from the new government. A man who had given so much for his country should have received honor for his family name, but criticism, jealousy and prejudice had destroyed a valuable soldier. He was not worried that the defection had hurt the fight for freedom, he had only injured himself and along with the painful limp that would forever remind him of the country he had once served, he would suffer defamation in the hearts of all who heard his name, in his lifetime and beyond.

He had also been aware that his fighting general had appealed to the Continental Congress many times to regain his seniority over the younger men promoted over him, younger men with meager ability and no fighting experience. The same favored few had been bent on destroying Arnold's reputation and the pain of his shortened leg and the agony that Congress had ignored his appeals for so long, had pushed him over the edge. Washington was sure that Arnold had lost faith in the new government, believing, (probably rightly so), that it would not abide by its promise of equality. Coming from a family that had lost its fortune and prestige, the man had fought valiantly in every battle, but had succumbed to the idea that independence from mighty British rule was impossible. He wondered if Arnold would ever realize that his defection had helped the Patriots' cause. The hue and cry of "Traitor!" had spurred the non-committed to enlist in a rush of patriotism, and the army quickly swelled in number with the additional troops and they fought with a new fervor.

The acute disappointment in a man he had trusted would not have been so profound had he not been so gallant a warrior in the quest for freedom. Having suffered much the same hardships at Valley Forge as Arnold's troops suffered in the Wilderness Campaign, he had felt a comradeship with the young officer he rarely enjoyed with other officers. Too many undeserving young men with varying grades of inefficiency, some with lack of training, some with lack of courage, had been undeservedly promoted. Arnold was a gentleman, his troops disciplined, and he had been ferocious in battle. Disappointment, injury, injustice and exhaustion had tainted his mind. He felt a great loss in losing his fighting general, more deeply did he suffer the hurt that allowed anger to control his feelings for a man he once loved and respected.

Yes, Benedict Arnold had become a detested symbol, but in the final analysis, his actions had helped the new nation more than they had damaged it. He hoped the man would someday come to realize his contribution to the freedom of a land to which he could never return. He would personally see that Arnold's new wife and infant son were sent to join him either in Canada or across the ocean. That chapter closed, the Commander of the Colonial Forces returned his thoughts to the problems at hand.

PART IV

1778

Chapter I

As the war years progressed from the beginning salvos in Massachusetts to the events that saw the coming resolution of the conflict, so also were conflicts and struggles being endured on a personal level in the far northern reaches of the country. By circumstance the inhabitants of Amitie le Christ were drawn into the outside world. With Merci's departure they had been forced to acknowledge that there was, indeed, life beyond their convent. Following their sudden decision to send her to the coast when the opportunity arose that she might experience a different culture before making a life decision, they became increasingly aware that her life might be fraught with danger. They were beginning to feel that they had perhaps been too hasty in their action. Unbeknown to the Sisters, the one most affected by her leaving was Thomas. He had expected Merci to return in only a few years. At first he had been fearful that he would not have the house finished before her arrival. Now he was concerned. What if something terrible had happened to her? It was spring and he decided if she did not return by the following spring he was going to begin his search. He began to ready the house and make plans.

Sister Margarite also began to worry. She thought she would hear news of Merci. Jacques Renault had not returned, had not passed their way, or if he had, he did not stop at Amitie le Christ. She considered that perhaps he was journeying and trading elsewhere, causing him to by-pass the convent. When the girl left Margarite assumed her venture into the outside world would be successful and she would return, at least for a visit, bubbling over with excitement and gratitude for the opportunity that had been afforded her. But years had passed and no word of Merci had reached the Sisters. She wondered how she should go about an inquiry as to the girl's whereabouts. She had expected Mr. Renault to return with a report on her welfare, but it had not happened. Anguish that she had perhaps sent the girl away too quickly, that she had been too trusting slowly crept into her mind. She had received knowledge of the war raging between England and the colonies from the various trappers and travelers that had stopped by the compound, but had received no word of Merci.

The events surrounding Merci made Sister Margarite also wonder if Thomas might wish to return to his own people. He had grown from a boy to manhood and though she had thought at one time he might become a priest, she knew that he spent a lot of time in the village of his native people. Some of his hunting trips had taken more than a week and at first she had been frantic that he had been harmed and might never return, but gradually she came to realize that he was searching for himself, perhaps even his birth parents. As she had accepted Merci's leaving and hopefully found her place in the world, so should Thomas be free to do the same.

Thomas had a busy morning. He had cut willow sticks about 15 inches long to use for spouts on sugar maples. Cutting each in half lengthwise, he carefully cleaned out the pith, making a smooth channel from end to end. He also cut some thick, strong sticks. His chore was to tap the many trees near the compound. He was thankful for the small auger that Sister Margarite had purchased from a visiting trader, making his job much easier. He carefully drilled a hole about three inches deep in the trunk of the first sugar maple and inserted the spout, then drilled a hole above and inserted the sturdy stick, carving a notch that would hold the bucket handle. His stack of buckets were soon securely hanging on the trees and the spouts were beginning to bring forth the sweet sap, drip by drip, slowly filling the buckets.

There was a fresh smell in the air, as though cleansed by the spring rains, and the earth had been washed of any residue of the previous year. Sister Margarite would soon be boiling down the fragrant sap into syrup, and some into sugar. He recalled how thrilled he and Merci had been with their "brick" of maple sugar at Christmas. When they were young they hadn't realized how much labor went into the making of their treat, but now he was more appreciative. He carried the filled pails for Sister, and knew what a labor of love it had been for the limping nun in past years, and he remembered the times he and Merci had raided the sap buckets (and the shout that went up when they were caught). For two young children the sweet liquid had been just too tempting. Now he was sure that Sister Margarite was probably amused by their transgression, though they had to stack firewood until dark in penance for their wrongdoing.

But it was late in the month of March, and he knew he could complete his house in the woods this year. The inside was finished and the outside walls were carefully fitted with rock, the windows were covered with full deer hides as the framed windows would not be incorporated until all else was completed. He had worked on clearing a garden spot and cleaned out a small spring near-by, and even built a stone walkway to the privy behind the house. He did not plan to move into his house, as he did not build it for himself. His room at the convent would remain his living quarters until the day arrived that he had planned, had dreamed, had built his heart around, the day of Merci's return.

Jean Edwards

When

When all the diamonds have been found
        and all the gold is gone,
How will the fancy ladies feel
        with nothing to adorn
Their throats, their hair, their dainty hands,
        no sparkles set in gold?
What tokens will their lovers bring
        their fealty to hold?
No rich, no poor, just people,
        finding friendship on life's way
Without dividing class or caste,
        it'll be a better day.
Perhaps things will be better
        with all on level ground,
When all the gold had disappeared,
        And all the diamonds have been found.

CHAPTER II

Mercy had put in a long day. It was Monday and the wash had been especially large. All the petticoats and pantaloons were heavy with ruffles and lace and were difficult to wring out, and the pieces that had been dipped in the starch they had cooked in the big iron pot over the fire in the back yard laundry area were slippery and hard to hold onto and hang on the line. Sweating and tired, she knew she must feed Pierre before she returned to her room to bathe and put on her nightclothes. The days seemed longer than before she was told of Jeremiah's marriage. Life did not have the same meaning as when her heart had been full of love and hope for the future.

Removing her wet apron and folding it over the edge of the laundry tub, forgetting that the knife she carried for protection was still in the pocket, and gathering some scraps of cabbage left over from preparing the evening meal she resignedly approached the hutch and was startled to find the door was open! She felt inside among the straw and bedding where he slept and no Pierre was found. Frantically looking about, she thought, "Oh, Pierre, I am so tired, why have you chosen today to escape?"

Reasoning as to what direction he might have ventured she ran to the edge of the near-by woods and entered by the large maple tree from which they gathered sap in the spring. Taking a few more steps and thinking she heard a rustling sound that could be the pet rabbit, she went deeper into the woods where to her horror she found Pierre hanging from a small wild cherry tree by a knife in his throat. The dying animal was still squirming as blood poured from the wound and ran down his soft fur. With his eyes bulging he took his last breath as Mercy ran to him.

"Oh, Pierre! Who has done this awful thing to you!" she cried, and grasping the knife she tried to pull it from the dying creature. As she raised her arms she felt a hot body pressed tightly against her back. A guttural laugh preceded her being thrown to the ground where she was roughly violated. No amount of effort freed her until the deed had been done, and Osmond Buck stepped back, re-positioning his suspenders on his shoulders.

"There, Little French Missy, that is what you needed to put you in your place! And you thought you could get away with threatening me. There's no use squawking. No one would believe a little French tart like you!"

With a guffaw he left her there by the tree where Pierre had died, where her own pride had died, also. Rolling onto her stomach she pounded the ground with her fists and cursed. "The name of Buck I curse! I curse the name of Buck! I'll dance on your grave you pig, I'll dance on your grave!"

Mercy did not move from the place of sorrow until she finally stopped crying, then she slowly rose and straightened her skirts. She knew that she could not prove she had been violated, she could not prove that Osmond Buck had been near her, and she could not prove that he had killed Pierre. Pierre was all she had left of Jeremiah and now he was gone. With an unworldly feeling of utter despair she found a small flat rock with which she dug a shallow grave and lovingly laid the animal to rest, then placed the rock over the freshly dug earth. Walking slowly back to the house she washed her hands and face and straightened her hair at the outside laundry tub where she had washed laundry earlier. Entering the kitchen Allie met her and offered her a bowl of corned beef and cabbage, and holding back from vomiting she quietly declined and said she only wished to bathe and get to bed. There was no point in telling Allie all that had happened, it would only open up old wounds. She would tell her the following day that Pierre had simply died. For now, she could only think of bathing, and bathing and bathing. She wondered if she would ever feel clean again.

In the days that followed Mercy could think only of working out her bond and being free. There would be few pleasant memories that were not clouded by the events that had robbed her of happiness. She pondered that if flowers were brave enough to blossom when they might be trampled or plucked, why was the plucking of her innocence something of which to be ashamed? Of course, flowers bloom, she reasoned, not just for the pleasure of onlookers but to attract bees to pollinate them to propagate the species, a completely different situation from hers. She had tried to present herself as clean and pleasant looking, never giving any thought that someone might misconstrue her actions, and never thinking her behavior would ever make anyone want to "put her in her place." But she had threatened Osmond Buck following his attack on Allie. He was to be considered outside normal civilized association with most people. She had desired to be liked and appreciated as a person or a friend, someone others would be proud to associate with, and she certainly entertained no ideas of physical contact with the opposite sex. Her thoughts had been filled with innocence and her thoughts towards love were romantically pure. Her concept of love was of the idealistic variety, of knights in shining armor that saved maidens from harm. Now she believed there were no knights in shining armor. What had happened to Allie had now happened to her, and she had

Jean Edwards

no way of making things right for Allie or for herself. Her experiences revealed the fantasy of what she had assumed to be an attainable state of love.

Weeks went by and Mercy realized that the horror of her attack was not yet over. The Clarkes at first thought the pale girl was merely overwrought from being rejected by their son, but soon they realized the problem was much more serious than that. They did not voice their suspicions, but waited for Mercy to reveal her condition.

Mercy knew she would be shunned, as though her sins would rub off and attach themselves to an innocent, or perceived innocent, righteous person, whereas the perpetrator of her downfall was free of any taint of evil for his actions. She would be deprived of any and every pleasure she might have desired because of the tragic events she had endured, and there was no choice but to live with her misfortune, working as long as she could at Clarke House, and then be forced to give the fruit of her womb to some honorable, barren, married woman who was probably no less pure than herself. Only then could she escape and begin a new life far away where no one would ever learn of her embattled past. When her time was up at the Clarke's she would go and live somewhere in a cold garret if necessary. What would it matter? There were many poor, and being deprived and penniless would not be a burden among acquaintances in the same state of poverty.

Mercy pondered all these things, and then considered the lioness. The lioness had things figured out. They mated if they desired but raised their cubs by themselves, did the hunting and providing, and the males were used merely for breeding. That was all they did. Oh, and roar about the forest. Mercy had not wished to breed and she was not ready to become a mother, married or not. The event had been forced upon her, now she must suffer an illicit pregnancy and then she would have to suffer giving up her flesh and blood. She didn't think it would be a difficult choice. If the child belonged to Jeremiah she would treasure it forever, she would die to protect it, but Jeremiah had chosen another, and for some reason he had chosen the Tories over the Patriots. She could not understand his position though she knew there must be a reason beyond her comprehension. The name Jeremiah Clarke was embedded in her heart but she knew he would never be hers. The unbounded love she had held that resounded with every beat of her heart was fading. There was nothing she could do to reverse her bad fortune. She planned to never venture out at night again. When darkness approached she would remain behind the locked door of her room where her weapon was handy. With nothing left to lose she would not hesitate to use it. Osmond Buck had not been near her since the attack and she was fairly confident he would keep his distance for fear that even an accusation by a loyal servant like Mercy might cost him his job. He spent most of his time at the stables attending his duties and the remainder drinking in town or in his loft room. Mercy was sure he would lose his job eventually because of his inebriety, but it was already too late for her.

All these things kept coursing through her mind, and as time passed she became more and more somber. Her feeling for Jeremiah slowly changed with the hopelessness of her situation. Gradually she came to the realization that there was a place for her, a place where she would be accepted, where she would be protected with no recriminations—a place where she could heal. As soon as she could leave Thomaston she would return to the Friends of Jesus.

Rumor had it that Jeremiah was a traitor though the townspeople never breathed a word of their feelings to the Clarkes. The store and market were too important to their own lifestyles to jeopardize their ability to trade with Albert Clarke. Lives were being lost in the war and lives were being destroyed on the home front, also.

Hidden Casualties of War

We sadly face the loss of life
As tragedies of war,
We mourn for lives that were too short
Their dying we deplore.
And then the ones that limp on home
And those with vision lost,
How valiantly they gave themselves
Regretting not the cost.
But there amongst the payments made
For ringing freedom's bell,
The silent penalties are paid
In ways no one can tell.
For tragic are the lives of those
Affected by the fray,
And how their lives were crushed and torn
Reach not the light of day.
Broken bodies, broken hearts
loneliness and desperation,
The hope for peace and freedom
Their only consolation

CHAPTER III

Being called to the library by Mother Clarke was not a good sign. With her clothing beginning to reveal her condition, Mercy had known it would be just a matter of time before suspicions would become obvious facts.

"Are you sure you have not dallied with one of the village boys, Mercy?"

"No, no, Mother Clarke. I was violated. I was forced and I did all I could to resist. I suffer greatly from the attack but I find no way to escape my predicament."

"I know you wanted Jeremiah. Are you sure you did not find a substitute because he is married and you feel he has betrayed you? Perhaps you are feigning innocence now that you are caught. It would be very wrong to accuse an innocent man of such a terrible thing, Mercy."

The attitude Mother Clarke exhibited was just as Mercy had expected. The tight lips, the stiff back, the curt accusations.

Mother Clarke continued, "You have been dishonest, Mercy, for you are far along and now you wish to excuse yourself. If there had been a crime you would not have waited until your condition is obvious to all. You shame this house. You may continue your duties but do not expect pity for your actions."

"But, Mother Clarke, I tell you the truth. It was the day Pierre disappeared. I was tricked when I went hunting for him. Osmond Buck was hiding in the woods. I can show you where. Oh, Please, please believe me."

"Osmond Buck has been a good worker and has caused no trouble that I know of."

"Oh, but he has. He did the same thing to Allie but the baby dropped from her body. I took care of her myself!"

"Now you are overstepping your position and expect me to believe your fabrications. How can you stand there and continue making up excuses when there is no way I would not have known if Allie had been attacked, became with child and then lost the babe from her womb. There would have been much bleeding and I would have known. Your wild tales are becoming more unbelievable by the minute. I will decide what to do about you later. You are dismissed."

"But, it is true! I washed the cloths and did her chores so she could rest. I beg of you to believe me!"

"Did you not hear me? I said you are dismissed!"

Prudence was angry that she had ever considered Mercy as possibly becoming part of the family. Now she could see it would have been a mistake as the girl had proved to be untrustworthy. Luckily, her Jeremiah had found a girl of higher class, and also English. It was indeed fortunate.

Stricken by the harsh words from a woman she had admired and respected, Mercy returned to the kitchen and began peeling potatoes, determined not to shed a tear until after she finished her work for the day and could go to her room. The pregnancy was hard to bear, but even harder was the rejection by the lady of the house.

That night Prudence Clarke informed her husband of Mercy's condition. When probed for more information she became tight-lipped.

"Well," he thought. "She has wanted to get rid of Mercy since the day she decided the girl was too close to Jeremiah, and now the opportunity has arrived. He decided Mercy should be sent home early as he did not approve of bonded servants in the first place and Mercy had been acquired before he had a chance to make any other arrangements.

He would have hired the girl and paid a salary so she could stay or leave at will. What surprised him was his wife's acrimony that showed a side of her personality that until now, he had not been aware existed. He would prefer that Mercy be lovingly cared for until the child was born and be allowed to make her own choice. Could Prudence still be afraid of the attraction between Mercy and their son? If Mercy said she had been forcefully violated he believed her, though he would never voice that opinion to his wife. He wouldn't want to cause trouble in his own marriage over a servant girl, but it did seem unfair. His marriage was of first importance and he did still love Prudence after all these years. He decided to allow Mercy to return to the convent and he would attend to passage himself to be sure the girl was returned to her destination safely. Jeremiah would want her treated well, though it was a little late for that.

His daughter-in-law must be very special, he surmised, to have stolen Jeremiah's heart away from Mercy. He had been so sure they had a love that was unique and strong, but perhaps he had been mistaken. Things usually worked out best for all concerned, in this case at least it would be best for the Clarke family as Mercy should not be there when his son and his wife came to Thomaston. However, things did not seem to be working out too well for Mercy.

Albert Clarke continued to sort out his thoughts. Jeremiah's leaving the militia did not seem rational. He had always had a close relationship with his son, an honesty and openness that few parents enjoyed. He was sure the boy had left Maine with all intentions of contributing to the struggle for independence, and he was sure that his son's feelings for Mercy were honorable and true. To have deserted all that he had held dear did not seem possible, and to marry so suddenly was unlike Jeremiah. He had always weighed his actions carefully. It seemed that either he had taken a fever or a blow on the head or some other strong influence that had taken over his senses. Albert began to suspect there was a logical reason for his son's actions but he had no idea what it was. His letter informing the family of his marriage had included concern for Mercy's feelings, which led him to believe there might be an ulterior motive, not just concerning his patriotism, but also the marriage. If he was not sick or injured in some way Albert felt he would eventually be enlightened. Perhaps the boy's hormones had clouded his judgment and forced him into a situation he had not planned. What a shame if both Mercy and Jeremiah were to live lives apart because of illicit sex acts. At any rate, he would make every effort to make some atonement to the girl he had expected to become part of his family.

Morning brought the opportunity he needed. His mission to deliver supplies to Garrison Island gave him the chance he needed to talk to Mercy and tell her he would assist her in her plight. It was necessary that arrangements be made for her confinement. Prudence was angry with the girl although he was sure Mercy was innocent of any wrongdoing.

"Come, Mercy, ride with me to Muscongus. We will have lunch in Meduncook and be back by nightfall. It will be good for you to get away from the house for a day!"

"But, Monsieur Clarke, Mother Clarke will be unhappy with me if I leave my work."

"No, no. I have already informed her you would be going on this trip. Just get your cloak as the ocean breeze can be chilling, and hop aboard the wagon. It is loaded and ready to go. All it needs is a pretty young girl on the seat to complete the load."

Reluctantly, Mercy retrieved her cloak from the hall closet and walked down the front path to the waiting wagon. She was very nervous because her troubles were so overwhelming she had not yet finalized any plan for future action. Her servitude would not be accomplished for two more years and her child would be born before that time was served.

They rode quietly for some time, following the ocean's winding shoreline, watching the gulls diving for fish in the sparkling blue ocean, listening to their call. The primrose was blooming along the rocky banks and the air was fresh and clean with whiffs of spruce and pine riding on the air. Mercy forgot her troubles for a time and enjoyed the pleasure of the day. She finally broke the silence between them.

"Monsieur, I must tell you that I am with child. I was forced one night when I went to feed Pierre. My rabbit was killed and I was robbed of my honor."

"Mercy, I know what has happened to you, but there is no proof. I also know that Jeremiah cared for you very much. There must be a reason for his marriage, but it must be honored and it cannot be changed. Would you like to return to the convent?"

"Oui, Monsieur, but I still owe two years time as your servant."

"I think we can dispense with that time under the circumstance. You have been a loyal and hardworking house girl and I will arrange passage for you back to the Amitie le Christ as soon as possible. When Jeremiah returns I will explain to him that you were assaulted. Let it be a comfort to you that I believe you and so will Jeremiah. This is all I can do for you."

"Oh, thank you, Monsieur Clarke," she cried as tears welled in her dark eyes. "If I am only to have your respect, that is enough to satisfy my heart. You know that I cared for your son, and I wish him happiness. If I am not to be his true love, then so be it. Please tell him that I understand

and will cherish the time we had together, but that is all in the past. I appreciate your generosity and concern, but if I go back to the convent I will find peace."

Mercy and Albert arrived at the shore at low tide and the horses easily transported the wagon of goods and its passengers across the rock ledge road out to the island where the garrison awaited the provisions. After unloading they journeyed back to Thomaston. Not only was the wagon lighter without its load of goods and supplies, but also Mercy's heart was lighter. Going home was what she wanted, what she needed, and she was anxious to begin the trip northward.

The following day Albert Clarke made secure arrangements for Mercy to return to the northern reaches of Maine, back to her home where she would be loved and cared for. He would forever live with the guilt that he had not protected the innocent girl; that her childhood had been wrenched from her, and her heart had been broken. He wondered if he would be punished for his sin of failure. There was nothing more he could do for the gentle girl who had graced their home for over three years. She had given them her love, kindness and uncomplaining service and her reward had been injury and disgrace. He suffered from the pain of his failure, but there was nothing more he could do for her except to give her the freedom she deserved.

CHAPTER IV

The small life Mercy carried did not prevent her enjoyment of the journey on which she embarked. Albert Clarke had booked her passage by sea and river to St. Stephen and the captain of the small packet had papers and payment to place her with a reliable trader with as much comfort as possible back to the convent. She had gathered her few belongings and took only the one dress she wore, some undergarments and a wool sweater of many colors she had knitted for herself of leftover yarn from the gifts she had made. Gathering the heavy boiled wool cloak she had brought with her when she first came to Thomaston about her body, she hugged a tearful Allie good-bye and quickly left Clarke house. Mother Clarke did not bid her farewell, though Mercy thought she saw her at a window when she took a last look back at the house she had once loved, a house she now associated with heartbreak.

The dock was crowded when she arrived, the crew was loading the last of the traded goods and supplies aboard and they patiently waited until the captain appeared at the rail and motioned them aboard. Albert carried her small bag and at the last moment before returning to the dock he suddenly threw his arms about her and quickly wished her well, then hurried down the gang plank and swiftly walked to his wagon, urging the horses up the gravel road away from the docks and away from his failure. Mercy thought she saw a tear in his eye and she was not mistaken. There was something in his kindness that was part of Jeremiah.

Somber-faced, she stood at the rail of the ship she had boarded and looked seaward. The same cool breeze she had first felt when she came to Thomaston whipped strands of her hair across her face. Brushing it back with her hand she pulled her hood over her head and clutched the cape closer to her body. Somehow the sea and the wind and the calling gulls had a calming effect. She felt she had been through enough misery for a lifetime, but the stirring of the child she carried reminded her that her future was forever changed. She would be responsible for another human being; she would no longer be the same girl that had come to the rocky coast, and she vowed she would cherish every good thing she could find in her life, no matter how small. Mayhap it was all a lesson given from the Supreme Being, that she should calmly face adversity and wait for the solution to come to her, to avoid flailing but to approach difficulties with peace and absence of fear.

The ship hauled anchor and the sea journey began. They headed northeast around Vinalhaven, east to Deer Isle, then headed past Swan's Island to open sea well away from the shore.

She had been quartered in the first mate's tiny cubicle, which she found comfortable, though the smell of male sweat permeated the room. That was the way of ships, she concluded, as women did not sail often unless as a passenger. Men never seemed to notice things like the odor of sweat, even though they were very capable in keeping things neat and orderly. Women were more fastidious in keeping their bed linens clean, as they were more conscious of odor. All in all, the small quarters proved very satisfactory, especially since she had no choice in the matter and would have slept in the hold with pigs if necessary to get back home with her beloved Sisters.

The rolling of the ship rocked her to sleep and by morning they were approaching the bay that separated Maine from Canada, slowly sailing up the inlet past St. Andrews to the east, then dropping anchor. In a small dory she, along with the captain, were rowed ashore at St. Stephen. The kindly Captain found a place for her to stay for the night at a boarding house for travelers and traders. The buxom woman who ran the house took her under her wing and assured the captain of her safety with her. Making several inquires in town he found and hired a reliable trader who was heading north, a family man who was returning to Montreal. His twelve year-old son was traveling with him and they were happy with the generous payment for Mercy's conveyance north. They had stopped at the Friends of Jesus on their trading trip earlier and were happy to deliver the girl to the Sisters.

Informing Mercy that her passage had been secured for the following day she bade the Captain farewell, offering him her most polite appreciation for his kindness, and settled for the night following a fine meal of cornbread and soup beans. She still felt the movement of the ship, and the room seemed to be rocking up and down as the ship had, so she closed her eyes and the sensation was gone by morning.

The overland trip was exhausting and nerve wracking. It brought back memories of the trip several years past when she had trusted Jacques Renault that she was going to a wonderful home and a wonderful future. How trusting she and the Sisters had been! It was confusing. She wondered if her unfortunate circumstance was her fault, the war's fault or the will of God. She had always believed that God was a loving and merciful God. That was what she had learned from Sister Margarite, so certainly her misery was not from Him. Trying to remember what she had done or not done to cause her own misfortune brought no enlightenment, so she decided the fault belonged to the war. If Jeremiah had not gone off to the war they would still be sitting on the riverbank discussing the latest book they had read, he would not have given her Pierre and she would not have been in the woods at night where she could be attacked, and Jeremiah would not have found a wife in Philadelphia. She could blame a lot of things but that would be as silly as blaming Canada.

She hoped all was well at the convent. She had heard of the Wilderness Campaign under the great hero Benedict Arnold that had fought its way to Quebec, and certainly once the trail had been marked troops or scoundrels could follow it more than once.—And all the pestilence and disease that the militia had endured, (or not endured, with the many deaths they caused), could have been carried to the small convent. The idea that ruffians might have raped and pillaged the convent made her cringe, then realizing that such a dastardly event would have been on the lips of every trader and trapper diminished that possibility. The news of such evil would have traveled quickly to the ports on the coast.

The jogging of the wagon made her back ache. The driver told her they would reach her destination in two more days, so she relaxed and tried to enjoy the scenery. Small lakes and streams, tall pines and fragrant firs, lacy cedars, fluttering butterflies, chirping birds and bees buzzing about gathering nectar for their winter food. It was late August, and Merci thought about the butternut squash that would be glowing golden in the garden at the convent, and the way the leaves on the deciduous trees would begin their shrinking just before bursting into brilliance, white puffs of clouds would be floating lazily across the sky, casting random shadows on the fruited fields and orchards, the drying grasses and timothy hay turning pale, pumpkins not yet orange but with traces of gold in streaks on the green orbs.

Eighth Month

Air whispers in August
In anticipation of the coming cool,
And the sky moves
Alternating sun and shade,
Making competing patches of gloom
And dazzling sunlight in the trees.
The lonesome caw in the stillness
Of the dew of morning,
Contrasted by the happy chirping
Of birds,
Anticipating
Their journey south,
As they observe the omens
In the sky
Of the coming winter.

As promised, the wagon arrived at dusk at Amitie le Christ. A tired and aching girl dismounted the wagon and tentatively approached the home to which she had returned. A stunned Jolene was sweeping the steps of the chapel and when she saw Merci she stared wide-eyed for a moment, then disappeared inside. Immediately, Sister Margarite and Sister Catherine immerged from the building and embraced their returning child. They realized her unmistakable condition but did not mention it or give any sign that they had noticed, but ushered her inside. Catherine returned to the yard and assisted the kindly tradesman and his son in feeding and watering the horses, then led them to the travelers sleeping quarters, promising a good meal as soon as possible.

Asking if any payment was due, the affable trader replied, "No, No, I have been paid handsomely to return this girl to you. I will be traveling on to Montreal on the morrow. I hope all is well with the girl. I did my best to care for her."

"I am sure of that, Monsieur, we appreciate your kindness. You have stopped here before and we are always glad of your visits. We will have a good breakfast ready tomorrow shortly after the crowing of the cock, and we will provide food for your trip."

"Thank you, Sister, but I have plenty on my wagon and when the cock crows I will already be on my way. I have been away from my family in Montreal much too long, so *Au Revoir*, and God bless you all."

With that, Sister Catherine returned to the dining hall where the excited Sisters had gathered around their returned child.

Exhausted, but happy and relieved to be home at last, Mercy glowed in the attention of the ecstatic Sisters who fussed over her and brought food to the table in celebration of the return of their darling.

"Thomas will be so excited when he finds you are here at last!" Sister Catherine exclaimed. He spends a lot of time in the woods hunting and working on his projects. He has been working with stone and who knows what he is thinking up these days. He works hard to keep all the chores done and still he works and traverses the woods. He has always kept busy and doesn't always express his thoughts to us."

"I'm really very tired," Merci quietly confessed, and as she arose from her seat at the table she immediately fell to the floor. The sisters quickly cleared the table and lifted their child onto the plank platform, as the obvious condition of their dear one presented itself. Some ran for clean cloths, Sister Margarite held her hand and Sister Catherine stroked her brow as the low moans at regular intervals told the story of what was to be. Lamps were brought closer and as the baby emerged it was Jolene that received the child while Margarite soothed the exhausted Merci.

"It's a monster! It's a monster!" Jolene exclaimed. "See the mouth that cannot suckle! This child will die and the sooner the better!" As tears splashed down her cheeks she cried, "This is the payment for her sin! No righteous girl would give birth to such a creature!"

As she stood holding the pitiful newborn Margarite quickly attended the needs of Merci who had fortunately remained in a faint from the exertion of her travail and went to Jolene. Taking the babe from her arms she could see there was no help for the tiny creature whose soul had left the deformed body.

Covering the baby she put her arms about Jolene and admonished Catherine to remain and care for Merci. Together Sister Margarite and Jolene entered the small chapel where Jolene tearfully revealed her own past, how she had given birth to a deformed stillborn and her husband had cast her out of his house for presenting him with a monster, declaring the child a result of unfaithfulness and that only sin could create such a disfigurement. Finding a haven with the Friends of Jesus had saved her from ostracism and she would be forever grateful. "I am so sorry for my outburst. I hope I have not hurt Merci. I'm so very sorry!"

"Jolene, perhaps this tragic situation was God's way of giving you the peace that you deserve. These things happen and no one is to blame. We do not yet know what has happened in Merci's life these three years, but the deformity of a child and its death is not a punishment, it is merely an act of God that we do not understand. Dry your tears. We must attend Merci. Her healing will be your healing."

Upon returning to the room where the birth had taken place they explained the condition of the baby and Merci asked to see him. Gazing at the still form she cried out, "The grave of Buck will bear the mark. Perhaps the one that is to blame, perhaps not, but it will be a reminder of this hateful day! There will be dancing on the grave of one who wronged an innocent girl!" With that she fell back into a deep healing sleep.

The following day Sister Margarite called Jolene to the sanctuary. "Jolene, take this child to the stream and baptize him, then bury him in the corner of the field near the giant oak and place a large stone on the grave. This poor babe is innocent of this unfortunate tragedy. By doing this you will free yourself from your own traumatic past as Merci will also be free. You both deserve to find peace, but you must do this. As you pour out your tears you will cleanse yourself of these sorrows."

Jolene took the bundle from Margarite and went to the stream. Pulling back the covering from the child's head she dipped her fingers in the cold water and sprinkled the tiny misshapen brow. "I baptize thee "William the *Pitoyable.*" With the wooden shovel she had brought from the barn she made her way to the far corner of the cleared field as she had been told. She tenderly placed the bundle near the base of the tree and dug deep. When the grave was finished she carefully placed the baby in and slowly covered him with the soft earth. When it was filled she stood for a long time, then smoothed the earth and patted it down firmly. Tears streamed from her eyes, but she went to the edge of the cleared space and found a large stone. It was too heavy to carry so she knelt down and pushed against it until it rolled. Slowly and laboriously she worked until the stone was placed on the grave marking the spot where she had buried Merci's child, and the child of her own past was sealed with William the *Pitoyable.*

Some days later when Merci awoke, Sister Margarite took Merci in her arms. As Merci tearfully blurted out the whole story of her years away Sister Margarite also shed tears. "I'm so sorry, Merci, so very sorry for all you have suffered. My remorse in ever sending you away weighs heavily on my heart. I thought you would find a better life and I beg your forgiveness. We have buried your stillborn child. He was baptized "William." As soon as you have strength we will take you to his resting place. Please forgive me for causing you pain."

"Oh, Sister, of course you are forgiven. I thought I didn't want to live but I do, I do. I want to be a Sister like you, and give my life to others."

Merci, there are many ways to serve God and you will find yours."

"But Sister, I cannot help cursing the name of Buck. I swear that when I am dead and gone I will leave my mark on the grave of someone with that name, so the name will be disgraced forever. Perhaps someone will stop there and think and wonder and reform any evil in their hearts."

"Now, Merci, you have been through a very bad time. You must ask God's help in learning to forgive. Perhaps you cannot forgive now, but you will later when your life is repaired, and God will help you repair it. You only hurt yourself with cursing so you must let time heal your wounds and let the Grace of God enter your heart."

"Sister Margarite, an innocent child is dead, he could not live for being fathered by a scoundrel."

"Merci, you were violated, but William's death is something we cannot understand. Only God knows the reason. You will see things differently in time. You must first heal your body, then your soul will heal and eventually His plan for your life will be revealed. Come, now. Eat this good soup that Delphia has prepared for you."

Silently, Merci ate, but she could find no way to erase the curse she had placed against Osmond Buck.

Sister Margarite had done all she could to calm Merci and accept the results of her own decision to send the girl to a place where she had been so traumatized. The taunts of her own childhood followed her, leaving scars on her heart. She had learned to accept herself as she was, limping through life was her lot, but she had vowed to never allow a physical deformity to hurt a child if she could prevent it. Unfortunately, little William was beyond saving, and she knew she must help Merci to recover from the injury that had been thrust upon her.

Pezhik Onindj

CHAPTER V

Thomas Pezhik Onindj returned from his hunting trip carrying several game birds tied together by their legs and strode to the kitchen where they would be welcomed for the evening meal the following day. His trips were always a great joy as he loved to hunt and the Sisters were always so appreciative of anything he brought to them. Even if his hunting was a failure they would cheerfully encourage him with, "Next time, Thomas, you will have a good hunt next time!"

Fetching his cup from the shelf above the burning fireplace he poured his cup full of steaming water from the kettle hanging on the spit over the hot coals. Dipping some honey from the honey crock and some ground birch bark from its bowl, he stirred them into the hot liquid, then sat at the table on the side near the fire. He had been away two days and having hunted near the lake the previous day he had returned to his nearly finished stone house in the woods and had camped there overnight.

He sensed that there was something different in the air. The smell in the kitchen was not the same. It usually smelled of freshly baked bread or stew or the earthy smell of freshly pulled vegetables from the garden. This was a different smell, some human smell he could not decipher, though he tried to place it.

Sister Catherine stepped into the room.

"Thomas, there is something you must know. It is very serious."

"Has someone died? There is something wrong here, and you must tell me what it is."

"Let me bring Sister Margarite to you. She can explain it much better than I."

Leaving a stunned Thomas, she quickly brought Sister Margarite to the room and left as abruptly as before.

"Sit down, Thomas," Margarite commanded in a serious tone. "Do not let your emotions rule your mind. Merci has returned."

"Merci? Where? Where is she? I must go to her! Why is everyone behaving so mysteriously? We should be celebrating! Where is she?"

"Thomas, you may see her in good time. But first there is something you should know."

Jumping to his feet he cried, "Is she injured? Is she dying? Oh, let me see her, I MUST see her."

"All in good time, Thomas. Sit down. I said, SIT DOWN!"

Thomas sat in the chair, against his will, but he sat. Never had Sister Margarite been harsh with him, and he was becoming frightened, frightened that Merci was going to be lost forever, frightened that she was dying or had some dreadful disease.

"Thomas, we made a grave mistake in sending Merci to the coast. Her new life was very unpleasant and I will always suffer remorse for being foolish enough to believe she would find a better life elsewhere. Merci was sold as a bonded servant and though she worked and learned and tried to make her life bearable until she could return, she was badly treated and neglected."

"In what way? Is she maimed?"

"No, not in the way you are thinking. She was violated by a terrible man, and the attack caused a child to grow within her. The child was born here last night. It was sadly deformed and did not live. It came much too early because of the difficult journey to return to us. Jolene has buried it in the far field by the oak tree."

Thomas was quiet for a moment, then he spoke softly. "Please let me go to her. She must be suffering."

She will heal in time, both body and soul and we must help her. The trip from Thomaston was long and tiring and the birth was difficult. She needs rest and comfort, so be very gentle and stay only minutes. Can you do that, Thomas?"

"Yes, Sister. I will only hold her hand for a few moments and then I will leave her to rest."

"Very well, Thomas. She is in her old room next to yours. We watch her closely and she seems to be healing. She is very bitter but glad to be safely at home."

Thomas went to the stream and washed the soil of his hunting trip from his body and then returned to the compound, entering his own room first to change clothing. Crossing quietly on the wooden floor he made his way to the room he knew so well, the room where he had stood and looked at the empty bed every night for the years she had been away. Slowly approaching the bed where the frail girl rested he knelt by the bed. She was asleep, pale and drawn, but she was his Merci home again at last.

Reaching out he took her small hand in his and pressed it to his lips.

"Merci, It is I, Lone Wolf."

She stirred slightly and softly moaned, "I cursed the name of Osmond Buck. Sister says I must forgive, but I can't, not yet. Oh, why must I forgive that evil one? Oh, why?"

"Merci, it will be all right, I promise. I will help you. I promise I will make everything all right."

Holding her hand he bowed his head, knowing what he had to do. Merci had drifted back into her dreams and Thomas quietly left the room.

When Thomas left, Merci was not all by herself, Rudy had secretly crept into the room and had hidden under the bed.

When all was quiet he came out and put his head on the edge of the bed and silently kept guard over his returned friend. The herd dog was more than a worker at the convent, he felt he was the guardian of all his people, and no one was happier to see Merci or more compassionate toward her illness.

The following morning there was no trace of Thomas Pezhik Onindj at the convent Amitie le Christ. He had packed Chavalier Noir for a very long journey, but first he made camp on the ridge overlooking Eagle Lake. Quickly making a small lean-to of fir branches he then gathered some wood and lit a campfire. Sitting with crossed legs before the fire his eyes watched the flames dancing above the burning embers and became entranced by their constant change as they leaped and rested, leaped and rested. Throwing his head back he closed his eyes and softly chanted, "I will wear the skin of the deer that I might be quick as I pass through the woodlands. I will eat the eggs from the eagle's nest that my vision will be sharp and clear, and I will eat the meat of the rabbit that I will be watchful of those who would do me harm."

Standing, he continued in a strange mixture of religion, that of the Holy church taught him by the Sisters and all that he had gleaned from the natives who lived beyond Eagle Lake. Thomas un Main, Pezhik Onindj, Lone Wolf, raised his fist to the sky as he prayed.

"Oh Mighty Holy Spirit, lead me in the way I must go. Let your light shine on me as the sun shines on the wings of an eagle, give me the strength of the mountain lion. Let me be wily as a fox and fierce as a badger. Do not let me falter as I seek justice for my injured companion. Be by my side, Oh, Great Spirit and lead me to the villainous monster that has caused such pain, that I might return with freedom in my heart. In the name of the Father, the Son and the Holy Ghost, Amen.

Standing on the ridge by the fire Thomas wondered how such terrible things could have happened to Merci. He stood there for hours with arms raised toward the night sky, crying out in anguish throughout the night. The smoke from the fire blackened his face until only his eyes were shining in the darkness, calling on the Spirits to lead him in the paths of righteousness and serenity.

Just before dawn he mounted his horse and headed southeast. The August weather was balmy and the days saw no rain and when the purposeful young man reached the coast there was no doubt in his mind of the unwavering purpose of his mission. Only when it was accomplished would he be free to return to the Amitie le Christ.

CHAPTER VI

Thomas was not the only person suffering. Sister Margarite spent the night in the chapel praying. They had bound Merci's breasts to stop the flow of milk that would have no use, and Margarite felt responsible for Merci's discomfort.

"Oh God,
    Our child has suffered more in her young life than most in a lifetime. It seems to us that she should have been blessed with happiness, we love her so much. We understand that your ways are beyond our knowing, but we ask your forgiveness for any sin we might have thought or done, and pray you will show us, in your infinite wisdom, the paths we must take to comfort our beloved Merci. We have made some bad choices for her that led to such terrible pain. Joy has been taken from her life. Help us provide safety for her, help us atone for our past failures and return her joy of living. We understand now the frustrations of child rearing, but please don't give up on us. We are forever your servants, Lord, and will try to follow your guidance more clearly, that we do not fail again. In the name of the Father, the Son and the Holy Ghost, Amen."

When Merci was able to leave her bed, she and Jolene went to the marker where William was sleeping. As Margarite had foretold, when they returned with reddened eyes their hearts had been cleansed and they were free to start their lives anew.

A few days later Merci felt up to walking about the compound. She observed many changes. The front of the chapel had been covered with stone, smooth gray stone gathered from the fields where the glaciers that had rounded the mountains millenniums before had dropped them in their slow passage south. They had been carefully selected for uniformity and lovingly matched for size and texture. A mixture of clay, water and straw had been used for mortar, and the effect was quite beautiful. Merci ran her hand over the cool surface, wishing she had been there to help.

The wooly sheep frolicked in the fields, fields well fenced with wooden posts and cross bars to keep them from straying and Rudy watched over the flock to keep predators away. She was amazed at the increase in number. The spring shearing would yield all the wool they could wash, card, spin and knit or weave into garments in a year, and even enough extra lambs for mutton stew and chops.

Wandering back up to her room she was surprised that it had changed very little. They had kept it clean and dusted awaiting her return. Glancing into Thomas's room she found a different scene. It was no longer a small boy's room. The walls were hung with the gray hides of wolves, a large bow with arrows placed neatly in a leather quiver, a rack filled with knives of varying sizes, their curved handles of deer horn holding them securely in grooves cut in the rack. Several pairs of moccasins sat against a wall, some of ankle height and some that would reach above the calf, with leather fringe adorning the tops. A leather vest with the same fringe hung on a peg by the door, and there by his bed rested his La Crosse stick and a leather bagataway ball. His bed was covered with the usual wool blankets woven with stripes of dyed yarn. The whole room had a different feel and smell than she remembered. It was obvious that little Thomas Pezhik Onindj had grown up.

Merci had a vague recollection of what she thought was a dream when she was confined from the birth of her poor child. She wondered if Thomas had been there. Was it possible that he had held her hand and spoken to her? He was not at the convent, he had left on one of his trips the Sisters had told her, and that he would return soon as always. They had no idea how badly she wished to see her childhood companion.

At night she slept peacefully listening to the brook that ran behind the buildings, bubbling its way to Eagle Lake.

At night I hear a little stream,
softly sighing as I dream.
It gathers raindrops from the sky
and water from the fields nearby.
It gathers all the drops together,
and sings along in every weather,
Loudly, following a storm, quietly on a summer morn.
When winter comes it cannot sing, as frozen there it
waits for Spring.
It sings in Summer, Spring and Fall,
but where I sleep,
Sings best of all.

CHAPTER VII

Dear Jeremiah,

Realizing that you have a business that takes much of your time in Philadelphia and that you planned to visit us at war's end, I implore you to change your plans. Your mother is not as well as I, and I am sure, you, would wish her to be. Although she still supervises the household affairs she is generally less strong than in the past. I convinced her to see a doctor in Biddeford, (with so many joining the war ranks we are short of personnel in the medical field). She would be dismayed if she learned I had informed you of her health concerns. The trouble is of a feminine nature and has progressed beyond a cure. If you delay your trip 'til war's end which may not be accomplished for several more years I fear you may arrive too late to kiss her good-bye.

Please consider my plea. If you were serving your country I would not ask this of you, but since you are living the civilian life I see no reason you cannot spare the time for this important family concern.

Your loving father,
Albert

Incidentally, Mercy has returned to the convent Amitie le Christ.

Jeremiah was heart-struck upon reading his father's letter. There was no way he could reveal his true mission in the fight for independence. Thankfully, Providence had allowed him an excuse for not leaving his post. If Abigail did nothing else for him, she had at least provided him the means to protect his secrecy. It was with great remorse he answered his father's letter.

Dear Father,

It is with a broken heart I must deny your request. I am unable to leave Philadelphia at this time. My wife is in the final weeks of a very difficult pregnancy and she cannot travel under any circumstances. I am well but feel it is my duty to remain by her side. I assume that Mother is unaware you have informed me of her condition, so I will write a separate letter to her with only cheerful news. Please forgive me for being unable to fulfill your wishes. I'm sure you understand my position and that you will forgive my non-compliance.

Your loving son,
Jeremiah

Albert's first reaction to Jeremiah's letter was anger. He was sure he had failed to express the urgency of his request, but soon calmed himself lest Prudence suspect there had been correspondence behind her back. The last thing he wanted was for her to lose faith in her husband, and she would be furious if she knew her illness had been revealed to Jeremiah.

He destroyed the letter from his son, but he delivered the letter addressed to Prudence.

Sitting by her chair as she opened the wax seal he listened as she began to read aloud.

Dearest Mother,

I have wonderful news! When independence is gained and it is safe to journey home to Maine with my wife there will be a third party traveling with us. Abigail will soon give birth to your grandchild. By all indications it will be healthy and robust. If it is a boy his name will be Andrew Albert Clarke. My hope is that he will bear the blue eyes and blond curls as do my sister's children. I can't tell you how much I miss you and love you, and I will be anxious to see my son, (or even a daughter), in your arms. If Abigail likes the area we may give up the store in Philadelphia and rejoin the family there in Thomaston. There is much here to hold me for a few more years, but then we could come north and raise our child by the rocky coast away from this big city.

Until then, I send my love,
Your son,
Jeremiah

Albert was relieved. He should have realized his son would be diplomatic. The only course to take was that of much prayer that the war would end swiftly. He could forgive Jeremiah's leaving the militia if only he could come home before the inevitable occurred. For Prudence to hold her son's child before the end would bring her much comfort. Jeremiah's not leaving his wife at this time was understandable, but having to wait until the war's end gave him second thoughts. Somehow, he had the feeling that there was more to the grocery business in Philadelphia than met the eye. He knew his son so well he had developed suspicions, suspicions that he could not, would not, reveal to anyone.

Sad as it would be if their son could not return before his mother's passing, Albert knew the reason was more complicated than words had described, and time would tell all.

As Merci recuperated, far away in Philadelphia another woman lay in childbirth. Her agonizing screams echoed thoughout the halls of the large house on the avenue. Abigail's husband waited for news of the results of his work by the apple tree in the back yard. Work it had been, to please Abby, not his own pleasure. He had mixed emotions about fulfilling his marital duties. There was always the guilt over using Abby's body when it was Mercy he loved. Whenever he murmured "Mercy" during their intimacies the silly girl had assumed he had been thanking her in French, and thought he was being romantic. He was forced by circumstance to keep her happy. Now he would be forever tied to a family of British sympathizers with whom he could never be honest. His sacrifice for his country was unimaginable to others, and must remain a secret. Would anyone in Massachusetts ever trust him again even if they knew the truth? He was sure they must doubt his loyalty. Trust was probably gone forever, as was his life with Mercy.

He entertained thoughts of leaving Abigail when the war ended. He could return to Maine and explain it all to Mercy. But could they live together without the sanctity of marriage? It would go against his morals and would be even more devastating to Mercy. What would the consequences of such a liaison do to the way they felt about each other? Would the guilt destroy them both? What about his parents, would they accept such behavior from their son and wouldn't they turn against Mercy for causing his transgression? To live outside the church and abandon the principles he had been taught since childhood was impossible. His sacrifice was a sentence he would have to live with. His anguish, loneliness and desperation sometimes overwhelmed him, especially deep in the night. With Abigail pawing at him he had given in and satisfied her, then contended with his guilt for hours, guilt that he could not love the simple girl that was his legal wife, and guilt that he was not only betraying Mercy, but also himself. His morning exhaustion from sleepless nights had been ignored by Abigail's parents. They assumed his amorous attraction to their daughter had taken its toll, and their ignorance, to Jeremiah, was bliss.

The thin wail of a new life entering the world was both a sound of wonder and a death knoll to all his dreams. Slowly he rose and walked into the quiet house. Entering the door at the rear of the house he felt a strange quiet, too quiet. Putting his hand on the bottom post he climbed the stairs to the second floor. Finding no one, he was halfway down the hall when he heard sobbing.

Following the sound he entered the room where his wife's mother and a servant stood by the bed where the ashen face of his dead wife rested.

"It is a boy," his mother-in-law sobbed.

Looking about the room in disbelief, he saw a newborn baby sleeping in a cradle, his motherless son. He was not surprised that Abigail had difficulty birthing their child. She had used the pregnancy as an excuse to gorge herself, happily eating "for two." It seemed that she was eating for eight, heaping her plate several times at every meal, then calling for dessert. She cheerfully consumed it all, and all the sweets she could find between meals, even sending him for 'just a tad" in the middle of the night. He felt the overeating was unhealthy but at least her bulging body had released him from his nocturnal duties. Mounting that mound was too much for any man.

As her time had approached, she had become more listless and begged less for food. Her ankles had become so swollen her feet would not fit into her shoes and she spent most of her days in a chair with the pitiful limbs propped on a footstool, her face reddened and her breathing labored. He knew she would have a difficult time losing the weight following the birth, but he had not imagined that she would die.

A weird sensation came over Jeremiah. Sadness that Abigail had to die such a painful death, gratitude that she had given him a son, realizing that she had given her all to him and he had given her nothing in return. He had only used her to his own advantage. Now she had given him freedom from living a lie.

Thoughts of Mercy ran through his head. His guilt was crushing and it would be months before he could reconcile his place in the world and find his peace with God. He prayed for the help of the Almighty God to lead him in the path he should follow.

Jean Edwards

Lament

How many children died in those days,
How many mothers cried?
How many mothers to their babies were lost?
And those children paid the awful cost.
Mothers that late in the night did weep,
For the stillborn babes they could not keep.
Sad. Sad, was the time when there was no keeping,
Those mothers and children
                    now in their graves sleeping.

Dear Father,

At the birth of your grandson, Andrew Albert Clarke, my wife Abigail was lost. There is much sadness here, but be assured Andrew will be well cared for. I have found a wet nurse for him and he is very healthy. I will bring him to Maine as soon as it is feasible. I pray that all is well there and that Mother will enjoy holding him when I return. He is blond and has blue eyes as I had hoped.

Your devoted son,
Jeremiah

Dear Jeremiah,

I regret to inform you that your mother passed on to her reward yesterday. She suffered much the last two months, so I cannot wish her back. As I held her hand at the end she said, "Andrew Albert Clarke, what a beautiful name," just before she drew her last breath. I cannot tell you how much she meant to me and how much I will miss her. I am sure you have suffered with the loss of Abigail, though you were not together as long as your mother and I have been. She had a happy life, I believe, at least I did all I could to make her happy. If ever an angel went straight back to Heaven it was my Prudence.

I anxiously await your return to bring my grandson to the land of his heritage.

Your loving father,
Albert

Jeremiah sat a long time after reading the letter from Maine. Tearfully he went to the crib where Andrew lay sleeping and stroked his pale curls. How sad that his mother never had the opportunity to hold, to touch, to love their son. He had given up Mercy, less painfully he had given up Abigail, and now he had lost his mother without being able to say good-bye—but he had Andrew. Yes, he had his beautiful son and he was doing his duty. He was beginning to wonder what else would be asked of him. He prayed that Andrew would be safe. If he could raise his son perhaps it would be worth all the pain he had endured.

The sad days following the passing of Abigail Worthington Clarke had been busy and confusing. Jeremiah had never imagined the affection he would have for his son. His pale hair and blue eyes stamped him as his own, and he loved him from the moment he first saw him and took him in his arms. He was sorry Abigail would never feel the love of the son he named "Andrew Albert Clarke," never hold him, never be able to see his first smile or play with him and hear his laughter. That his union with Abigail could have created such a miracle was a thing of wonder, and it was unfathomable that he might have callously left after the war without any consideration for Abigail or of the child she carried. He knew the moment he held him in his arms that he would have remained with Andrew and his mother had she lived, and now he would have to decide what path to follow for the good of the small wonder whose eyes held his with such trust.

Knowing that his duty to his country had not ended, he continued his stay in the Worthington household, gathering any information he could, and allowing the grandparents the pleasure of knowing their grandson. He made the decision that when the war finally ended he would be wrenching Andrew from them and returning to his homeland in the North.

Jeremiah hired a wet nurse for his son, a voluptuous woman with seven children that had the ability to feed her own newborn and Andrew as well, in fact, she could have fed several babies if the opportunity presented itself. Jovial, kind and appreciative of the generous stipend offered, Andrew was content in her loving care and developed a happy and outgoing humor. It was going to be difficult to tear the child away from the only nurture he had ever known when the war ended, but he would cross that bridge when he came to it.

CHAPTER VIII

In the native manner Thomas Pezhik Onindj had removed his facial hairs as they emerged one by one in his early teen years, using two sharpened muscle shells to tweeze them, until his face was smooth and no trace of growth was seen. With his shirt with the crocheted lace edged jabot and his Sunday suit neatly packed in leather saddle bags by his bed roll he traveled the usual route south, following the trails and rivers on the northeast boundary of Maine. As Providence would have it, in June, a trader stopping at the convent for an overnight stay had ridden into the compound on a fine bay, and Thomas had greatly admired the saddle and saddlebags as he fed and watered the animal before securing him in the barn for the night. Thomas had always ridden Chevalier Noir bareback in the native fashion, but the next week he was hard at work fashioning his own saddle and saddlebags. His horse didn't seem to mind the change, and now he was grateful for the circumstances that had instigated his project, allowing him to be prepared for the mission at hand. His horse was accustomed to Thomas riding either with or without the saddle, and the new paraphernalia made carrying his food and supplies much easier. He preferred the freedom of bareback riding, and he thought Chevalier Noir preferred it also. There was something about a man and his horse riding like the wind unencumbered by any artificial aid. He had made sure to reserve time for pleasant rides over the hills and around Eagle Lake, but the business at hand called for the formality of the saddle and attached storage bags. "When this trip is over, Chevalier Noir, we will take a freedom ride," he told his steed, "but for now you must help me carry out my mission."

Before leaving the convent he had cut large squares of white birch bark on which he wrote this message. "Jacques Renault, liar, cheat, kidnapper. Do not trade with this man." He planned his trip to insure passing settlements and trading posts in the night, posting his notices silently, to be discovered and hopefully heeded in daylight. He did not plan to physically harm the man, but he meant to take away his livelihood. An innocent had been sold into bondage, injured until near death and he planned to punish those responsible and then protect the one he loved until his dying days.

There was only one man he planned to permanently remove from the earth, an evil infection that he felt must be eliminated.

Reaching the outskirts of Thomaston, Thomas found a stream winding toward the ocean. Bathing, he washed his hair and wound it in sections onto reeds and tied it in place with riverside grasses, knowing it would dry overnight and when he untied the grasses his hair would fall in curls. The results would place him as a Frenchman, not a native. Smoothing his clothing and hanging it on a nearby bush so the final wrinkles would hang out, he camped for the night and slept soundly, knowing the morrow would soon be upon him and he wished to be ready.

When morning came he tended Chavelier Noir then rode around the outskirts of town, always keeping out of sight of the townspeople. Thomas prepared his noon meal of hard cornbread and dried venison, and then as the shadows began to fall he folded his buckskins and placed them, along with his moccasins, into his saddlebags. Dressing in his dark suit with the lace at his throat, he donned his oiled and polished black boots. After untying his hair and letting the curls fall about his shoulders, he entered the town. Making several inquiries as to taverns he was told that there was only one in Thomaston, narrowing his search.

The tavern was a crude structure at the end of town, the opposite end from where the church stood, which was appropriate. The patrons of the tavern were, indeed, separated by culture from those who attended church, the tavern patrons being, for the most part, as crude as the structure that housed their patronage.

The rough plank exterior was study, as was the rail at the front for tying horses, though most who frequented the establishment walked, rather than rode to the building they enjoyed. Inside the iron hinged door one entered a darkened room with only one whale oil lamp hanging from a chain in the ceiling, covering the lack of cleanliness. A fireplace in the back corner was the heat source and it had smoked black the stones that surrounded a low burning fire. Four tables, some round, some square, had been placed carelessly about the room, each table with several rustic chairs placed beside it, and a deck of cards sat in the center of each table, cards that often caused fights and arguments as the evenings wore on and drinking began to cloud minds, causing some to become suspicious of cheating, (often with just cause). The atmosphere of gloom went unnoticed by those who spent their evenings at the tavern, as with each drink the surroundings became more acceptable. To this place, Thomas came to find the person responsible for the misery of the one he loved.

He was sure the man he was looking for was probably a drinker, so he tied Chevalier Noir to the hitching post outside the establishment and stepped inside.

Thomas requested a glass of rum, always speaking either in French or an affected French accent. Sipping it slowly, not knowing what effect it might have since he was not used to strong drink, he listened to the talk that inevitably occurs in such surroundings until he heard the name "Buck". A rowdy looking man was cajoling with another, slapping him on the back and telling bawdy stories, the like of which Thomas had never heard. When one mentioned the stables and "were the colts any more safe than the sheep", he knew he had found his man.

The group had eyed Thomas carefully, noting his dark suit, and also the careful way he kept his right hand in his pocket. They wondered if perhaps he carried a lot of money or possibly a weapon. Since he spoke only French, they, along with the proprietor, assumed him to be a Canadian French gentleman. The French were sometimes of a dark complexion, and the man's obvious wish to remain undisturbed was honored for a short time while the town riff-raff decided where to draw the line. No one could have suspected such a fine gentleman of the mission he planned.

The rowdy group began to talk quietly among themselves, occasionally rolling their eyes and glancing toward Thomas. Becoming louder they slapped the particularly rough looking fellow on the back and laughingly offered, "Hey, Buck, how would you like a pretty suit like that? You could catch yourself a pretty little miss with those clothes."

"No need," the man identified as Buck replied. "I find plenty of little misses just the way I am, sometimes little French misses!"

Upon hearing Buck's statement it was all Thomas could do to control his rage. His native instincts urged him to draw his knife and kill the man on the spot. The smell of evil that hung over Buck caused Thomas' nostrils to flare in hate and distaste.

"Hey, Buck, why don't you challenge this fancy fellow. Maybe he's as tough as you are. Maybe he's escaped from the English army. Give him a try!"

Thomas turned to the group, and in a falsified accent exclaimed, "I beg of you, I am not *ze fugitaire!*"

"Here, here," the proprietor interjected. "No trouble in this tavern! Let's calm down."

"I wish no trouble, Monsieur, so I will leave. I must be on my journey."

As he left he heard the guffaws of the rude bunch in the corner. They continued with slapping the table with their fists and much laughter.

"I guess we scared that fop. It would be no fun fighting a cowardly dandy, but it would be fun to see his pretty clothes in the mud. Not much of a challenge, though."

"Maybe we should go after him," Buck replied, "I'd like to have that black horse he rode in on. One more round and I'll go after him for sure!"

When Thomas left the tavern he rode toward the river. No one in that ocean town would ever see him again, but Thomas was there. He found a vantage point and waited until the ruffians left their drinking for the night and watched until Osmond Buck made his way to the stables where he quartered with the horses.

Mounting Chavalier Noir, Thomas smiled as he turned his horse toward the road heading southeast, riding swiftly towards the wooded coast. He had found his man and he would deliver the message he planned, but first he would exchange his clothes for his buckskins and braid his curled hair out of his way. There was work to be done. Thomas un Main, Pezhik Onindj, had become "Lone Wolf" once again.

Osmond Buck did not hear the soft padding of moccasins as Thomas climbed to the hayloft where the pervert lay sleeping. Plunging his knife deep in the chest cavity of the evil one, he withdrew the blade and dragged him to the edge of the loft and threw him over, impaling him on the sharp edge of an upturned plowshare. The final death squirm plunged the metal further into the wound that the knife had opened in his chest. No one had seen Thomas as he quietly began his trek north. No questions were asked. After all, accidents do happen.

There was a rumor in Thomaston that a renegade wolf had approached the town as a strong resounding cry was heard late that night, and the townspeople were watchful of their small children and newborn livestock for weeks, but it seemed to have disappeared as mysteriously as it had arrived.

CHAPTER IX

Thomas did not return by the same route he had taken to the coast. Though he doubted anyone would think he had been the one to rid the town of the villainous Osmond Buck, he took no chances. Riding southwest he followed the Penobscot River, riding in the woods out of sight of any trappers or traders, always choosing unbeaten paths but following the sun as it traveled west each day, camping at night in the deep forests along the way. He thought about the canoe he had built when he was younger, thinking that he would rescue Merci and bring her home. It was amusing to recall all the things he had done in anticipation of her return. She had returned by herself, and now he had avenged her honor.

The best thing he had done in her absence, besides growing from childhood into becoming a man, was the building of the stone covered house in the woods. He planned to keep it a secret until it was completed. When the last stone was in place, the windows set and wood for the fireplace stacked, he would show it to her.

These thoughts entertained him on the trip back to Amitie le Christ. He had not considered the teachings to which he had been exposed throughout his childhood, especially, "Vengeance is mine, sayeth the Lord." In his anger and hatred all thoughts of compassion, understanding or forgiveness had left his being. The pain Merci had endured because of the inhumanity perpetrated on her being had completely consumed him, and now, with the deed accomplished, he still felt no guilt. Whether it was the emergence of native instinct or simple uncontrolled wrath he was not sure, but on his return trip north he had gradually settled the event in his mind. He reasoned that he had been chosen as the instrument of the Lord to wreck vengeance on the deserving Buck.

It was with a clear conscience he traveled north, traversing the wilderness and changing direction several times, even crossing the trail of the Patriots under Benedict Arnold in the ill-fated trek to invade Canada. The Sisters had indeed been fortunate that their convent was unknown to the forces struggling towards Quebec. Had the convent been found, the Sisters, in their compassion for the militia's pitiful condition, would have opened their doors and shared all they possessed with the needy troops, to the point of their own suffering and great want, and probably many would have contracted small-pox and died of the disease. That they were unknowingly passed by was a Blessing of which they were unaware.

Leaving the trodden trail he calmly returned to Amitie le Christ. Before returning to his quarters above the shed he fed, watered and brushed Chevalier Noir, patted Mer Pain who had been cared for by the Sisters in his absence, as usual, then walked slowly up the hill to where William the *Pitoyable* was sleeping.

Dropping to his knees he brushed a few pebbles from the stone over the new mound of earth, and tenderly smoothed the earth with his hand.

"I'm so sorry, small one. Your body was weak because of the terrible creature that sired you. If you had lived I would have embraced you and cared for you as my own. I will guard and protect your mother as long as I live. This I vow before the God that made us both."

Bowing his head he remained in the kneeling position as the evening dew began to fall, then he silently arose, bathed in the near-by stream that flowed toward Eagle Lake and entered the conclave.

SADDLE

(1) CUT ALL PIECES OF HEAVY LEATHER
(2) PAD WITH HORSEHAIR
(3) LACE TOGERHER WITH LEATHER STRIPS
(4) WHITTLE WOODEN BARS FOR STIRRUPS
(5) CARVE LEATHER DESIGNS

CHAPTER X

Thomas had returned to a different atmosphere at Amitie le Christ. The good Brothers had brought six new novices to help with the enlarged convent. He immediately moved his personal possessions from his quarters above the shed and transferred them all to a space in the barn loft where travelers usually slept. Quickly walling off a small section he placed his rugs and paraphernalia in his new chamber. It was crowded, but he didn't mind. He hoped to finish all the small details of his stone house during the winter and planned to show Merci the home he had built for them to share in the spring.

Although the health of the Sisters was excellent as their activity and manual labor along with a healthy diet was extending their youth, the new faces were welcomed. The animals had multiplied and more feed was needed to be prepared for the winter and help was also needed to assist with the daily chores of tending the larger flocks and pens. The wooly bear caterpillars had been in abundance, signifying a long hard winter ahead. They would burst forth in the spring as tiger moths flying about in the sunshine, but their significance as forecasters of a hard winter was unmistakable.

Following the departure of the jolly monks who were on their way to Riv'iere Du Loup to investigate the possibility of a monastery and convent there, Sister Margarite lined up the girls in the kitchen. It was the warmest room in the compound and there was an autumn chill in the air. She was not worried about the extra mouths to feed although it had been quite a surprise. Since they had arrived she had watched them closely and studied their attitudes. She had been sent a short biography of each novice, written by their supervising nun in Montreal and sent in a sealed envelope.

She chose Marie to assist Delphia in the kitchen, Ophelia and Ruth to help Catherine with the animals, Evangeline to assist Sarah and Iris with sorting and packaging seeds for spring planting, Joanna to help Marti with weaving and Jolene with general housekeeping. Elizabeth she chose for her own personal assistant. She was sharp and quick and had a cheerful nature, was very literate and could help with the record keeping. She lovingly cradled the small animals and Sister Margarite could sense the healing touch in her hands. She would assist in the nursing and the gathering of apothecary supplies.

With training in husbandry, weaving and cooking, religious studies, spinning and planting, they would be prepared for the attrition that time would provide.

The extra help released Sister Margarite from chores that tapped her physical ability. She and Elizabeth spent several hours a day gathering herbs from the woods and fields and they made attempts to cultivate some. Part of the herbs was used for seasonings and flavoring drinks, but more important were the medicinal herbs. Sister Margarite had compiled a ledger of all the information she had gleaned from books and added the knowledge discovered from the native peoples. Jars of dried herbs comprised her apothecary.

Taking her new assistant under her wing, she explained all the remedies she was accustomed to administering.

"Some of these are native remedies, but I find them extremely useful."

"But aren't the natives wild and superstitious? Surely we are not to dance and shake rattles over the ill," the girl exclaimed.

"No, Elizabeth, we do not, but we do understand that the natives have been here much longer than we have, and they know much of the herbal remedies. At this far outpost it is wise to take advantage of any help available. They discovered that chewing tiny cones from spruce trees can cure a sore throat and that boiled wild mint will assuage nausea. If anyone has an asthma attack a small dose of powdered skunk cabbage roots can control the wheezing and whistling from the lungs. As we age we will need oil of wild primrose for swollen and painful joints, and willow will calm a fever. Many ills are in the mind and a cheerful attitude accomplishes much. The natives have much confidence in their medicine men, and their rites are helpful to them because they believe it is so. Do we not pray to God and have trust in him to aid us in misery?"

"Oh, Sister, I have much to learn."

"Our own discoveries are that a salve made with yarrow will heal cuts and bruises and willow bark contains a cure for headache. We grow horseradish here, a great aid in relieving hay fever, and we make our own yogurt to stop diarrhea. We also make our ink from pokeweed berries. You may find out how great horseradish is during haying season. There are many others and you will learn about them all. I am sure you will be a great asset to this convent. I must warn you, however, that I am aware that the natives south of Montreal roast chestnuts and peel and grind them into flour, which they make into very delicious bread. The chestnut trees here are of a different variety and the nuts are inedible. They bloom with beautiful flower clusters but one must never consume the fruit. The leaves are in clusters of five and seven, while the trees south of here with the good fruit have singular leaves."

"Oh, Sister Margarite, I always wanted to be involved with medicine, and I prayed I would be of service to mankind. I can hardly believe my prayers were answered with such clarity."

"That is God's way, my child. Sometimes when we least expect Him to answer a prayer, He does. Perhaps you are also an answer to my prayers. Come, it is time for vespers. We have much for which to be thankful."

Chestnut Trees

Edible American Chestnut

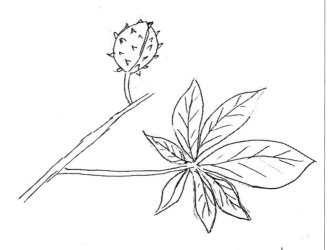

Inedible Horse Chestnut

CHAPTER XI

Weeks went by and Thomas was well satisfied with his room in the barn. He didn't mind the cold, though it really was not that cold at all. The heat from the animals below provided enough warmth in the building to keep it comfortable, and he didn't spend a lot of time there anyway. Once his work was done he mounted his horse and rode to the woods to put the finishing touches on the stone house.

He returned from that pastime one day and entered the barn. Petting the horses, brushing them and checking the cows and sheep to be sure there was plenty of feed, he heard a rustle behind him, followed by arms thrown about him from behind.

"Ay, what is this?" He removed the hands from his chest and turned. It was Ophelia.

"What is it you need, Ophelia? You mustn't grab me unaware. You could have been mistaken for a vandal or a robber. I could have injured you. Do not play dangerous games."

"Oh, Thomas, you are being silly. There are no robbers here, only lonely girls! Don't you like me?" And she removed her headpiece and began to remove her frock when Thomas shouted, "What are you up to? Replace your habit at once!"

"You must be lonely, too, Thomas, or do you visit all the Sisters here?"

"Return your clothing to its place. I fear you are not ready for this life. In this place vows are taken seriously. Perhaps you should renounce yours and return to Montreal. The life at a convent may have seemed glamorous and you had sincere intentions. However, you are ill prepared for Sisterhood."

"But you must think of spending time with a girl, and I am here, right now. Do not shame me by refusing my attention!"

"You shame your own name, Ophelia. I am bound to Merci, and will forever be so."

"Merci? But she is so bland! She seems weak and hardly carries her weight around here. How can you be interested in Merci?"

"You know nothing of Merci. I pray you have an easier life than she has had, but back in MONTREAL !"

"How can you be bound to Merci?"

"We are not of the clergy. We are orphans raised here, but that is not your concern. Go to Sister Margarite at once and I will forget this incident."

"If you do not give of yourself to me I will tell Sister Margarite that you attempted to attack me! I promise I will!"

"No one will believe you—

"And I am witness to that!" Sister Sarah came from behind the stall where the milk cow was stanchioned. "Come, put your habit back and fix your headpiece. I have never witnessed such actions in all my born days!"

Tearfully, Ophelia left the barn with Sister Sarah and they headed for the sanctuary. On the way Sister Sarah cautioned the girl.

"You must simply tell Sister Margarite that you have made a mistake. If you blame anyone but yourself for your decision, you can be sure that I will bear witness against you. I hope you understand the seriousness of your actions. I fear you will be sorry if you do not state your position simply."

The tearful Ophelia pleaded, "I will behave from now on if I can stay, I promise."

"My dear, there are some things that sorry doesn't fix. Lascivious thoughts are banned from our minds. I think that perhaps your calling is not to the Sisterhood. You can return to Montreal and find a life outside of the church. You were probably born to become a wife and mother. It is obvious you will never be satisfied with our kind of life, and that is not a bad thing. Life here would cause you to suffer and stifle your instincts. Renounce your vows and be free to live the life you were meant to lead. It is not here. We live closely together in the winter and cannot tolerate such behavior. The snows are light now but the deeps snows will be here soon, and then it will be too late to travel. You do not have the self-discipline to live in close harmony with others without sinful thoughts and actions. You must save yourself now, and in Montreal you can find your chosen calling."

The loving Sister Margarite accepted the pleas of the girl who was obviously too young to have made her life's decision. Ophelia did not mention the incident in the barn, nor did Thomas or Sarah ever reveal having any part in her decision. When the Brothers returned the following week she joined them on their journey back to Montreal. The Sisters knew Ophelia would be safe with them, but secretly, Sarah wondered if the Brothers would be safe from Ophelia.

Margarite wondered what had prompted Ophelia's sudden decision, but she had noticed something in the girl's personality that did not seem compatible with the Sisters at Amitie le Christ. She decided to let sleeping bears remain in their den.

Sarah did not offer her knowledge of Ophelia's transgression, nor did she reveal Thomas' revelation of his feelings for Merci. Time would tell if it had any truth or if he had been merely controlling a difficult situation.

CHAPTER XII

Merci was content with her life. As days and weeks passed she decided she would remain in the safety of the convent and let the past fade from her being as she basked in the love of her true family. She sealed the past away, as ashes in an urn are sealed and buried, to perhaps be remembered at times, but safely entombed and unable to inflict any damage to her emotions. So now she could live, she could find her way in the world and create her life with greater expectations. Nothing in the future could be as bad as the hurts and sorrows of the past. The freedom of thought she enjoyed was a healing balm, and her face began to show the peace she had found.

And Thomas Pezhik Onindj, Lone Wolf, was there. Her return had changed their lives in that she no longer saw him as a younger brother, but as a man. His bronzed skin and flashing dark eyes seemed out of sync with his kind and gentle ways. Tall and slim and muscled, quietly working with the animals and mending the fences and housing to protect them against the harsh winters, he found time to spend hours in the woods hunting and bringing fresh game for evening meals.

December

The silvered fields of winter
Sport their crystal coats of white,
As snowflakes silently come creeping
To frost them in the night.
When morning sunlight wakes the earth
That did rest so soundly sleeping,
Now gives diamond sparkles bright,
To make a wonderland our keeping.

The Christmas celebration was as Merci had remembered, and there was never a gift so loved as the maple sugar brick she received. She felt young and untouched again, and never was there a happier Christmas than that of her homecoming. Although she was still weak she was fast becoming healthy in body and spirit. Thomas had given her a book of poetry he had traded pelts to obtain, and tearfully she confessed, "I have nothing for you, Thomas, and no gifts for the Sisters. What shall I do?"

"Do not fret, Merci. You will soon be well and you will be knitting and cooking and helping with the chores. I will make sure that you do your share," and he playfully poked her in the ribs.

"Thomas, I will promise to do all that, if you can catch me, that is."

"Catch you! I can out run you any day!" And he picked her up and held her off the floor until she began to shout, "Put me down, put me down! Just wait, I will pay you back for that!"

"I can hardly wait, but for now, sit beside me and read to me from the book. I have not opened it as it has been waiting for you."

Margarite and Catherine exchanged glances. Their children were back to their old ways. It was a wonderful Christmas gift.

Thus went the winter, Merci continually becoming stronger, Thomas donning his snowshoes and hunting rabbits, spending time in the woods and secretly finishing his cabin, and soon it was time for Rudy to leave his warm spot by the fire to survey the fields that sported only patches of white leftover snow from the bleak winter. Thomas let the cattle and sheep into their pastures to stretch and romp a few hours each day before whistling for Rudy to round them up and return them to their barns.

Following breakfast on a sunny morning he put forth an invitation.

"Merci, would you like to visit with Mer Pain today? She and Chevalier Noir are in the lower pasture. I think it is time for you to become reacquainted."

He placed his fingers to his lips and whistled for Rudy to come and join them.

"Thomas, show me how to whistle, that I may call Rudy as you do."

"Here, Merci, put your fingers on either side of your tongue and blow."

Time and again she tried, to no avail. Only air escaped with nothing more than a slight wheeze escaping from her lips.

"Never mind, Merci. I will make you a whistle. You are wearing yourself out with effort. I will make you a willow whistle and you can call Rudy, and even Mer Pain. Today we will just visit the horses. I think you will be surprised."

"Do you think she will remember me? Oh, Thomas, I hope so."

Taking her hand he led her to the pegs where his jacket and her cape hung.

"Here, the winter chill is still upon us and Sister Margarite would be angry with me if I let you become fevered."

Helping her with her cape and putting on his jacket, they left the compound together and visited the lower pasture. The stream was still partially frozen but not enough to allow easy crossing. Thomas swept the slender girl up into his arms and carried her across. She was amazed at the warmth of his body, his smell, the feel of his hair blowing across her cheeks, stirring emotions she had not felt before. Little did she realize the feelings Thomas was holding at bay.

WILLOW WHISTLE

(1) Cut a six inch willow stick in early spring when willow is soft and moist, (ends should be flat).
(2) Make a cut all around near one end. This is the holding end.
(3) Tap bark all over with knife handle until bark loosens.
(4) Slide bark off in one piece.
(5) Cut an indented hole near the end.
(6) Cut a flat area from the indent to the end, (blowing end).
(7) Slide the bark back on the willow stick.
(8) Cut a matching notch in the bark over the indented hole.

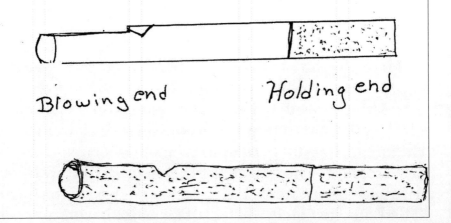

Blowing end   Holding end

When they crossed the near pasture to the rail fence of the lower pasture, Thomas tendered, "Merci, le petit bon Mer Pain has waited for you, but see, she has found love with Chevalier Noir. Now she presents you with her children! Chevalier Noir is their proud Papa, and they are both spirited and beautiful. Big brother thinks he is boss but petit Bon Pain has his heart. Look at how they play. The convent will soon be known for the beautiful horses bred here, as we will find a little competition for Big Brother. Come, come with me. We will see if you can ride after your years of town living!"

Merci did not know what to think of this amazing person. She was awestruck by his size. He was a man and a very handsome one, an incredibly handsome man with a muscled body that had carried her as though she was light as a feather. He had the sinewy body of a native warrior and the gentlemanly manners of a French nobleman. She wondered if she had changed too much from all the tragic events of her life, and if they would ever truly feel the same camaraderie they had felt as children. Since her strength had returned she was beginning to put the past behind her. Her golden streaked brown hair had regained its bounce and she felt at peace with herself. As she recuperated she had even sorted out her feelings about and forgiven Jeremiah, knowing he had made no promises. It was as though the death of Pierre had somehow foretold the end of that phase of her heart. Never anticipating any feelings of love to return after the years of horror and sadness she had endured, the peace and serenity of the commune had promoted great healing. She was free to renew the friendship she had shared with Thomas in their youth. He had raised their riding ponies and cared for them and their strength and beauty astounded her. Closing her eyes she could imagine herself as only fourteen again, and the wind against her face was cleansing, exhilarating, and her freedom was complete.

Mer Pain came to Merci and as she put out her hand the horse came to her and gently nibbled her ear.

"Oh, Thomas, she knows me, she knows me! Oh, how can I ever thank you for taking such wonderful care of her!"

"We have all been waiting for you—Mer Pain, Chevalier Noir, the Sisters, and most of all, Merci, I, Lone Wolf, have waited for you. He helped her onto her horse and she rode slowly around the lower pasture, and returning to where Thomas stood, he lifted her down to her feet.

"Come, we must return and have a hot drink. If the weather is warm tomorrow we will ride to the lake. We will ride every day, and there is much I want to show you."

Carrying her back across the stream again, they entered the sanctuary and sat for a few minutes before making their way to the warm kitchen for hot tea and corn bread. Delphia came in and took a bowl of fresh butter from the cupboard and said, "Here, it is better with butter", and they all had to laugh. "Scat, now, supper will be ready soon, and you will spoil it with too much nibbling."

"Now, Sister Delphia, have I ever been without appetite when you cook?"

"Well, no, I don't think you are ever filled, but scat, anyway."

Thomas took Merci by the hand and they left together. Delphia wondered if they were childhood friends again—or something more.

Chapter XIII

Sister Margarite found much happiness in the sound of laughter whenever Thomas and Merci were together. Their happiness was hers, and she wondered how she could ever have thought of keeping them apart. Their zest for life and the joy they found in being together again was wonderful to behold. They eagerly worked together accomplishing their chores. Sometimes she thought that perhaps they were a little too eager to finish quickly to allow time before dark to ride their horses. She wasn't sure where they went but presumed they rode to the lake to watch the sunset, but they had always returned for vespers and the evening meal. With the warm weather the yellow blooms of spring had burst forth as though there would be no spring days following their arrival, shaking their heads in fear that the hot summer sun would wilt them to their knees. Birds happily chorused as they fluttered about, singing loudly with exuberance for life, mating on the wing in exultation. They scavenged small twigs and grasses with which to build their summer homes and searched for early dandelion fluffs to soften the beds of their anticipated hatchlings.

When the spring rains ceased and the weather became balmy, Thomas Pezhik Onindj, (Lone Wolf) and Merci rode to Eagle Lake and after dismounting they stood side by side, hand in hand, transfixed by the land, the water, the sky—all of the wonder of the earth that God had granted them to enjoy.

"Merci, you are free. The man called Buck is receiving his reward in Hell and he will never hurt anyone on this earth again. Do not ask about this ever, but be assured, my love, you will always be safe with me."

Merci was stunned. Her emotions confused her, and as she entered his arms and the safe haven offered there she knew her life had turned a corner. No place on earth, no one on earth could ever give her the beauty of love she had found.

There was much to think about as Merci lay in her bed that night. Her thoughts were only of Lone Wolf and wondering if he, too, was having trouble sleeping, wondering what the morrow would bring and if it would be as wonderful as their day at the lake, and wondering what the future would hold. The following day would be Sunday, and perhaps they would ride again if the weather permitted. The sky had been red at eventide, signifying good weather. She longed for his arms about her again, and was anxious for the dawn.

Following services and eating the noon meal with the Sisters, Merci and Thomas mounted their horses and followed the stream thought the woods. They stopped and Thomas told her all about the woodland creatures, their habits and their homes in the forest, then they rode on through the tall pines and spruce trees, following the stream as it meandered until they again reached the ridge overlooking the lakc. That night they did not return to the convent, but made their bed of soft reindeer moss and slept under the stars in the quiet summer night, watching the heavens and listening to the sounds of the nighttime forest. Their love blossomed and as their passions overtook them their completeness was found in each other.

Mercy, Merci

My love is like a mountain stream
Endless flowing, never ending.
My love is like the ocean wide,
Deep and strong,
Reaching far beyond the horizon.
My love is as the stars,
Ever bright and glorious,
My love is like the sun,
Forever warming my soul.

Jean Edwards

Consummation

Two horses ride into the sunset glow,
Two riders side by side with hearts as one.
As with the wind they ride, but do not know
That love will find them 'ere the day is done.
Now through the mountain pass they quickly ride,
Now splashing through the roiling bubbling stream.
Through field and glen the stalwart ponies stride,
On through the day 'til lost is daylight's gleam.

And pausing there atop a barren hill,
Two hearts in two young breasts are beating fast.
As all the forest sleeps, the earth is still,
Two souls reach out and find their love at last.

While stars nod their approval from above,
Their hearts combine and consummate their love.

CHAPTER XIV

Sister Margarite was not surprised when Merci and Thomas came to her asking permission to marry. She had never been more certain of anything than that the two belonged together, and with much joy the Sisters planned the legalization of their union.

While the Sisters bustled about making preparations for the joyful occasion Thomas took Merci to the forest and with much pride presented her with a wedding gift, the stone home he had built in anticipation of the day she would belong to him. She was astounded when she saw the fine woodwork, the wonderfully smooth wooden floors, the fireplace and cupboards, the soft down filled mattress and fine wool blankets. The light dispensing windows were like none she had ever seen. Tears of joy ran down Merci's cheeks as she envisioned the many hours Lone Wolf had spent working on the house while waiting for her to return. She could not bear to think what would have happened if she had not done so. The awful pain she had suffered that brought her back was nothing compared to his suffering if she had failed to come back to him. Even pain has its purpose, she decided. Never had she expected she would ever live in such a home, or ever feel so loved.

"Oh, Lone Wolf, I have nothing to give you in return!"

"Merci, your love is all I have ever wanted, and it is the finest gift I could ever want. To live here with you is my heart's desire. *Cheri,* to lie beside you at night and hold you and keep you safe is my desire."

"Oh, Lone Wolf, have the Sisters seen this?"

"No, *Cheri*, it is for you alone. Only Rudy and Chevalier Noir have been here with me. It has been waiting for only you."

"After we are married we must have the Sisters come for a dinner! Oh, I can hardly wait to show it off!"

"If I can stand to control myself once you are truly mine I guess we could have company, but let's not make plans yet!"

"Very well. But we can tell them about it, can't we? Oh, Lone Wolf, I never believed I could be this happy!" And she fell into his arms.

Chapter XV

There was much bustling about at the convent. Marti brought out the finest sheer wool she had woven, and had crocheted a veil of matching thread, Delphia supervised the planning of the wedding feast, and the rest gathered evergreens and dug up wildflower plants and re-planted them in the sap buckets that were not in use. The anticipated wedding of their children was the most exciting occasion they could imagine. They had tried to convince Thomas to let them make him a new suit but he insisted that he wear the buckskins that he had made for the occasion. They reluctantly gave in, deciding that a man should be allowed to wear what he wished on his wedding day.

Jolene scrubbed the sanctuary while the other Sisters made new tallow candles to fit holes made by Thomas' auger in small birch logs that had been split in half. They were determined to make it the most wonderful wedding ever. Thomas and Merci would have been happy with simplicity, but they could not discourage the Sisters or take away their joy. After all, when the wedding was over the Sisters would have nothing but the cleaning up, while they would have each other.

In accordance with church doctrine Mary Catherine Merci and Thomas un Main were united in Marriage by sister Margarite at Convent Amitie le Christ at noon, June 30, 1779.

The sunlight filtered through the isinglass cross and was reflected back from the many candles lit in honor of the occasion. No more beauty could have been found than that of the rays of light that touched those God held in his care.

Tears came to the eyes of Sister Margarite as she spoke.

"I take thee, Thomas un Main to be my beloved husband, and as Merci repeated the vow, "I take thee Thomas un Main" she hesitated, and with her eyes holding his she silently mouthed, "Lone Wolf", then continued. Neither Margarite's nor the other Sister's happy tearful eyes saw the reason for her hesitation, but Thomas did, and his dark eyes sparkled with pleasure, and at the completion of the ceremony his powerful arms clutched her to his body and he began kissing her face, her eyes, her lips, until Sister Margarite sternly announced, "Enough! Now we must celebrate!"

Hand in hand the two stood together while the Sisters rushed forward to congratulate them. It was as dramatic as any wedding before a large congregation could have been. Though they were few, it was a congregation of beloveds filled with unbounded happiness.

Thus would the Sisters pray and bless the union of their children, binding their hearts in the Blessing of God's love, and give thanks for the food they had prepared for the wedding feast.

The blackberry and elderberry wine was brought forth and with toasting and laughter the little commune enjoyed its happiest of days since the founding of the convent. With tables laden with venison, squash, potatoes boiled and mashed, flavored with wild onions and fresh herbs, bowls of cottage cheese, corn bread, boiled eggs, cored apples filled with honey and baked to a crispy covering served with whipped cream.

The Sisters did not understand the glances exchanged between Thomas and Merci or realize their longing to escape the celebration to be alone with their love. The newly vowed couple knew how much they owed their very lives to these dedicated and passionately kind women and they understood their delight with the marriage and the carefully planned celebration. They deserved more than Merci and Thomas could ever repay, so in their appreciation they put aside their longings and remained until the occasion reached its very end.

As the Sisters threw daisies and buttercups at the departing lovers they mounted Chevalier Noir and Mer Pain and rode off into the deep woods where their first night together as husband and wife would be spent in the balsam bower Lone Wolf had created.

In the fulfillment of their dreams their pasts had proven that each moment of happiness must be held and cherished, heightening the sweetness of the time spent in each other's arms. Time and again their overwhelming desire was quenched until all the unhappy misfortunes of the past were completely obliterated.

They awoke to a gentle frosting of dew that had fallen during the night, decorating the balsam branches, making a glistening wonderland of the forest. All was clean, all was quiet, all was beautiful.

Chapter XVI

Soon after the excitement of the wedding had passed Sister Sarah approached Sister Margarite and asked for a private meeting that would not be overheard or disturbed. The event in the barn back in the winter had laid a burden on her heart. Though she had vowed not to reveal the incident, it had spurred her concerns.

"Come, Sarah, let us go berry picking," Margarite offered.

Fetching two of the sap buckets that had been emptied and washed following their use for the wedding flowers, Sarah agreed that it was a beautiful day for such an outing, so off they went.

They picked the field strawberries for awhile in the pleasant warmth of the day before Sister Margarite inquired, "What is it you have on your mind, Sarah? Let's discuss any problem that worries you."

"Sister, I am concerned that the new novices are too young. I am afraid they might not be ready to make their life choice at such an early age. They are still in their teens, and we will be wasting our time with their training if they are to leave us one by one."

"Sarah, I understand how you feel and your observance has much merit. Ophelia was not only young, she was unsuited for this lifestyle. Her leaving was of her own doing, her temperament was explained in her biography. It was hoped that being sent here would help her make a choice, and it did. We were all older when we made our vows, and many of us had experienced unhappiness. This life suits us, but it may not suit the new novices at all. Please consider that they have come to experience this life of service, and perhaps they will leave when they discover that it is not as glamorous as they had expected, but perhaps it will make them kinder, more loving and more moral persons than they might have been without our influence. We will be returning them to society where they will make wonderful devout wives and mothers. Perhaps that is the service with which they will be charged, as we are charged with making them better suited to whatever their choices might be."

"Oh, Margarite, you are so wise. I feel much better,—and look, there is a large patch of berries there on that little hill!"

Happily, Sarah ran to the hill and Margarite hobbled along behind her to the knoll. The day proved to be a Blessing beyond expectations.

The days of summer passed happily. Crops ripened and were harvested and stored, wood for the fires cut and stacked, meat smoked, and all the other preparations for winter in the normal cycle of living in the isolation of the northern Maine wilderness were accomplished. The calves that had been born in the spring were fat and healthy, wooly lambs were growing back their coats following their shearing, the wool was being washed and carded and bagged to be spun into thread for weaving and knitting in the winter months when they would be snowbound, plentiful feed for the animals had been gathered and stored.

Merci and Thomas came to the compound often, attending service on Sunday and sometimes vespers during the week. One particular Sunday they were leaving the sanctuary to mount their horses and return to their home in the woods when they found Rudy waiting on the sanctuary steps as they were leaving. He held a small bundle tightly in the grip of his jaws, a very small bundle of black, white and gray fur.

"What is it that you have there, Rudy?" Thomas asked. "Have you been hunting on your own and brought us meat for our supper?"

As they approached the herd dog he rolled his eyes imploringly toward his master.

"Here. Rudy, let me see what you have brought."

Carefully Thomas removed the bundle of fur and discovered it to be a small pup.

"Where have you found this, Rudy, are there more?"

Rudy kept his eyes on Thomas and sat back on his haunches and whined softly.

"I see a familiar look to this pup. What have you been up to my good friend? This pup has the look of a wolf but has your fur. I think you have been busy a couple months ago."

"Merci, see what Rudy has brought us. I'm sure it is his own but looks too young to have left its mother."

On closer inspection they realized why Rudy had taken the pup from its mother. It had not been a matter of "taking" as the small animal had a badly bent front leg, and in the wilds a deformed animal would have been left to die and only the perfect nurtured and raised.

Merci exclaimed, "I will find Sister Margarite. She and Elizabeth will know what to do!"

They entered the conclave and took the pup to the kitchen, with Rudy following closely behind.

"Do not worry, Rudy, we will save your offspring if it is at all possible."

Merci found Sister Margarite and Elizabeth and with the pup on the kitchen table they carefully inspected him. It was instant affection for the afflicted animal and Margarite announced, "This poor creature has been abandoned by its mother. It is obvious that his father has rescued him from certain death. Merci, warm some milk, he must be hungry and if you wish him to live you must feed him every few hours until he is old enough and strong enough for solid food. It will be quite a chore."

"Oh, Sister, I will gladly tend him. He can sleep by our bed and I will feed him whenever he whimpers!"

With a small rag soaked in the milk they put it against the tiny mouth and immediately he began to suck the warm fluid from the soaked cloth. Time and again they soaked the strip of cloth and time and again the hungry pup suckled it dry until with a round filled belly he slept soundly in Merci's arms.

Everyone was beaming with success except Sister Margarite.

"We are not finished, Merci. We will let him rest a few days and then we must attempt to straighten his leg. An animal cannot survive in his condition, and we may have to break his leg to make it straight. The sooner we do it, the better, before he begins to grow."

"Oh, Thomas, I hate to think of this little creature suffering more pain."

"Merci, it must be done. His pain will be much greater when he cannot run and play with Rudy. Come, let us fix him a basket to put by our bed and in a few days he will be strong and Sister will make him whole."

They bundled him up and held him tenderly on the trip back to their stone house and in four days they brought him back to the compound and placed him on the kitchen table again, where they fed him warm milk with a tiny bit of laudanum. Sister Elizabeth held the pup while Margarite forcefully straightened the tiny limb. There was a small "crack" and Merci winced. The drugged puppy whimpered but remained still. With wooden splints on either side of the fractured leg, they bound it tightly with rag strips.

"What a good scout he is," Thomas exclaimed.

"Oh, Thomas, that will be his name,—"Scout." Oh, I do hope he heals well!"

By the end of summer Scout was romping about, getting into everything and chewing all he could find. He was scolded, but tolerated. His happy scampering about was a joy to all and his visits to the convent were much anticipated, and his papa was the proudest of all.

"We must teach him to help Rudy," Thomas Lone Wolf declared. "Rudy knows what to do by my whistle. A long low whistle sound means he should bring the cows to the barn for milking; on hearing two short whistles he brings in the sheep: three whistles means danger and he brings all the animals into the barn. If I whistle sharply Rudy knows to come to me. You must remember this so you will not blow the whistle I made you and confuse the commands."

"I have decided to never blow the whistle unless you are away, Lone Wolf. You are Rudy's master and I would never interfere. I will write down the whistle calls so I will not make a mistake."

"Yes, Merci, You don't want Rudy to think you are crazy!"

"You are right. Probably he would know what to do without any instruction from me. I only hope Scout will be as clever as Rudy."

Merci was silent a moment, then softly said, "Lone Wolf, there is something I must tell you if we can be serious for a moment."

"I am serious, Merci," and he grabbed his wife and carried her to their sleeping room.

"Stop! Stop! First you must hear me out!"

Stunned, as Merci had never before halted his attentions, Lone Wolf whispered, "What is wrong, have you stopped loving me?"

"Oh, Lone Wolf, never will I stop loving you. But I fear I must share love with someone else."

Disheartened, he cried, "Share? With whom will you share yourself?"

"I already share and you have not noticed!"

"Taking his hand, she placed it on her body. "Here, this is where your child grows, Lone Wolf, and you will share your love also, won't you?"

"Oh, Merci, Merci. You carry our love within. *Cheri*, is it a girl or a boy?"

Laughing, Merci responded, "Only God knows that, Lone Wolf. The only thing I know is that our life will be complete."

"Do you think it will be whole, and not like me?"

"Oh, my darling, you are the most complete person I have ever known and if it happened I would not be sad, but my heart tells me it will be strong and perfect."

Tenderly, he took her in his arms and they lay together in complete happiness.

Chapter XVII

The cabin in the woods was the happiest of homes. Merci blossomed with health and happiness, and Thomas was the most elated of all. He could hardly believe he could be so fortunate to have joy beyond any dream imaginable. Merci assured him she was well and strong and he should not worry, and must refrain from spoiling her so. The Sisters prayed continually for her health and the well being of the infant she carried.

When the blustery March winds had blown themselves out and the fields were beginning to peek through the snow again, the time came for Thomas to ride to the convent and bring Sister Margarite to the stone house in the woods. The other Sisters spent the night in the chapel in constant prayer. The novices were unaware of the tragedies of the past, but they had come to love the couple in the woods and prayed for their well-being and that of the child about to enter the world. In anticipation of the event, the Bible was open to the recording page where they planned to write the name of the awaited child.

"Aiyana" (Forever Bloom) was born April fifth, healthy and beautiful, with her father's snapping dark eyes and her mother's smile. When Thomas Pezhik Onindj held his daughter in his arms and the small fingers reached out and clutched his forefinger in her grip, he looked down at his smiling wife and asked, "May I name her Aiyana? That is "Forever Bloom" in my native tongue, the language of the Algonquin. She is the symbol of our love that forever blooms in my heart." As Merci began to drift off to sleep she murmured, "Aiyana, what a beautiful name for our daughter."

The pride of the Sisters over their "grandchild" was surpassed only by that of her ecstatic parents. Their unbridled joy glowed in their eyes and their hearts were light with happiness. Thomas Lone Wolf's love for his wife and his daughter shone in his eyes and he was the most loving of husbands and fathers. Aiyana was dressed in the softest of doeskin and she had outerwear of rabbit fur for cool weather, warm sweaters in abundance as each Sister felt compelled to knit and weave the finest of their wool into clothing for their darling. Merci could hardly believe God had granted such peace and happiness and love after the trials she had endured. The past was erased as she realized the fulfillment of all her dreams in her life with Lone Wolf. Between the love and care of the Sisters and her Beloved, she was completely happy.

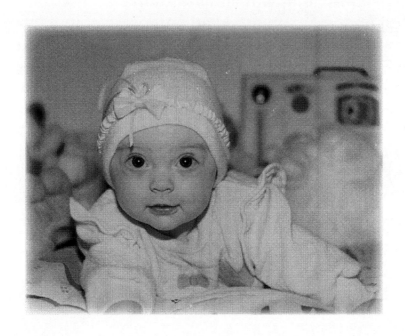

Aiyana

Rudy

Chapter XVIII

Philadelphia

Bodie Thompson was worried. The bartender at Tolliver's Tavern was becoming suspicious of his drinking habits. He had pretended drunkenness on too little rum too many times. Today would be the last time he could receive coded information as he was sure he would be apprehended should he attempt the mission again.

When Jeremiah arrived and ordered a small glass of rum and then sat down at the table Bodie started to tip over beside him. Bodie said loudly, "Take a leak, take a leak! I need to piss!"

Jeremiah put his arms about the so-called drunk and to the bartender he volunteered, "I'll help him outside. I fear the poor man is inebriated and may smell up the establishment. It would be best if he relieves himself out by the trees in back and perhaps sleep it off there."

"Thank you, Mr. Clarke. I don't need his kind discouraging customers here."

Once outside Jeremiah slipped the order to Bodie and helped the "staggering" messenger to a spot behind the tavern.

"Jeremiah, this is my last mission here. I am under suspicion and if I am apprehended I fear they might suspect you of espionage also. Find another method of delivery as soon as possible. I will inform the General that you will accomplish that. I have great confidence in your ability, as does he."

With that, Bodie Thompson left in the dark of the night and never returned to Philadelphia.

Bewildered and worried, Jeremiah went back to the Worthington's and sat long into the night. There was to be another gathering Saturday evening and he was sure his father-in-law and some of his officer friends would be in Philadelphia secretly visiting their wives, and they usually met at the Worthington's for a drink before their clandestine rendezvous. Surely this late in the war some valuable information would be available, and he intended to gather all he possibly could. A plan was forming in his mind and he needed to think long and hard on its execution.

By midnight he had decided what his course would be. He would deliver the information directly to General Washington. If the English caught him his "list" would be merely a merchandise order and he would be released. Being stopped by Militia might be more problematic. He would have to request to be taken to General Knox, the Marquis de Lafayette or General Washington himself, and just pray they would oblige. Of course this was all conjecture, in the hopes that he would, indeed, be able to secure information of such value as to make the attempt imperative.

The gathering of English officers occurred as Jeremiah has anticipated. They were in a jolly mood as they felt the war was going well and soon they would be returning home to England.

"As soon as Cornwallis takes the South it will all be over," one declared. "I hear we will be marching inland soon. When he takes Wilmington he'll go on to Virginia."

Jeremiah had brought some spiced sausages and more wine and rum, along with a tray of pickled eggs. He intentionally dropped a couple of eggs on the floor as he was taking them from the crock to place on the platter on the table. The small splat of vinegar resulting from the dropped food allowed him to remain in the room to clean the carpet. One of the officers that had not been at the Worthington's previously looked askance at him, but the host quickly informed him, "Do not worry, he is my son-in-law and he is no problem," and he rolled his eyes, in a way of letting him know the clumsy man serving them was no threat.

The group continued, "I hear he will be marching to Virginia and will probably make Yorktown his base. He expects to have seven thousand men at his disposal. He is quite the warrior and plans to destroy everything in his path."

"Too bad to have that beautiful country destroyed. There are some fine homes and farm buildings there."

"Such is war. If we wipe them out and destroy their property they will have learned a good lesson and we won't have to repeat this in another twenty years. I am anxious to get this mess over with as my wife is homesick for her family and jolly old London."

"It won't be long now, boys," Worthington promised. "Much as I'd like you to stay, you'd best make your visits and return to your regiment before daylight. But first—and he raised his glass. "To England!" They repeated, "To England", and one by one they silently left the house by the back door and disappeared into the night.

CHAPTER XIX

Leaving Philadelphia was not as easy as Jeremiah had anticipated. He had become accustomed to the calm security of living the civilian life away from the tragic horrors of the battlefield. As he rode through areas where the trees were riddled with musket ball wounds and others with shattered limbs hanging from the tree trunks by bark alone, he felt the chill of death about him. Realizing that the men who had fought there were also bullet riddled and with shattered and missing limbs reminded him of what the General had said, "but you will live" and he had spoken truly. In spite of the heartbreak of losing Mercy, he had a son who was healthy and unscathed. His constant guard against detection was the only fear he had been forced to endure, and until now he had not felt the horrors of battle and the ghosts of the lost ones. The air was chilled as he rode through the night, over streams, through pastures and following trails through the woodlands. He considered what he would do if his horse stumbled and he was thrown on the rocks where he would suffer and die unless some kind soul came by and saved him, and what if that savior was some blood thirsty soldier who needed a steed to take him home and away from the fight . . . . then what would become of Andrew? Probably he would go to England with the Worthingtons and his own family would never hear of him again.

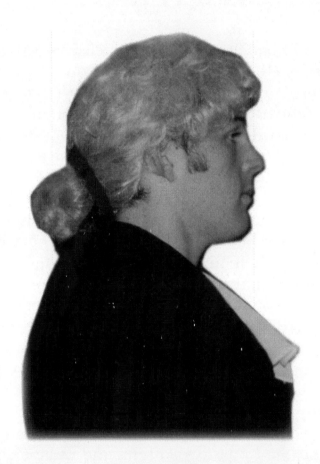

Jeremiah

Andrew

"My God," he thought. "I have become a coward living a life of luxury while my comrades are dying!"

With renewed determination he spurred his horse onward and as morning light crept over the horizon he continued towards Delaware only to be suddenly stopped by an English patrol.

Adopting his air of inefficiency that had become easy behavior due to constant practice, he halted his mount.

"Dismount, I say," the patrol sergeant demanded.

"Oh, yes Sir, of course, Sir," Jeremiah stammered.

"Where are you headed and what is your business?"

"I am a mere grocer from Philadelphia on my way to Charleston to see what merchandise is available there. How far is Charleston from here?"

"Young man, you are several days from Charleston. We must empty your saddlebags and inspect all you carry."

"Of course, Sir"

Knowing they would find his coded provisions list and only bags of tea besides his travel clothes, along with some corn bread, he was still slightly nervous. He could think of no way they could suspect the list of anything subversive, but still he worried. He hoped they wouldn't notice the sweat that was trickling down his back under his jacket.

When the tea spilled out the guards began to laugh. It was Dutch tea and they chided him about it being poor quality compared to English tea. The sergeant looked over the merchandise and grocery list, then put it back in its packet with his other paraphernalia and placed it all back in the saddlebags.

All Jeremiah had heard was confirmed when he was told to hurry on his way as the area would soon be too dangerous for travelers, especially an unarmed grocer. They could hardly believe anyone would travel with no firearm for protection. They shook their heads and sent him on his way.

Jeremiah's decision to bring the tea had been wise. Planning to give it to settlers if he became lost and needed help in directing him to General Washington, it had provided amusement for the English guards and had helped him escape. He feared that Washington's guards would not be so easy to convince. Riding on slowly at first lest the British hear the urgency in the hoof beats, he gradually urged his horse on faster as he put distance between himself and the enemy, hoping no more English guards would accost him before he reached his destination. He feared the tea might be a hindrance with the militia, and that it might look foolish. It had served its purpose so he hid it in the brush as he approached the area where the Army of the Potomac camped.

"Halt," came the command. "In the name of the Continental Army, halt!"

Jeremiah reined his horse.

"Show us your papers," was the demand.

"I have no papers, but an urgent message for General Washington."

"Let us see the message."

"I cannot allow that, but if you will get word to either General Washington, Knox or the Marquis de Lafayette that the grocer from Philadelphia seeks an audience, I will be admitted."

There were a few controlled smiles, then a decision.

"And what would they want with a grocer? I see no provisions."

"I implore you to contact them. Your failure to do so would do great harm to the cause, whereas you have nothing to lose by honoring my request."

Following another discussion the men spoke to a corporal in the group who immediately turned his horse and galloped away.

"Remain here, grocer, until the corporal returns. When he does and you are exposed as a fraud, or worse, we will decide what to do with you."

"May I dismount and rest my horse? It has been a very long ride."

"You may, but first I must be sure you are unarmed and carry no contraband."

Obliging, but holding onto the packet containing the order, Jeremiah waited over an hour. He began to sweat again. If they demanded or confiscated the packet they would decide he was a lunatic trying to gain access to Washington's camp. He would be considered a spy and his fate would be in their hands. He had contemplated hiding the packet along with the tea as he hoped to report directly to Washington, but with no packet to deliver they would never have admitted him to the Commander in Chief.

When the corporal returned it was at a rapid gallop.

Saluting the sergeant of the patrol he exclaimed, "I must deliver this man safely to General Washington as soon as possible!"

Awestruck, the sergeant turned to Jeremiah. "Mount and be on your way," he ordered, and the subdued sergeant watched as they rode out of sight toward the command center.

The sergeant shook his head. One never knew the complete workings of warfare. He would never have guessed the pale grocer was of any value to the war effort.

CHAPTER XX

Real War

In the days of shortened childhoods, propelled into the adult world, young boys were forced to take the role of "man of the house" in the absence of their fathers while other boys of twelve went off to the war when they knew nothing of real war. They emerged from playing childhood games of pretending to be crusaders with wooden swords or fighting Indians or Normans, battling pretend foes with make believe muskets.

Real War is difficult to describe. How can the horrors be presented in their truth? No one with a loved one that joined the battle wants to hear that their son or father is dying or dead or lying bleeding, moaning in agony, trying to stench the flow of blood leaving their body, trying frantically to put their own limbs back in place in a futile effort to make themselves whole again. They did not wish to envision them searching the battlefield for a lost arm in an anguished frenzy as life drained from the open stub or crawling blindly to escape without the aid of seeing eyes, their faces now with dark gaping holes where once the orbs had been attached. Nor do they want to hear of the maggots in the spoiled food, their only fare; disease from contaminated water, and as their sustenance was infected, so were their wounds until they sank into fever, gangrene and agonizing death.

They had dreamed of glory, but there was no glory. They fought for freedom and vowed no cost too great, no sacrifice would they deny their country. But ask them, as they lie mutilated in the throws of agonizingly painful dying if they knew what they were giving. Their lives were so shortened they would never be sitting in a rocking chair claiming, "life is too short." This is the price that must be paid to achieve victory, giving up their youth in the bloom of their beginning maturity. When victory is achieved those who survive will reap the harvest of their sacrifice. To those who live it was worth it all—but what about the lost ones? Was the agony welcomed? And what of the bereaved families that must suffer the hardships caused by their loss? Those brave souls offered up their lives, but most believed they would be among the survivors. How pitiful that they would never hear the cheers of victory.

When old men sit in their rockers playing checkers with their cronies, hashing over their past trials, tribulations, aches and pains, how often will they remember those who had died on the fields of battle. They had not lived long enough to have much past, and they certainly had no future. It was all lost so that those who survived might have theirs. Attitudes change swiftly once the battle drums are silent.

War changes everything, women robbed of the men they loved and children robbed of their fathers and brothers. Every generation assumes they mature at an earlier age than the previous generation, but it is not their doing. It is war and the effects of war.

CHAPTER XXI

Soon after Jeremiah's brief visit with General Washington events escalated at a rapid pace. General Morgan's troops defeated Cornwallis at the Battle of Cowpens where the Patriots stormed the cannons, followed by General Nathaniel Greene fighting him to a draw at Guilford Court. Cornwallis marched on to Wilmington, then with fifteen hundred men he advanced on Virginia. Greene and his troops, assisted by the forces of Francis Marion, Thomas Sumter and Andrew Pickens pushed the British back into Savannah and Charleston. Rawdon defeated Cornwallis at Hobkirk's Hill and General Alexander Stuart gave him a thrashing at Eutaw Springs.

Obtaining seven thousand more men Cornwallis razed the countryside, inflicting much damage on the land and made Yorktown his base. The French Fleet arrived and penned him and his army in by sea and Washington's army, with seventeen thousand men led the siege on Yorktown by land, forcing him to surrender October 19, 1781.

Anxious as he was to return to Maine, Jeremiah Clarke decided to stay in Philadelphia until the treaty giving the colonies the independence they desired was signed in 1783.

Chapter XXII

Maine

Autumn had arrived in all its glorious hues but had quickly faded. The geese had honked their way south and fields had turned from crystal frostings to light snow coverings that fell softly in the night, large flakes clustering together and falling in pairs and triplets, their whitening proclaiming the rapidly approaching winter. The little family in the woods cuddled in their woolen blankets and fur robes, not dreading the onset of frosty days, but relishing their warm togetherness.

Wood had been split and piled in anticipation of its need, meat had been smoked and dried, fish salted, apples, potatoes, carrots and other root vegetables stored in dirt bins below the frost line. All was well.

For Lone Wolf, life was idyllic. His only ambition was for one more good hunt before the snow deepened and made travel impossible. The snow would be five feet deep in another month and his hunting would be over until the spring thaw.

"Oh, please don't go," Merci cried. "We love you here with us!"

"I will not stay overnight, *Cheri*. I will leave at dawn and return before you light the candles. Come to me, let me love you once more before we sleep. I will leave quietly just before the sun begins its circle in the sky and you and Aiyana will have a pleasant day by yourselves."

Lone Wolf enjoyed the crisp morning air. He passed a mountain stream that sparkled and splattered over a cliff in a sheer crystal waterfall making rainbows in the morning sunlight. As he neared the river that flowed into Eagle Lake he noted the strange way a river freezes in early winter. First, only the very edges along the bank congeal, just a sugary icing that slowly builds, followed by smooth roundlets of ice, tiny floes that dance and swirl in the current, then finally holding hands until they touch the frosty edge where they cling until they are incorporated into the advancing ice cover and only the center of the river has visible moving water. Approaching the lake, the gently moving waters were churning crystals in a rolling motion and further along the lake sat still,—still and quiet, waiting for the freezing cold that would soon freeze a translucent skin, then slowly cool deeper and deeper until the lake would be frozen over solid with all living things below sleeping until the return of spring.

How he loved the woods, the streams, the carpets of dark green moss with its small spore cases moving in a gentle breeze; firs and spruce and cedar trees, the winterberries whose cheerful red fruit promised hope on the dark days of winter, the first arbutus of spring, daisies and buttercups of summer and the goldenrod of autumn. It was a part of his being, and now he had Merci and Aiyana. How Blessed he was!

Hearing a noise in the brittle wintry brush behind him, Thomas Pezhik Onindj turned and met his destiny.

As evening shadows lengthened Merci poked the fire causing it to glow brightly, not wanting to light the candles until Thomas Lone Wolf returned. Finally she lit one and sat it on the table. Aiyana was sleeping peacefully in her crib and Rudy and Sport were napping by the fire. Usually Rudy went on hunting trips with Lone Wolf but this time as Thomas had strapped on his snow shoes he instructed Rudy to "Look after them, Rudy, until I return," as he left on his hunt in the woods.

Merci sat by the burning candle and watched as it flickered in the slight shift of air that managed to breathe from under the door. Finally she heard a noise, and the door burst open.

"Merci, help me!"

Jumping from her chair, Merci ran to his side and assisted her husband to the sleeping room. Blood was dripping from his shoulder and arm and over his hand. Quickly she ripped some of Aiyana's wrappings into strips and bound his wounds to stop the bleeding. The pale skin made it obvious that he had lost a great amount of blood. She tied a piece of bloody cloth to Rudy's collar and sent him to the commune.

"Go to Margarite! Fetch Margarite, Rudy!"

She opened the door and the dog disappeared into the night. Merci prayed he would be safe and bring Sister Margarite and Elizabeth back quickly.

While at evening vespers the Sisters were interrupted by whining and barking outside the sanctuary door. Opening the heavy iron banded portal they found Rudy staring at them imploringly. The blood soaked rag was immediately recognized as a call for help. Elizabeth and Margarite grabbed their medical supplies and made their way to the barn, mounted the bay together and with Rudy in the lead were at the stone cabin within the hour. Bursting into the room they hastily stoked the fire to heat water to boiling, found cloths and a pan and entered the sleeping room.

A tearful Merci was on her knees beside the bed holding Thomas' wrist.

"Oh, Sister, he is so injured. Please save him. I could not live without him!"

"Let us see the wounds. What did this awful damage?"

"It was a bear, Sister. He fought a bear and he killed it but not before he was mutilated. He keeps saying, "You are safe, the bear is dead." "Oh, Sister, I fear he could have escaped but he felt he was protecting Aiyana and me. Oh, you must save him!"

"First we must clean the wounds. He has lost much blood. Pray he will have enough left to fight infection."

Carefully Sister Margarite and Elizabeth washed the wounds. "We cannot sew the torn flesh of wounds from an animal or he will surely infect. Elizabeth, hand me the wine. The alcohol content will help clean the wounds. Merci, give him three drops of this laudanum every three hours for pain. We must watch him carefully for fever. We will take turns. Elizabeth, sleep by the fire while I take the first watch. Merci, you must rest also."

"No, I cannot leave his side."

"Then lie beside him. Knowing you are near will give him strength, but first he must drink this willow tea even if you have to spoon it between his lips. He must replace the fluid he has lost and it will help control the fever."

As soon as she had fed him all the tea he would drink, Merci lay beside her husband and tried to warm his cold body, he was so very cold.

By morning he was no longer cold. He was burning up with fever. Elizabeth helped Sister Margarite prepare poultices of crow garlic, feverfew, black alder and spicebush, hoping to draw out the infection. They changed the poultice, they brought snow from the yard and made cold packs for his forehead.

The fever raged for three days. Merci refused to accept the severity of the situation. She had been sure Sister Margarite and Elizabeth would save him, but by the end of the week the inevitable was obvious. Sister Margarite sadly announced that the only hope was to remove Thomas' arm.

"No, No! Do not take my arm! I have been "one hand" my whole life and I could not live with no hand at all. My life would be over but with much more suffering! Let me remain in the hands of God as I am. He will decide my fate." Exhausted, his eyes closed.

The Sisters crossed themselves and left the sleeping room and knelt by the fireplace and prayed. They prayed for strength to accept what was to come and that God would put his loving arms around the little family that they loved.

Lone Wolf opened his eyes and looked at the wife he adored and with effort softly uttered, "*Cheri*, I must leave you, but you have our little flower, Aiyana, and she is part of me. She is the symbol of our love, so do not weep for me. Our love has been stronger in our few years together than most have in a lifetime. I will always watch over you. You must find happiness for yourself and Aiyana, it is the way of life. My body fails but my spirit will be with you always."

As his eyes slowly closed, a vision of the doe and fawn standing alone in the forest flickered in his mind, and his gallant spirit fled his body as it began its journey into the unknown hereafter. His soft sweet breath ceased to caress her face as Merci lay by his side. The peace of his countenance could do nothing to stem her tears or prevent the breaking of her heart. She remained beside him for a long time, then she went to the cradle, and raising her child she held her to Lone Wolf.

"Look closely at your father, you may not remember his face but I will always keep him alive unto you. We will find our own way, as he would wish, and he will follow and protect us until the end of our days.

Thomas un Main, Pezhik Onindj, Lone Wolf, was buried high on a hill overlooking the river, a fitting place for him to rest. Day after day Merci rode to the grave while the snow was still without depth, until one day an unusual early December rainstorm gathered and the sky began to drop its cleansing power and washed over the sad figure kneeling there.

Rain

Rain, wash my tears away.
Rain, wash the pain from my heart.
As the river flows and carries chaff to the sea,
Let this pain be washed from my soul.
Have I not suffered enough in my life
That I must bear this loss also?
How can I heal from this wound?
My only comfort is the small one given,
As a forever blooming flower of our love
That shines as a rainbow in my heart.
I clutch her to my breast and hold tightly
Lest I lose the last remnant of our great love.
Forever in my heart you will remain,
My darling Pezhik Onindj,
Lone Wolf, Thomas un Main.

CHAPTER XXIII

Merci could not stay in her beloved home in the woods by herself and sadly she packed their belongings and she and Aiyana returned to the convent. The Sisters rearranged their rooms giving Merci her old room once again. The only furniture she brought from her home was the carved cradle Thomas had made for his daughter. The room across the hall that had belonged to him bore no resemblance to the room he had occupied most of his life. It was now filled with the bunks of the novices. The compassion of all the Sisters was not enough to heal the wounds of her loss. Only time and God's mercy could accomplish that. The Sisters also mourned, as Merci's happiness was their happiness. Their delight in the little family that was body and soul part of their own beings was now crushed.

Christmas came and it was the saddest Christmas since the inception of the convent. They fashioned toys and gifts for Aiyana, but as she toddled about the compound in melancholy, calling, "Pe're, Pe're, Seul Loup", their hearts were broken from the pitiful refrain, knowing that she would never find the father she sought. Time would erase the pain, and her plaintive pleas would cease, but for a while they would all have to suffer with the mother and child.

Aiyana

The blustery winds of March evolved into the torrents of April. Thunder and lightening shook the compound and upset the livestock that were waiting to escape the confines of the barns and pens. The Sisters worried when a lightening strike in the woods burned brightly into the night. The convent was untouched but later they discovered that the cabin in the woods no longer stood. Only a pile of rocks remained with occasional flecks of mica glinting in the sun.

Chapter XXIV

Philadelphia

Jeremiah's guilt over his lack of grief at the passing of Abigail had not been apparent to the other mourners. They had assumed it was his northern upbringing that prevented him from showing emotion in times of grief and stress. He had tolerated his marriage to serve his country but at times Abigail's ignorance and silliness was almost more than he could stand. Now he did feel compassion for her, as his love for Andrew grew. His recent trip to "purchase provisions" had aroused some consternation. He explained his absence of several days as being caused by the militia, that they had stopped him and questioned him, delaying his arrival back in Philadelphia. He did indeed look harrowed but it had been his fear of the British patrols that had caused him to find refuge in the woods. He was glad to return to the safety of Philadelphia and to his son.

As time passed the successes of the colonial troops south of Philadelphia became apparent. There was a great upheaval in the Worthington household when news came of the surrender of Cornwallis. It was a great relief to Jeremiah as he was released from his duty. The Worthington's made plans to return to England even though they were not forced to do so. Any British sympathizers that wished to remain in the colonies could do so with impunity.

Jeremiah made his decision. He did not want to hurt Abigail's family. They had been kind to him and the truth would be painful, and he hoped they would never discover his deceit. Approaching his father-in-law he stated his decision to remain in the colonies.

"Sir, I regret that I will not be traveling with you. I understand and sympathize with your position, but Maine is my home. My mother has passed on and my father is not young. My duty is there. I will remain in Philadelphia until I find a shopkeeper to take over my store, and then I will return to assist my father."

"Jeremiah, are you sure you do not want to journey to the homeland with us? We should raise Andrew in the land from which his blood flows."

"I understand your feelings, Sir, but my son and I will eventually travel north, away from the politics and related skirmishes that will surely be rampant with the new government of this struggling country. There he will be free to make his own choices as we have made ours."

"Jeremiah, you are like a son to me. We will miss our grandson but not stand in your way."

"I appreciate that, Sir. Rest assured I will take good care of him and he will grow up strong and proud in the hardy hills of Maine. I am also sure he will want to visit you one day."

With hands clasped and each with an arm around the other's shoulder they bid their adieus, with Mrs. Worthington in tears.

It was more than a year before Jeremiah closed his store, sent the list of goods left in the store and all the money from his business except traveling money to General Washington. He suggested that perhaps the store would not need to be closed following the signing of the peace treaty, but whatever the decision, he wished to be released to return home. There were many men looking for work since the cessation of fighting, and perhaps the store could aid someone in need.

When his discharge papers arrived Jeremiah was surprised to find a special commendation for his devotion to duty signed by General Washington.

Jeremiah was relieved. He had managed to complete his duty with the Worthington's none the wiser about his wartime activities. He wished them no pain. They had lost their daughter because of him, and they had not held him responsible. He had betrayed their generosity with his subversive activities and used them to the advantage of his military missions. He felt no real guilt as he had carried out his orders at the expense of his own desires. The colonies were free of tyranny and he had helped in the fight for freedom,—and he had Andrew. The boy was nearly four years old, with tumbling blond curls. He was bright and good-natured. He would explain it all to Mercy when he returned to Maine and trust she would understand. God help him, he hoped she would understand.

Jeremiah arrived in Maine at October's end. The treaty of Paris had officially ended the war. With the turning of the leaves, so turned the country's government. It had taken longer than he had planned but he was free of his obligation at last, and he had returned a hero. His identity as a spy for the Patriots was not revealed but he carried a certificate of commendation for his loyalty and service in aiding the fight for independence signed by George Washington himself. Whenever his mission was questioned he simply answered that he did not wish to discuss the horrors of war, which was accepted, as many men who returned did not wish to open old wounds.

Albert was elated over his son's safe return and Andrew was his pride and joy. He revealed his failure to protect Mercy and Jeremiah suffered for her pain and the additional anguish his marriage had caused the girl he adored. Together they asked God's forgiveness for all the hurts their actions and omissions had caused and for guidance in the course of action to take. It was decided that Jeremiah should leave Andrew in Thomaston with Albert and Allie and journey north to Amitie le Christ and try to make amends for their transgressions. Jeremiah noted that his father and Allie had grown close in the years since his mother died and would not be surprised if their need for companionship bound them together. No one should be lonely as far as he was concerned.

It was November and soon there would be snow so Jeremiah traveled by chebacco boat as far as St. Croix and then bought a horse for the overland trip. He located a trader who knew of the convent and with a little gold in his hand he agreed to take Jeremiah to the commune.

It was with much trepidation he approached the convent. How could he believe Mercy would forgive him—what if she had taken vows or blamed him for the attack, and what of the child resulting from the attack?

His first contact was with Sister Sarah who answered the door at his knock and took him to Sister Margarite. He explained his identity and he begged to see Mercy.

"I will ask if she will see you, but I make no promises," she said. "Do you realize what she has been through?"

"Yes, Sister. I know that she was raped. Is the child here also?"

"Yes, Monsieur Clarke, William lies in his grave on the hill. He died at birth and we nearly lost Merci. Later she married her childhood companion and they had a wonderful love that presented them with a daughter. She is only now ending her year of mourning for her husband. She may not wish to see you who betrayed her."

It was almost more than Jeremiah could absorb. His mind reeled and he thought he was going to embarrass himself by fainting, but managed to keep his senses intact.

"Please, Sister. Please ask her to see me, I beg of you. I will be very careful not to upset her and I will leave upon her request."

Merci agreed to the visit, and with mixed emotions she received him in the sanctuary. Sister Margarite remained and busied herself cleaning wax drippings from the alter candles, clipping wicks and other small chores. She wanted to be near if Merci had difficulty with the meeting. She knew of the pain he and events in Thomaston had caused in the past and would not allow any new anguish.

Jeremiah was struck by Merci's beauty. She was more lovely than ever even though she still wore her mourning black. How often had he longed to see her in her simple frock with her hair blowing in the wind off the ocean. The locks now covered by her headscarf peeked out at the hairline and flowed in waves down her back.

Softly he spoke to the girl who had become the loveliest of women.

"Mercy, our freedom from British rule is now secure, and I beg you to understand that you were with me each moment of every hour. My commission is resigned and now my only commission is to implore, nay, beg you to understand that I was forced to do things against my will to aid the fight for freedom. I will not go into detail, but I have a motherless son, the only good thing resulting from my forced liaison. I could not tell you or my parents of the demands put upon me. The years of deceit to gain access to military information to aid the war effort were a constant weight upon my soul. My forced marriage was a complete sham, but Andrew is precious to me. I did not love his mother and I must carry that guilt, but my love for my son is sincere. I have told no one these things, but here in the sanctity of this Holy place I reveal my war mission and it cannot go beyond these walls. No one must know the clandestine nature of my service. My wife is dead and I would not hurt her parents who were very kind to me, not knowing of my deceit."

"Jeremiah, my heart was broken when you married another and it was a crushing blow. I thought what we had most precious, but it seemed to be easily discarded. The personal tragedy and humiliation I endured in Thomaston left a pronounced scar on my life, but I was rescued from despair by a love so profound and pure that it cannot be described. I am not sure I will ever be able to love again. My daughter is my first concern, she is the light of my life and her father will always shine from her eyes. You must know that it was the most wonderful love imaginable, and I don't think it will ever leave my heart, and I am not sure I will ever want it to leave me."

"My darling Mercy, whatever the years of war imposed on us, it is past. We both have children we love dearly from our unions. Let us not live in that past, but savor the good things life still has to offer. My love for you can accept that you may never love me as you did your child's father. I deserted you to serve my country and it was unfair to you and it was unfair to me. We have our children and I will be happy to be just your friend if that is possible, but please consider the good from our past relationship, and let me try to erase the pain we have endured since those happy days so long ago. Each day we start out lives anew, and we have a new country with new liberties. Without the control of the British Parliament we are free to travel beyond the great mountain ridge to the West. We could build our lives beyond the reach of the injuries and injustices and sadness that we have suffered. My father's wish is that I find some measure of happiness, and I will gladly accept whatever small consideration you can give.

My father had secretly considered the possibility that I might have been a traitor, but then later suspected that I might be on a secret mission. He was greatly relieved when I presented him with my letter of commendation signed by General Washington for my service to my country. Service in secret is a new method of warfare, I believe, at least it was new to me. I did what was asked of me but you will never know the anguish I suffered. Abigail was silly and simple and my guise as an attentive husband was a constant sore. Our contact was as seldom and brief as I could make it without arousing suspicion."

"I understand, Jeremiah. You have always been a person of great moral fiber, and I appreciate your coming for me, but it is much too soon. If you come back in the spring perhaps I will feel differently. I will have the winter to sort out my thoughts. Time is a great healer but I cannot promise I will ever recover from losing Thomas."

"I would be happy being second or third in your life. I want to take care of you and your daughter if only as a friend. Father would love to have you visit and Allie will be ecstatic when I tell her of your daughter, and that you are as beautiful as ever. She and my father have become great friends since Mother's passing and are a great comfort to each other. Life goes on. You must at least visit even if you cannot find it in your heart to accept my love."

Suddenly Aiyana came running into the sanctuary and hid in her mother's skirts, hugging Merci's legs but peeking around at Jeremiah with dark inquisitive eyes.

"This is my daughter, "Aiyana." Say 'Bon jour', to Monsieur Clarke, Aiyana."

As the tall slim man knelt on one knee in order to better see the dark haired child, Aiyana hesitated for a moment, then she ran with outstretched arms into Jeremiah's, and he clutched the child to his chest. His tearful eyes met Merci's and the poignancy of the moment touched them both.

"I promise to visit next spring if you come for me, perhaps I will have searched my heart by then. You are my dear friend, and I will consider all you have presented."

"And my promise is that I will return for you. I will leave on the morrow but I leave my heart with you. Just remember, I have always loved you, Mercy, Merci.

Dare I

Dare I love again?
Dare I risk the pain?
Each time I gave my heart
I've loved and lost.
Am I strong enough to weigh the cost
Of giving my heart again?
How much do I have left to give?
Should I take the risk and try to live
Forgetting heartaches of the past?
Could I find permanence at last,
With someone who has suffered, too
And sacrificed for justly cause?
We both have these reminders dear.
Together we can salve our wounds,
And with these small ones find our way,
To love and build a better day.
God grant me strength and vision clear
To serve these that I now hold dear.
The sweetness of lost love remains
Within my heart, and thus will stay,
And be with me both night and day.
I'm given now another chance
To find a more sedate romance.
So now again my heart I'll give
That we might heal and love and live.

Epilog

In the mountains two hundred miles west of Front Royal in the shadow of a peak aptly named "Wolf Mountain," the hills and valleys became inhabited by a family of stalwart mountain hunters and trappers, with strong women by their sides, raising large families of freckle faced red haired children. Some say they were descended from the Scots, but there is a legend that a young Englishman and his wife of mixed native blood immigrated from the North and settled in the Appalachian hills. They rode black and white horses attesting to the tales of a black stallion and his white mare that commanded and populated the mountain passes.

If one listens, on the full of the moon the lonesome call of a wolf can be heard resounding over the valley, and when the sun rises over the hills on a misty morning, a rainbow sparkles across the ridge, encompassing the hills with glorious promise of a great protective love.

The Curse Confounded

As here I stand twixt land and sea
The morning mist envelops me,
And hides the yard where souls doth sleep.
Some sleep in peace, as they are blessed
In their long journey of slumber there.
While some, nay, one, will always bear
Witness to the curse she gives.
Though she is gone, the symbol lives
And time cannot erase the fame,
Of one who chose to shame her name.
Now the stone, with tracing casting
Displays the dancing everlasting.
But all was not in vain, the warning stain
May keep someone from injuring
another pure in heart.
The one who cursed has now been blessed
With love and happiness unbounded.
The evil deed is thus confounded.

Finis

Lindsay Cameron

Lindsay Cameron, who portrayed Mercy, Merci, is a five time YMCA All Around state champion gymnast from Rhode Island. She is pursuing an education degree at Rhode Island University.

Jon Ross Caron

Jon Ross Caron, portraying Lone Wolf, the star soccer goalie and basketball playmaker at Mt. View High School in Maine, is pursuing a career in law enforcement at Unity College.

Chris Utley

Chris Utley, portraying Jeremiah, is base player, back-up vocalist and recording engineer for the band "Hollowday" and is a music tech major at Belmont College in Nashville, Tennessee.

FRED

Lindsay Cameron and Matthew Cameron allowed their early childhood photos used to portray Aiyana and Andrew.